The 13

CW00515043

Frank Malley

For Carole and Michael

The only thing necessary for the triumph of evil is for good men to do nothing.

Table of Contents

Prologue

1

2

3

4

5

6

7

8

9

10

11

12

13

14

15

16

17

18

19

20

21

22

23

24

25

26

27

28

29

30

31

32

33

34

35

36

37

38

39

40

41

42

43

44

Acknowledgements

Prologue

January 20th, 1961.

Henry Winter emerged from the grey stone walls of the Foreign Office, carrying a brown leather briefcase, misty breath rising in the cold air.

He was an unremarkable character, a man of exacting routine, each day a mirror of the one before. Grey suit, black overcoat, sallow complexion, neat moustache perched atop a thin mouth full of imperfect teeth. His fedora, stingy brim pulled forward to mask his appearance, by some distance his most interesting feature. It was almost as if Henry had worked hard to hide behind a cloak of blandness. The epitome of the British civil servant.

Not that the man across the street in the shadows was here to judge. As Henry edged down the steps and scurried along Whitehall, towards Charing Cross station, the man crossed the street. He fell in 50 yards behind, immediately blending into the city landscape. Purposeful stride, youthful air, scarf muffling his mouth A tightly-rolled newspaper under his arm.

At the top of Whitehall, overlooking Nelson's Column, Henry turned right, stopping briefly at a newspaper kiosk. The man closed in, studying Henry as he purchased his usual tobacco, while a throng milled around the entrance to a nearby cafe listening to an authoritative American voice with a Boston-Irish twang emanating from a crackly radio.

"Bit chilly tonight," said the kiosk keeper.

"Yes, first outing for these." A thin smile as Henry raised a hand to show off the black leather gloves his wife had bought for Christmas. He stuffed the tobacco into his briefcase, pausing for a few minutes to evaluate the stirring rhetoric.

The radio blared. "Let the word go forth from this time and place, to friend and foe alike, that the torch has been passed to a new generation of Americans, born in this century, tempered by war, disciplined by a hard and bitter peace, proud of our ancient heritage …"

1

Heads turned, strangers nodded in appreciation. A glow of optimism all the way from Washington D.C., where a new president, young and vibrant, was swearing the oath of office, appeared to track Henry. The words, "And so, my fellow Americans, ask not what your country can do for you, ask what you can do for your country", rang faintly in his ears as he made his way into the Strand.

Good line, mused Henry. *Not a chance it will ever happen in the mad consumer-driven world of America. Sold its soul to capitalism long ago and there's no turning back.* He parked the thought.

"That Kennedy's a breath of fresh air, isn't he?" he heard one man say.

His companion nodded. "His wife's a bit of all right too."

Five minutes later Henry squirmed along the teeming platform to await the 6.20 Northern Line train to East Finchley, anticipating a reviving gin and a relaxing draught on his pipe when he reached his fringe of comfortable suburbia.

He worked his way to the front of the platform, not far from the mouth of the tunnel. When the train arrived, commuters jammed the nearest carriage. Henry jostled with a swelling virus of humanity, his stalker shoehorning into position behind him, so tight he could feel the texture of Henry's woollen overcoat.

Henry clung to an overhead strap. The train lurched forward, a passenger pressing hard against him. He could feel her heat and the thought occurred that this was probably the closest he'd been to a woman in years. His wife no longer had inclination for intimacy. He sighed. Sadness and resignation.

"Sorry," mouthed the woman as the carriage lurched once more, the jolt again forcing her to steady herself with an elbow against his midriff.

"Don't worry. Can't be helped. Everybody wants to get home at the same time for some reason."

The woman, no more than 30, looked into his eyes, radiating the sweetest of smiles, red lips a reminder of the buds he nurtured with loving attention all summer in his rose garden. Those lips were Henry Winter's final vision.

The lights flickered as the train approached Leicester Square station throwing the carriage into temporary darkness. The man seized his opportunity.

In one rhythmic movement he wrapped the scarf around his nose and mouth, reaching forward to thrust the rolled-up newspaper into Henry's face. A crack sounded, resembling a clap of hands, although the train's mechanical groaning muffled it beyond significance. In reality, the sound of death, the catch of the piston-operated aluminium cylinder concealed in the man's newspaper releasing a plume of spray into Henry's respiratory system.

Henry sensed cold, damp vapour on his cheeks, yet had no time to react, save to greet the reality he'd recognised for years. The price of betrayal has to be paid. Only time and place in doubt.

The assassin had chosen the venue for its intimacy, the weapon for its reliability at close quarters, paralysing the arteries that feed blood to the brain.

Death would occur within 90 seconds, yet after five minutes the killing agent's effect would dissipate, allowing the arteries to return to normal, leaving no trace.

Henry slumped silently, head lolled against the sweet woman's shoulder, still upright, wedged in a human sandwich. When the lights flickered once more and passengers shifted with the sway of the carriage, readying to alight at the station, he slid to the floor.

The woman screamed. As the carriage doors opened, passengers, inured by the whirl of daily incidents in the capital, stepped over Henry to amble to favourite restaurants in theatre land. A few caring souls fussed around the twitching body. One shouted to the platform guard for assistance.

The man, scarf hiding his youthful features, slid around the back of the commotion, doffing his hat to two concerned ladies who strained to see past the milling crowd.

"Who is it?" said one.

"No idea," replied her friend. "Poor man looks like he's suffered a heart attack."

The man smiled. He knew well enough the identity of the dead commuter. Henry Winter, the innocuous civil servant at the Foreign Office. Or, in another incarnation, Colonel Sergey Kuznetsov of the Russian security forces.

The man tapped the newspaper against his palm and with a nonchalant swagger disappeared into the night. Mission accomplished.

The office stank of musky perfume and faded ambition.

Thick and depressing, the scent lingered amid the humdrum chatter of girls sat in regimented rows, headphones and microphones ruining weekend hair-dos.

Emily gazed out of the window, raindrops blurring the London skyline.

The forecast? More rain and further outbreaks of widespread boredom. Twelve months and counting. That's how long she'd stuck it on the floor of the insurance call centre.

Insurance. Even the word sounded tedious, conjuring dreary phrases. Passenger liability, no claims bonus, professional indemnity. To a young engineering graduate with dreams of working on a space programme, it was a job without interest. Like watching an advert for double glazing.

But the job kept her father's disapproving looks at bay and would tide her over until she found something more suited to her talents. Emily was passing a few tips to the new girl next to her when a dumpy supervisor, red nose matching streaks in her hair, nickname Jobsworth, noticed her receiver on downtime.

The tone was scolding. "Earth to Emily Stearn."

"Oh, sorry." Emily broke off, adjusting her headphones.

"Concentrate Emily. Please."

A weary smile, a roll of the eyes. Emily connected the waiting call, answering tiresome questions in robotic fashion. Yes, car insurance was comprehensive. Included breakdown assistance and windscreen repair. A courtesy car, if possible. No, a 50 per cent discount on last year was impossible.

Several calls later, the scowling supervisor waddled by again to find Emily's headphones askew once more.

"Miss Stearn."

"I was helping …"

"I've warned you."

"But …"

"Don't take me for a clown."

Emily's eyes fixed on the nose and red streaks. A couple of nearby operators tittered.

"You're joking, right," said Emily.

"Pardon?"

"Nothing."

"Are you trying to be funny?"

"No, I'm trying not to be." More titters. Emily cast a disapproving sideways glance at her colleagues.

The supervisor thought it was aimed at her. She affected her most fearsome tone. "Miss Stearn, we don't pay you to sit there all day chatting away."

"Yes, you do, it's a call centre."

The supervisor sucked through gritted teeth before reeling off the pedantic terms of employment. Two breaks a day. Fifteen minutes only, at the discretion of the supervisor. Emily's green eyes glinted fire. She'd tried her best to bite her lip. Almost drawn blood. But, for once, her best wasn't good enough. Something popped inside her head. The circuit responsible for restraint blowing a connection. *I was only trying to help. Why won't this infuriating supervisor go away?*

"Miss Stearn, you need to brush up your people skills."

"Maybe I'd have better people skills if I worked with better people."

"That's enough, do your job or I'll have to …" The supervisor never finished the sentence.

"GFY."

"What?"

"I said, GFY."

"You can't say that to me."

"I just did."

Emily's heart was racing, palms sweating, mind fighting to unscramble a tangle of thoughts. She hated confrontation. Always had done.

Every other day she would have obeyed the supervisor, apologised, begged forgiveness, cringed in embarrassment. But this wasn't every other day. She was on her feet, the stand-off transfixing around 40 operators, gawping at the most interesting office incident in months. Perhaps years. Her cheeks burned bright crimson. Emily could be forthright but she wasn't sweary. Hardly ever cursed, always using abbreviations if she did. *That way it wasn't really swearing, was it?* She'd gambled on the fifty-something supervisor not being conversant with text speak. She'd lost.

"You can't swear at a supervisor. I know what GFY stands for. It's a sacking offence. Any more of that, and there's the door." The supervisor's jaw jutted as she motioned to the office exit.

Emily grabbed her bag and coat, demeanour stubborn, tongue spitting textpletives as if swearing were her first language. Colleagues gasped, but Emily's mind was in a curious state of slow motion. Thoughts dragged. Her voice distorted, demons created by a year reining in frustrations, conforming to mundanity, obeying inflexible bosses, spilling out in a heap. Right there on the call centre floor. She wondered if she was experiencing a breakdown, but then breathed deep, striding past rows of open mouths and bewildered faces.

No one tried to stop her as she stumbled to the lifts, jabbing the button for the bottom floor. Where she'd decided her life was heading. Hurrying out of the office block onto the London street, hunched against drizzle, she boarded a bus to King's Cross bound for an underground train to her parents' house in Highgate. She could have headed straight to the flat she shared with her boyfriend, Blake, but it was mid-morning and he worked 10 miles away in the south of the city. She wanted to speak to someone. Needed her mum to tell her everything would be all right.

Finding a vacant seat on the top deck, she tried to compose herself as the bus negotiated the inevitable series of road works.

Still, her hands shook, a knot of anxiety twisting in her stomach. She fiddled with the strap of her handbag. What would her dad make of her reckless departure from permanent employment? How would Blake take losing her share of rent on the new apartment they'd recently moved into? No point worrying. No going back. She blanked out dark thoughts and observed pedestrians scurrying in all directions. Another busy working day in the capital.

The bus stopped at traffic lights. Emily glanced at the throng crossing the road in front of a parade of shops. Normal people going about their business. No one hurling abbreviated abuse at each other, or so it seemed. A mother with two toddlers, probably twins, in a pushchair. A man in brown overalls, roll of carpet balanced expertly on his shoulders. A group of pin-striped businessmen, carrying briefcases, striding out as if they ruled the world. A young man with wavy blond hair, overcoat with collar turned up, navy and white striped scarf swung loosely around his neck. Like Blake. It could be Blake. *Oh my God, it is Blake.* Emily's spirits soared as she waved to attract his attention. It was good to see a familiar face amid the morning's trauma. But what's Blake doing on this side of town in the middle of the day?

He never mentioned anything at breakfast. Another ordinary day. "Can't wait to get home. We'll watch a film and open a bottle of red," is what he'd said as they parted.

Emily tapped the window but Blake was on the opposite footpath, too far away. The oncoming traffic had begun to roll. She slid back the window, thrust her face into the wind, sucking in diesel fumes, but as she shouted his name a lorry trundled past obscuring him. Reaching for her phone, she keyed in his number. Then there he was once more. Blond hair unmistakable, but face partly hidden. For good reason. He was kissing a woman.

Not a peck on the cheek. A full frontal, tongue probing clinch. In the middle of the street. The girl was gorgeous. Even amid the surreal awkwardness of the moment, Emily had to concede that. Long flowing hair, sweet features, model figure. Emily was as entranced as she was confused. For some reason, she took a picture of the scene with her phone. As the bus pulled away she fixated on that kiss. Willing it to end. All the while the knot in her stomach cramping, so tight she could barely breathe.

She heard the concerned voice of a fellow passenger, a middle-aged woman in the seat behind. "Are you all right? What is it? What are you looking at?"

"Nothing important, just my life falling apart." A pain in Emily's chest stabbed at random, like the twitch of a phantom limb.

By the time the kiss was complete the bus had travelled too far to decipher detail but Emily knew. Every woman would have known. This was no chance encounter. The body language plain. The clues in the carefree toss of the woman's hair and the way Blake hugged her close. Head nestled in her locks, her right leg cocked like a trigger as she leaned into him, arms coiled around his neck.

The bus turned a corner and Emily slumped into her seat. A tingling sensation crawled up her spine but her mind was firm. No tears. Emily didn't do tears. She surprised herself. She always thought she'd rage at betrayal, if only because betrayal comes from those closest to you. Yet there was no anger on the bus to King's Cross. Maybe that would come later. She dispatched another three-letter abbreviation to Blake's phone, along with the photo she'd taken, proud at her reserve, in contrast to the earlier incident that morning. A frown of disappointment clouded her features, but all was not lost. After all, she no longer had to worry about her share of Blake's rent.

That's my girl, she mused. Deep breath. Head high. Stay in control. No dark thoughts. *I was too good for him anyway.* Half an hour later she strode up the driveway of her parents' home, past the stone heron she'd helped choose as a youngster, grateful for the familiarity. She rapped on the knocker, sensing something wrong as her mother swung the door open. Eyes red and misty, weak smile failing to disguise a backdrop of pain.

"What's the matter, Mum? You look like you've been crying."

"It's Uncle Sebastian."

"What about him?"

"He's dead."

As the old Emily would never have said, *What a bitch of a morning.*

2

"Mum, I wouldn't be seen dead in a hat like that."

Most daughters would have kept such an opinion to themselves as they stood outside the crematorium waiting for the cortege to arrive. Emily wasn't most daughters. She took a step back, eyes sizing up her mother. "But I love your outfit, Mum. You look good in black. Makes you look slim and sophisticated."

Typical Emily. One moment sour. The next sweet as crème brulee.

It could be tough being Emily's mum which was what Eleanor was thinking as she gazed at the glowering March sky, wondering what had become of her husband, who was accompanying the hearse containing Uncle Sebastian from the undertaking parlour in the seaside resort of Weymouth.

Two weeks had passed since Emily walked out of her job, or was fired, she was still unsure which. Not that she cared. She'd moved back in with her parents after informing Blake he could send on her belongings at his expense. He didn't argue, although he did suggest Emily owed a month's rent.

"There's a good reason why I don't," she'd replied, surprising herself at how calm she remained. Seconds later she resent the kiss photo via her mobile phone, consigning Blake to history. She was about to do the same with Uncle Sebastian.

"Sorry, Mum, but I always thought Uncle Sebastian led a sad life. He never got married, never had children, never came to visit us. He spent his whole life studying stuff that happened hundreds of years ago."

"You didn't really know him."

"I know he had a heart attack in his own bed and no-one even knew. Not until his cleaner turned up two days later. That's a sad end to a sad life."

"Emily, it was no more than 24 hours later. Please don't talk like that when your father arrives. We might not have seen

Uncle Sebastian often but Harry thought a lot of him. He went so suddenly. It wasn't a sad life."

For the next few minutes they stood in silence, mother and daughter eyeing a small gathering, trying not to look self-conscious. Eleanor recognised Uncle Sebastian's cleaner, a wiry woman in her fifties with a kind face, chatting in whispered tones to a man Eleanor assumed was her husband but could easily have been a brother, a neighbour, a lover even. The rest were men and Eleanor thought she'd seen one of them before, a stout individual with rotund girth, balding pate and ill-fitting suit, but she couldn't place where or when. Another man caught Emily's eye for different reasons, this one slim, tall, silver hair, a confident air and steady gaze, although he waited a little way behind the others, leaning on a black 4x4 with dark-tinted windows.

The hearse proceeded at a solemn crawl up the long drive with Harry alongside the driver, a car behind carrying pall bearers.

No flowers or messages of endearment. No tangible sign that Uncle Sebastian had bequeathed any emotional footprint during his 83 years. The undertakers did their job. The haunting intro to *A Whiter Shade of Pale* piped up from a concealed recording device as mourners filed into the hall behind the coffin. Harry and Eleanor held hands, Emily trailed behind, while the cleaner dabbed an eye with a handkerchief.

The celebrant wore a grey suit and appeared well-preserved for a man in his sixties, honeyed voice inducing trust and solemnity. "For those of you who haven't attended a humanist funeral service before it's nothing unusual. It's based on humanity and reason, not religion. We're not here to worship but to grieve by celebrating the life of Sebastian Emile Stearn."

"Emile?" mouthed Emily with a perplexed grimace. Eleanor shrugged.

The celebrant proceeded to recite a litany of Sebastian's details. Born in London in 1939, worked for 50 years as a history professor at Cambridge University, wrote countless books on past civilisations. Emily yawned.

Where some perceived excitement in the threads of the Bayeux Tapestry, wonder in lichen growing on the ancient slabs at Stonehenge, Emily saw faded material and a pile of rubble. To Emily, history was a thing of the past, like Blake. She was more than happy to leave it, and him, there.

Harry fished reading glasses from his inside pocket, ran fingers through greying hair and read the eulogy from prepared notes. The prose was beautiful. Words befriended Harry. He helped run a London publishing house so they came with the territory. He spoke about history as a small step for man but a giant leap for mankind, mentioned the Wright Brothers, English longbow men at Agincourt, sappers crawling through mud at the Somme and children turning on laptops to let knowledge flood into their minds.

"History is also about people such as Uncle Sebastian. He loved history and encouraged many young minds down the years to do the same. Once, long ago, I asked why he'd devoted his life to the subject and his answer was more poetic than I anticipated. History is the twinkling stars in the night sky and dust collecting on our shelves. History is not only about yesterday, it's about all our days."

Harry removed his glasses, folded his notes, a catch sounding in his voice. "Farewell Uncle Sebastian."

Eleanor debated whether to clap, eventually seizing the moment, diffident at first, enthusiasm accelerating when others joined in, applause echoing around the airy chamber. Emily's hands remained thrust deep into the pockets of her overcoat.

The celebrant asked if anyone else would care to speak. Eyes lowered, feet shuffled, until the rotund man coughed, raised a hand and lumbered to the lectern.

"My name is Andrew and I worked with Sebastian. That sounds too grand. Actually, we worked in the same building, Corpus Christie College in Cambridge. I was a young assistant handyman, he was a famous professor, but I'll never forget his kindness."

Andrew explained that 15 years ago, travelling by train to a work assignment, he was talking on his mobile phone to a friend. Andrew admitted that he was struggling financially, unable to pay his rent. The call ended, Andrew falling into a deep, disturbed sleep.

"When I woke up there was a white envelope on the table. Written on the front were the words: A helping hand from someone who has been lucky enough never to have been there. Inside the envelope was three hundred pounds in twenty pound notes."

Emily sat up, intrigued.

"I know what you're thinking. How did I know the money came from Sebastian? Well, an acquaintance of mine happened to be further down the carriage and when the train approached Sebastian's stop, he saw him reach over from the seat behind mine and leave the envelope. You never forget that sort of kindness. That's why I came today."

Andrew shuffled back to his seat. A few moments of silence ensued before curtains closed around the coffin and the celebrant administered his closing address. As mourners filed out, Harry paused, head bowed, where the coffin had lain, listening to the soulful strains of *Blue Moon* playing from a wall-mounted speaker.

3

On the car journey back to London, Eleanor slept on the rear seat while Emily mulled over the details of the day alongside her father in the front. They hadn't long joined the motorway when Emily asked, "Why *Blue Moon*?"

"No idea. Don't think anyone knows. Uncle Sebastian left instructions for it to be played. Must have meant something to him, but don't think we'll ever know."

"Did he leave any other instructions?"

"Not for the service, but his will is detailed. He wanted to make sure all his books and music went to a good home. That's going to be a big job over the next few months. As the sole executor of the will it's my headache."

"What needs doing?"

"Thousands of books and cds, old vinyl records and tapes, all need cataloguing. Some will go to the university. Some need throwing out. Others can be sold with proceeds to the estate. It's a job for someone with a meticulous mind."

Eleanor, yawning in the back, sat up, alert and excited. She'd been listening in and detected an intrigued tone in Emily's questioning. Her daughter's future was uncertain. Emily had shown little regret over losing her job or boyfriend and Eleanor had encouraged her to follow her dreams. One of which was to do a post-graduate course in maths and physics. Emily loved maths. Partly because the subject involved asking questions and formulating answers. Mostly because there *was* an answer, rather than literature and art where everyone's opinion seemed uniformly valid and equally meaningless. Solving problems and finding solutions appealed to Emily. She'd landed a job in an engineering firm after gaining her first degree, although it hadn't worked out. Too much theory.

"Sounds perfect for you, Emily. Harry, why don't you ask her to do the cataloguing," said Eleanor.

"I don't think …"

"You know you can trust her."

Emily threw a black look. "I am here. I can speak for myself."

Harry sneaked a sideways glance at Emily, detecting a glimpse of interest. "It's not a bad idea. You'd have full use of his bungalow and I'd pay you. Or at least Uncle Sebastian would."

"I don't know. Sounds a bit boring. I'm not sure I'd be interested in any of Uncle Sebastian's stuff."

"Go on Emsy," said Eleanor, adopting her most pleading expression.

"Do you mind not calling me that, Mum. I'm twenty-seven, not seven. I'm not a child." Emily's green eyes, wilful and fiery, pierced her mother in the rear mirror.

A flood of memories invaded Eleanor's mind. Emily had been a *special* little girl. At least that's how her mother preferred to describe her, although occasionally she'd overheard neighbours whispering, pointing towards Emily, mouthing, 'What an odd child'.

Her instinct was to protect. Punch them on the nose. Draw blood. Let them feel the hurt. She would have done but for the nagging thought that it wasn't normal for a seven-year-old girl to sit at the end of the driveway each day of the summer holidays, recording car registration numbers in a notepad.

Eleanor had attempted countless diversions, including a selection of video games flooding the market. Nothing worked. Instead, day after day Emily filled her notebook with letters and numbers in pristine rows for no apparent reason.

"Don't worry, she'll grow out of it." Eleanor's friends dismissed the obsession as a schoolgirl fad. But Emily never did grow out of her lists and numbers, until Eleanor was convinced her little girl resided on a medical spectrum.

There was something else. As Eleanor gazed at Emily's reddish-blonde curls cascading onto her shoulders she shivered at a distant memory. The day Emily had sliced her knee to the bone on a shard of glass hidden under leaves in the local park.

As Eleanor ran to help, Emily pulled the shard from her knee, watching blood drip down her white socks. No panic or tears. No emotion. That can't be normal, thought Eleanor. The wound required stitches but the next day Eleanor phoned the doctor. *Why doesn't my child cry?* Tests followed, spectrums were mentioned, but no definitive diagnosis was forthcoming. Eleanor preferred to call Emily's behaviour a gift from God. She set about proving that by drawing up a list of her own, comprising famous people considered to be odd. Hans Christian Andersen. Lewis Carroll. Charles Darwin. Albert Einstein. Michelangelo. Mozart.

Eleanor recalled that list now, wondering whether they cried as children. She hoped they did. As she pondered the best way to persuade her daughter a few weeks paid work, courtesy of Uncle Sebastian, was a good idea, an unexpected sadness fell upon her. It lifted only when Emily barked out her decision.

"Okay, I'll do it."

4

She loved the seaside. Not those brash fairground resorts full of donkey rides, kiss-me-quick hats and dodgy characters queuing up to prise money from parents' purses.

Emily preferred natural beauty. As she turned her car onto the coast road she glimpsed a fleeting view of the ocean, white horses, whipped by the gathering breeze, glinting in the watery sunlight. "How beautiful," she gasped, distant memories provoking an unexpected gush of warmth.

On entering the town, she listened to the radio headlines before jabbing the off button when the newscaster droned on about the latest economic forecasts. Past boats bobbing in the marina, over an iron road bridge and into narrow, twisting, cobbled streets exuding charm, promising intrigue. As Emily had skipped lunch, she kept an eye open for a sandwich shop.

She'd visited Weymouth a couple of times as a child on the odd occasion her mum persuaded Harry to take a long weekend, but never as an adult, apart from the funeral. The town seemed smaller, more compact than she remembered, yet clean and inviting.

Pensioners, bald heads gleaming, strolled along the promenade. Some sat on wooden-slatted benches, putting the world to rights, shielding from the late spring wind inside wooden shelters. One steered a child's pushchair containing a Bichon Frise, or maybe a Coton de Tulear. Emily couldn't distinguish but it resembled one of those house dogs that demands cuddling, then barks the place down for no apparent reason.

Spotting Tasty Treat, a café cum sandwich bar, she squeezed into a parking space, and headed for the takeaway sandwich aisle. Something simple but filling. Tuna baguette with mayonnaise would suffice. She joined the queue to pay while two old ladies flirted with the check-out assistant.

"Alex, that's a nice name," said one of them, reading the assistant's name on his shirt badge.

"Actually, people call me Al," replied the lad, decked out in the café's brown and cream uniform, including peaked cap. Emily gauged he was around her age, noticing a mischievous smile light up his sun-tanned complexion.

"Like Pacino," chirped one of the ladies.

"If you say so."

"I love his films. He was in *The Godfather*, you know. And *Scarface*."

Her friend nodded. "I preferred him in that film when he was blind. What was it called, Janice? It's on the tip of my tongue."

"*Scent of a Woman*," said Al. He handed the lady her change, complete with another dazzling smile.

The ladies shuffled away and Emily deposited her baguette on the counter, opening her purse. "How much?"

"Do you fancy a drink?"

Emily glanced up. The cashier's smile was cheekier than ever, thick dark eyebrows raised and slanted in a questioning manner. The memory of Blake's betrayal was too recent for Emily to consider any fresh liaison. Her tone brusque. "I'm not going out with you. I don't know you."

"No, you don't understand. A drink's included in the meal deal. It says so on the shelf." The cashier chuckled, pointing at a sign in the sandwich aisle.

Most girls' cheeks would have burned red with embarrassment. Not Emily. "Just the sandwich, please." Handing over her money, she threw Al a suspicious glance and strode out of the shop.

She ate her baguette sat on a bench, enjoying condiments of salt-kissed air and the sea's iodine aroma, content to have escaped the stress of London but unsure what her unexpected sabbatical in Weymouth would bring. One week only had passed since Uncle Sebastian's funeral. Her father's brief was vague, but had convinced her to treat the time as a paid holiday.

She finished her meal, dropping the wrapper in a waste bin, scrutinised by a cohort of gulls ready to swoop on stray crumbs, jumped back in the car and made her way to Uncle Sebastian's bungalow.

Sea View Road was cut into the craggy lump of rock and earth that overlooks Portland Bay. Less grand than expected. On the high side, a row of three-storey Victorian houses, prominent chimney stacks standing resolute against the sea breeze, even if most had seen better days. A couple of overflowing rubbish skips littered the road while scaffolding scarred the face of several buildings, lending the vista a transient, unwelcoming ambience.

In contrast, modern villas, tidy and well-maintained, lined the low side, driveways falling away as they tracked the steep contours of the hillside. Emily edged through the gateway at number seven, appreciating the clean lines of the bungalow's grey stonework, although she noted the garden appeared overgrown and unkempt. A winter of neglect, as if gardening chores had proved irksome in Uncle Sebastian's dotage.

As she back-pedalled out of the car, grabbing her lightweight suitcase off the back seat, she glimpsed a man crossing the road, heading towards her. A kind-looking man with thinning grey hair. He wore a warm smile, classic Barbour jacket, corduroy trousers and gardening boots. In his hand he dangled a bunch of keys. His cheery greeting was sharp and refined. "You must be Emily. I'm Marcus. Your mum said to expect you. You're right on time. Good drive down?"

"Yes thanks. Not much traffic. I suppose it isn't holiday season."

"Not yet, but give it a couple of months. You know the madness has begun when they're queuing down the promenade to get into the fish and chip shops."

Marcus took the suitcase from Emily. "Come on, I'll show you around. Your mum said you hadn't been to the house before. You have a treat in store."

Marcus stepped into a roomy hallway housing a giant cheese plant. A variety of artwork adorned the walls.

Emily studied the predominance of seascapes, most in pale water colours, although an oil painting of the beach bedecked in summer splendour, striking blue and red deckchairs forming a pleasing impromptu sculpture, caught her eye. "I don't know much about art but these are good, this one in particular. Did Uncle Sebastian paint these?"

"Yes. The paintings are just one of the reasons I love this house."

Marcus dumped the suitcase and beckoned for Emily to follow him into the lounge, where he almost bowed in reverence to announce the view. Emily's eyebrows raised without conveying overt enthusiasm, although Marcus sensed appreciation in the way she skipped towards the window, affording a spectacular panorama of the Isle of Portland, the harbour below and Chesil Beach glinting in the distance.

Marcus joined her, admiring the sweep of the bay, white sailing boats tacking on a freshening breeze.

"Who needs television with a view like that?" said Marcus.

"What are the other reasons?"

"Pardon."

"For loving this house."

Marcus spun around, flourishing a palm this time in the direction of a baby grand piano, tree-trunk legs rooted in one corner, white teeth-like keys smiling as if appreciating the company. *Steinway & Sons of New York* embossed in gold writing on the polished wood.

"Sebastian's pride and joy. He loved this piano. It was wonderful to hear him playing at times when I knocked on the front door. Brought the house to life. He used to let my daughter come across for an hour or so each week to practise for her music exams."

"That's nice."

"That was Sebastian. Lovely man. Gentle and kind. This house possesses his aura. Soothing and calm. Something to do with being able to see the ocean from every vantage point. I do miss him."

"How well did you know him?"

Marcus pondered the question, brushing a film of dust from the corner of the piano with the sleeve of his jacket. "I knew his mother when I was a lad. She used to live here. Not in this house but on this plot of land. When she passed away twenty-odd years ago Sebastian knocked down her old place and built this. He wanted a home to retire to when he finished at

Cambridge, one with a few more mod cons than his mother was used to. A bachelor pad, I suppose, with a spectacular view. He still retained a study at Cambridge but in the last few years he came down here more often. I looked after the garden for him when he was away and we shared the odd tot of whisky on summer nights watching the sun go down over the ocean."

"When did you last see him?"

"A few weeks ago. Normally, I'd pop in every couple of days but Mary and I had been away for a while visiting our daughter. We're having building work done on the house and wanted to escape the dust. I feel terrible that we weren't here and he was found by the cleaner."

"I didn't see you at the funeral." Emily's statement was direct. It could have been construed as an accusation. Marcus paused as if deliberating whether showing up to mourn someone in death was remotely equivalent to being there for them in life. A gentle smile played on his lips.

"Mary doesn't do funerals. But my thoughts were with him. Have been ever since I heard the news. I'll leave you to unpack and have a mooch around. The instructions for the heating are on the kitchen worktop and there's fresh milk and stuff in the fridge but if you need anything, just ask, we're over at number ten." He handed over the bunch of keys.

Emily heard the front door bang as Marcus left, allowing peace and calm to descend, her gaze falling once more upon the ocean. The soft tick of a clock the only sound. Her nose twitched, detecting the faint, comforting odour of stale cigar smoke blended with wood polish.

She sauntered through to the kitchen, a generous space with an island worktop, dining table and large sliding glass doors, offering another jaw-dropping view of the bay. She smiled, noticing a ceramic three-foot version of one of the seven dwarfs gazing out to sea. A mural of the world, painted in vibrant colours, adorned one of the stark white walls. On another wall a framed water colour of a man's face drew her attention. Laughter lines formed the hint of a smile under a distinctive beaked nose, thick golden hair brushed back neatly. The blue-grey eyes, exuding vitality and wisdom, transfixed Emily. Piercing and hypnotic, they seemed to track her, Mona Lisa-style. She strained to decipher the inscription in the bottom right-hand corner, partly smudged as if clumsy thumbs in another lifetime had done their worst. She could make out the first three letters, *Seb,* while the date was clearly *1981.* A self-portrait.

Looks like a film star, thought Emily. Like Robert Redford in *Butch Cassidy and the Sundance Kid,* her dad's favourite film. Emily began humming *Raindrops Keep Fallin' on My Head* and grabbed a Diet Coke from the fridge before walking through to the study.

The daunting prospect of cataloguing Uncle Sebastian's belongings suddenly struck. One big wall supported floor-to-ceiling shelves, straining under the weight of cds, vinyl records and audio tapes, all in original plastic containers. Fortunately, Uncle Sebastian had arranged them in alphabetical order by artist. Emily calculated that would save days when cataloguing. If that wall was stunning, then the two other walls, forming a horseshoe of the world's most creative musical and writing talent, were also impressive. Every shelf filled with books, again in meticulous order. Perhaps as many as 2,000.

Emily whistled through her teeth. *Was this a good idea, after all? I don't even read books. I like maths and solving conundrums. Give me a Sudoku or a Rubik Cube, fine, but I wouldn't know a Salman Rushdie from a Jane Austen.* She glugged a mouthful of Coke, enjoying the metallic fizz on her tongue, and ambled along the shelves, drumming fingers on the books while perusing the collection. Most were textbooks Uncle Sebastian had amassed down the years, arranged in date order from *The Oxford History of Ancient Egypt* through to *The Official History of the Falklands Campaign.* Four shelves were reserved for classic novels. There were sections on sport, popular fiction, gardening, motoring, and two shelves for cookery books. *I wonder how many he read. It would take a lifetime to get through all these. If he read them all, there'd be no time for anything else. Maybe that's why Uncle Sebastian never got married. Wedded to his music and books. All that knowledge, all that education. Gone.*

She was ready to stroll down the hallway to pick up her suitcase when her fingertips alighted on the 16th Century and a curious volume in the textbooks section. No title, no picture on front or back, no come-and-buy-me lure. If it hadn't been for the unusual texture, the book would have remained unremarkable. But the leather-bound cover exuded quality and inset lay a black velvet rectangle. Intrigued, Emily plucked it from the shelf. Solid, encyclopaedic heavy. Depositing the book on the writing desk, she flicked open the pages, starting at the back. Her nose wrinkled, brow knitting as her eyes fell upon a sea of numbers, adorning every page, written by a tidy hand in what appeared to be fountain pen ink. The endless digits, similar in format but different in detail, triggered childhood memories, sitting for hours documenting car registration plates. As beautiful and random as a pleasing abstract artwork, yet unfathomable.

When she reached the first page, the only words in the entire book leapt out at her:

Sebastian Emile Stearn
The answer is blowing in the wind

5

The next morning Emily awoke at 5.30. She wasn't normally an early riser but she'd left her bedroom window ajar and as dawn broke hungry gulls screeched for breakfast.

By the time she reached the window to shut out the squawking she was wide awake and padded barefoot to the kitchen in her pink pyjamas to watch the shifting silhouettes and stark contrasts between sea and land as the rising sun coated a new day in refreshing light.

Flicking the kettle switch, she rummaged in a cupboard and found a jar of instant coffee. Most days began with coffee, stronger the better, one first thing, another around midday. She considered coffee elastic, allowing her to stretch her energy resources.

She carried the mug and her laptop through to the study, sipping as she went, pondering the contents of the leather-bound volume. Emily adored a puzzle. At first glance the numbers seemed random, single digits, in other places as many as seven digits before a space. Emily was steeped in numbers. She must recognise something, yet the longer she stared the more mystifying the pages proved. Not a formula, a theorem, or anything mathematical in her experience.

She scanned the book for almost half an hour, eyes flicking back to the only words. *The answer is blowing in the wind.* What answer? It made no sense. The binding served as the only clue. Would Uncle Sebastian have wrapped a work of insignificance in a cover oozing such quality? Surely not. What then? A secret code he shared with history colleagues. A manuscript perhaps that he'd never published. Maybe a controversial opinion on one of history's infamous leaders? But Uncle Sebastian was noted for quiet diplomacy. *History is the twinkling stars in the night sky and dust collecting on our shelves.* That's how Harry had recounted Sebastian's philosophy in his eulogy. It didn't sound like a man intent on shaking up his comfortable firmament. Irritated by her inability to solve the conundrum, Emily drained her coffee, formulating a plan of attack.

Where to begin? At the beginning, logic told her. She started documenting Uncle Sebastian's vinyl record collection from left to right, slipping each record from its sleeve, checking condition, noting title, artist and year of release before taking a picture of the front cover. Emily had never listened to a vinyl record but she'd read they were de rigueur with retro music lovers from the sixties, seventies and eighties hungry for nostalgia, as well as a new generation fascinated with old technology. Something to do with the emotional click of the stylus into the plastic groove and the hissy crackle of dead air. Emily didn't understand, but as she photographed a copy of *Ziggy Stardust* she conceded the covers were colourful and creative.

She ploughed on for almost four hours, entranced by Uncle Sebastian's breadth of musical taste. From jazz, not that she'd ever heard of Thelonius Monk and Blossom Dearie, through to more mainstream artists such as Frank Sinatra, The Beatles and David Bowie. Did Uncle Sebastian actually listen to all this music? Or was he merely a collector of trinkets tracking popular culture through the ages? Her phone rang. Mum.

"Hi, how's the job going?"

"It's only ten o'clock on my first day."

"I know, but you like to get stuck into a project."

"I've done a lot already. Uncle Sebastian may have been dull but he was neat, tidy and everything is positioned in date order. Makes the job a lot easier. I like his house. Feels safe and homely. Decoration's a bit clinical but that's probably to be expected from a man who never had a long-standing relationship."

Eleanor was relieved to hear Emily describing the job in positive terms. She'd gauged Emily capable of the task but feared the subject matter might stretch her boredom threshold. All appeared fine. "Glad you're enjoying it."

"I am. No need to worry."

Emily toyed with telling her mum about the strange leather-bound volume, but concluded there was no point. Her parents skimmed the surface of Uncle Sebastian's existence. The chances of them knowing fine details of his writing life were negligible. "Bye." She hung up and returned to sifting through the record sleeves.

A few minutes later the doorbell rang, a series of long and short chimes as if the caller were playing a tune. Emily skipped along the hall, throwing open the front door, forgetting she was wearing pyjamas. In the doorway stood a tall man with wavy black hair, carrying a large cardboard box.

"Yes?" Emily was a tad sharp as she noticed the man eyeing her nightwear.

"Oh, it's you."

"What do you mean?"

"The lady from the café. The one who didn't want a drink."

"Oh."

"I'm Al. I served you yesterday. You told me you wouldn't go out with me. Remember?"

Emily looked perplexed. She studied the man more closely. No café uniform, no peaked cap, but the confident air lurking behind the dark eyebrows and healthy tan was memorable.

"Oh yeah, Pacino, I remember."

"Nice to see you again." Al put the box down. He stood marinating an awkward silence.

"And?" Emily gestured, palms upturned.

"Sorry, I saw the car in the driveway. A courier delivered the box a couple of days ago, addressed to Sebastian. The driver knocked on my door when he couldn't get an answer and I took it in. Didn't know what to do with Sebastian having passed away. Thought I'd wait until someone arrived. Here you are."

"You live next door?"

"I'm the lodger. Or, more accurately, the house sitter. Jim and Jean are spending a year in South Africa. I'm looking after the place."

"And working at the café."

"That's right. Earning some money while I'm waiting to start a degree in October."

"What subject?"

"Maths."

"That's a coincidence. I'm thinking of doing maths and physics as a further degree after a few years out."

Emily smiled. Maybe she'd misread this café cashier. At first meeting she'd categorised him as a brainless lothario, adept at flirting and seducing women. Another Blake maybe. Perhaps she'd been harsh. The women in the café were on the north side of 80. Her demeanour softened.

"Did you know Sebastian?"

"No. I've only been here a month. I met him once over the garden fence. We chatted about his allotment. He gave me some handy tips about growing fruit. I thought I'd have a go at raspberries but all the staking and training sounded a bit like hard work. He seemed a lovely man, though, kind eyes and patient. I was looking forward to getting to know him better. He knew I was on my own, even invited me for a drink some time. Pity, we never got around to it. Anyway, do you want me to drop the box inside for you."

Normally, Emily would have refused, especially wearing pyjamas. She didn't embrace the impromptu, preferring organisation and routine. Change and strangers were unwelcome, but this felt comfortable. She stepped aside, signalling for Al to enter.

"Just drop it there," She pointed to a chair by the hall table.

"It's not heavy, just a bit cumbersome. You'll probably find the box is ten times bigger than what's packed inside, full of polystyrene and bubble wrap that'll take a hundred years to biodegrade. All delivered by a bloke who thinks he doesn't have a carbon footprint because he drives everywhere."

"Is that a joke?"

"Did you think it was funny?"

"A bit."

"Okay, then it was a joke."

Emily chuckled. "Thanks."

"No problem."

"I'm Sebastian's niece by the way. Great niece, in fact. I've come to help sort out his belongings."

"Let me know if I can help. I'd be glad to. I'm bored most of the time when I'm not working at the café."

Al turned to go, but as Emily made to shut the door she surprised herself. "There is something you may be able to help with. A book of numbers I've found. I can't make much sense of it and two minds are better than one."

"I can see why you're good at maths." Al dispensed another of his smiles, although the quip eluded Emily. "I'm working at the café in half an hour. How about if I pop over this evening. Say about seven."

"Seven it is." Emily shut the door and carried the box through to the study. She placed it on the desk, pondering whether she should leave it for her dad to deal with. A label on the box intrigued her. *Books – Handle with Care.* Felt too light for books, at least the books filling Uncle Sebastian's shelves.

Emily grabbed a letter opener to slice open the packing tape. She prised the lid ajar to find it contained another smaller box, surrounded by a duvet of bubble wrap, as Al had predicted. She put the letter opener to work once more, reached inside the smaller box, pulling out a book. A famous book. *The Grapes of Wrath* by John Steinbeck. She flicked open the copyright page. *First published in April 1939.* No mention of later printings. The price, $2.75, adorned the top corner of the dust jacket, although much of the cover was stained, while the bottom corner of the front flap proclaimed *First Edition.*

Emily took scant notice of the literary world, but realised this wasn't your average book delivery. This was a rare book, the author a Pulitzer prize winner. First editions, even far from pristine condition, could fetch a handsome price. She reached into the box again and pulled out a sheet of paper. A compliments slip from the book vendors, Carringtons of Chelsea, containing a simple printed message:

If you are reading this, I must be gone. Use the Wrath (wisely) - Sebastian.

Emily read the message again. And again. Around 20 times in all. *Did it mean Uncle Sebastian knew he was dying? But why had he sent a message to his own address?* Her stay in Weymouth amounted to no more than a day, yet the conundrums thumped an intriguing beat in her head. Time for breakfast followed by a peaceful sunbathe on the balcony overlooking the orchard. Time she read *The Grapes of Wrath*.

6

Emily was wriggling into a dress when the doorbell rang.

She didn't often wear dresses but she'd spent a sticky day in Uncle Sebastian's study, wading through his vinyl record collection. She'd reached a middle shelf, around the time The Beatles were revolutionising the music world, before showering in time for seven o'clock. She looked at her watch. Five to. He's early. How irritating.

She swung open the front door to discover a dazzling smile. Al, holding a bottle of red wine in one hand, brown paper bag in the other.

"Thought we might need sustenance."

"We're not having sex." Emily threw a guarded look as she eyed the wine, her nose detecting the sharp tang of hot sweet and sour sauce.

Al chuckled. "Fair point, well made, but you do eat and drink, don't you?"

"Yes."

Al lifted his arms. "Well then, let's eat and drink."

As Al unpacked the Chinese banquet, she searched for a corkscrew, rummaging through the utensils' cupboard. "God knows where he kept one. This house is brilliant and also infuriating. Everywhere you turn, another mystery."

"Sounds interesting. Have you made any sense of the book of numbers?"

"No, but let's eat first." She discovered the corkscrew inside a towel drawer, raising it in triumph above her head.

"Let's get the party started," said Al, immediately putting a finger to his lips and lowering his voice, pretending to apologise. "I mean, let's have dinner."

Al had chosen well. Lemon chicken, sweet and sour pork, beef in black bean sauce, mountains of special fried rice and vegetarian options also. Emily was surprised. She felt safe and relaxed, the pleasing mellowness not all induced by good food and a second glass of acceptable wine. She took another sip and looked him in the eye, not an everyday occurrence in Emily's existence.

"You know why I'm here. What brought you to Weymouth?"

He pointed to a full moon rising, the water in the bay shimmering as dusk gave way to night, while the headlights of distant cars flickered like fireflies as they hurried across the causeway. "Good question. But you only have to look out of the window. There's an uncomplicated beauty to this place. Not too crowded, not too isolated. Enough going on to hold your interest. I can see why Sebastian lived here. I could sit for hours watching the ebb and flow of seaside life from that window."

"But that's why you stay. What made you come here in the first place? Do you have family here or some other connection?" Emily approached conversation as she would an equation, each phrase requiring forensic examination to elicit a definitive answer.

"I saw the advert for the house-sitting job online and thought it a good way to spend a few months before starting my course at Bristol University. I get paid a bit by the owners, can work in the café during the day and when my course starts I'll be able to commute to Bristol for a while. Throw in a sea view and it's a pretty good deal."

"Where do you come from originally?"

"Ah, well, that's where you bring in the United Nations. I was born in Latvia." Al swished wine around the bottom of his glass, drained the dregs and reached for the bottle. He stretched to pour a top-up for Emily but she placed a palm across her glass. Al shrugged, filling his glass instead.

"I thought I detected a hint of something. Couldn't work out what it was."

"I didn't live there long but my mother taught me her own languages and I suppose it stirs up the accent a bit. My dad lives in Scotland, although I don't see him much these days. My parents split up when I was young and Dad does something protecting the environment on the Isle of Skye. Not sure what exactly."

"Saving the planet presumably."

31

"Something like that. He's passionate about conservation. Always told me if I met a woman to talk about global warming."

"Why?"

"Because it's an icebreaker."

"That's another joke, right?" Emily didn't know what to make of this new acquaintance. She'd known him barely two days. He seemed kind, thoughtful, attentive, as the impromptu banquet proved. He was also slightly irritating. Emily found solving mathematical problems easy. Differentiating nuances of irony, satire and veiled humour posed more of a challenge.

Al laughed at Emily's quizzical expression. "Sorry, yeah, it was a joke. But I am into conservation too. I marched to Downing Street once to protest against fracking. You may have seen it on the news. I can't believe that in the 21st Century some people think it's a good idea to blow up the ground, literally under our feet, with all the toxic baggage that involves."

"Nor can I."

Al sat up, sensing a connection between them. His blue eyes glinted, jaw jutting, words firing out, fast and sharp, like tracer bullets. "If I were Prime Minister I'd pump subsidies into wind and solar farms and get serious about the greatest threat to the human race since a giant meteor put paid to the dinosaurs. But it won't happen. Forget the promises. Politicians are too invested in lining their own pockets, second guessing how they can stay in power, looking after number one. Conservation? More like conserving corruption."

Emily felt his passion, her own eyes wide and glowing. "That's exactly what I think."

"But I can still joke about it. Now, how about showing me your book of numbers." Al's shoulders settled, mood relaxing in an instant, a smile replacing the vexed demeanour.

"Follow me."

Emily walked through to the lounge where she'd left the leather-bound volume on a coffee table. She sat on the brown leather settee, gesturing for Al, wine glass in hand, to join her.

"Lovely binding, that doesn't come cheap." Al parked his glass on the table, picked up the book, and sniffed the cover.

His first impression concurred with Emily's. If the contents matched the precision and quality of the cover then the book must be a work of significance. He pored over the numbers in silence wearing a quizzical expression. After a while he turned back to the first page and read the only words, Sebastian's name above *The answer is blowing in the wind.* Al tapped the line with a forefinger.

"Sounds like a line from a Bob Dylan song, *Blowin' in the Wind.* Almost as if that's the key to everything that follows. The answer to the riddle of the numbers. Maybe there's something in the record sleeve that will explain what it's all about. Have you looked through his record collection? Is there any Dylan?"

"I don't know anything about Dylan. I know he's supposed to be a great song writer but he's passed me by."

"You can't be a protestor and not know about Dylan. He was the king of musical protestors." Al's tone carried a hint of derision.

"When did he release that song?"

"What? *Blowin' in the Wind*?"

"Yeah."

"Early sixties, nineteen sixty-three I think."

"I don't think he's in Uncle Sebastian's collection then."

"Why?"

"Because I've been through all his vinyl records up until the break-up of The Beatles at the end of the sixties. I've not come across anything from Dylan."

"Maybe it's not in order."

"Everything so far has been. In date order from earliest to most recent."

"Even so, it could be on a Greatest Hits record or even covered by another artist."

"That's like searching for a needle in a haystack of vinyl records. It could take forever. I don't think Uncle Sebastian was the sort to buy Greatest Hits compilations."

"Maybe he bought Dylan on cd. Maybe the clue's hidden inside one of his plastic cd cases."

"Hope not, there are even more of them, although I've had a quick look. Most are classical music."

Emily took the book from Al, feeling the weight, pondering the secrets it may contain. "What do you think it might be?"

"Difficult to say. Sebastian was a historian so it could be his take on an ancient or medieval civilisation, written in number code to protect his thesis. I don't know. It's something exclusive to him or his name wouldn't be written formally on top. Maybe it's a diary or a memo pad and the numbers are hiding nothing more than shopping lists or old essays."

Emily drew a breath through gritted teeth. "You're a mathematician. Don't you know anything about codes?"

"So are you. A mathematician, I mean." A chuckle accompanied Al's riposte as he took a weighty swig of wine. He sat back, sinking into the leather sofa before making a pronouncement that sent a rush of anticipation surging up Emily's spine. "I know what sort of code it is."

"Really, that's great."

"At least I think I do." He took another sip of wine and Emily wondered whether the alcohol was talking.

"Go on." Her tone eager.

"A book code."

"If that's all you've got to say, then it's getting late and …"

"No, I don't think you understand. Most codes need a key. Some work by replacing the letters of the alphabet with a letter which comes further up the alphabet."

"Such as."

"I'll show you." Al grabbed a pen lying on the coffee table and pulled an old paper receipt from his pocket. He proceeded to write the letters of the alphabet in a single row. When he'd finished he said, "Choose a number between one and ten."

"Seven," said Emily.

"That's what's called the rotation amount. So now we start writing one to seven underneath the letters of the alphabet and when we get to seven we start using letters again starting with A, writing out the alphabet once more. When we get to Z, we go to the beginning of the alphabet line above this one and continue filling in letters until we've written the entire alphabet."

"I'm confused."

"You won't be. Watch."

34

Al proceeded to write until he came up with four rows.

"Voila."

Emily stared at the rows.

"Let's write something," said Al.

"What?"

"Anything. How about?" Al tore off a piece of paper, studied the rows of letters, before scribbling a message, handing it to Emily.

She unfolded the paper to reveal B EBDX TE.

"Gobbledygook," said Emily.

"That's the point. It's the sort of code kids use to write secret messages to each other. All it requires is for the writer and receiver to work from the same alphabet key."

"What does it mean?"

Al set down the four rows. "If we look at the top line of the bottom two lines, then, B becomes I, E becomes L, and so on until we have ..." Ten seconds later he had unravelled the encoding.

I LIKE AL

Emily threw a guarded look that melted into a coy smile.

Al explained. "Problem with such a simple code is that it's easy to crack by searching for repeated patterns. You can make it more complicated by changing the spacing and sections so those patterns don't stick out so easily but, to be honest, it wouldn't fool even an amateur codebreaker."

"But Uncle Sebastian's book is all numbers, not letters."

"That's why I think it may be a book code. I'm not being facetious. The numbers correspond to page numbers, line numbers, the position of the word on the line. So each group of numbers identify a different word or maybe even a letter. The key is the book. If you have the same book as the writer of the code, then reading the message is easy."

"How do you know so much about codes?"

Al drained his wine glass. "Did you ever watch *The Wire*?"

"No."

"I was fascinated by it as a teenager. It's a box-set about drug dealers and police trying to catch them by listening in to their phone calls. The drug guys came up with all sorts of clever telephone codes to try to elude the police and it appealed to me. Got me interested in the concept of encrypting and deciphering. I even went for a day out at Bletchley Park."

"That's where they cracked the Enigma Code. I've heard of that. I watched the film. *The Imitation Game*, with Benedict Cumberbatch." Emily looked delighted to have made a contribution.

"That was down to Alan Turing, the greatest code breaker of them all. A mathematician like us, yet the man most responsible for the defeat of Nazi Germany in the Second Word War. After Winston Churchill maybe. You should go to Bletchley Park. It's exactly as it was during wartime with all the massive old computers and codebreaking equipment. Looks primitive compared to technology these days but Turing's genius was identifying the puzzle and eventually understanding it. That's all we have to do with Sebastian's book."

"You make it sound easy."

"It will be, once we find the key."

"How do we do that?"

"If I'm right, then it has something to do with Dylan and that song title. If it's not in a record sleeve or a cd, and the chances are it isn't, because the sheer weight of numbers suggests sophisticated vocabulary has been used, then it must be a book. A weighty book at that. Maybe there's a Bob Dylan biography in his collection. A history of rock or protest music. Only way to find out is to search the entire collection."

Emily puffed her cheeks, expelling a slow, steady stream of breath. "That could take some time, especially if we're not sure what we're looking for. There must be more than two thousand books. It could take weeks."

"I don't think there's an alternative if you want to crack the code."

Al had gained Emily's attention. Cataloguing Uncle Sebastian's artefacts and belongings could wait. A puzzle required solving, one that appealed to Emily's world of order.

"I'll start tomorrow," she said, rising abruptly from the settee, leaving Al in no doubt the evening was complete.

"Want some help? I'm on early rota the rest of the week. I'll be done at the café by early afternoon." An awkward pause ensued.

"No thanks," said Emily, slicing through the silence. "Think I can take it from here."

"If you're sure."

They walked through to the hallway and Emily contemplated taking Al into the study to reveal the details of that morning's delivery of *The Grapes of Wrath*. She decided against it. It had nothing to do with Bob Dylan and she concluded one puzzle was enough to share with a comparative stranger. Instead, she led Al to the front door.

"Thanks for dinner and the wine."

"No problem. My pleasure. If you change your mind about needing help you know where I live. And work, for that matter."

Emily shut the door and headed for the study and Uncle Sebastian's bookcase.

7

A stiff breeze blew off the English Channel, tugging and wrenching at the marquee beach structures housing angled lines of folded deckchairs. Emily sauntered past them in search of a bakery.

The crooked finger on the promenade's Queen Victoria memorial clock was ticking towards 10am. Yet Weymouth's grey brigade already massed in force, old ladies and flat-capped gentlemen huddled together in their natural habitat on long walled benches or under protective shelters, watching the tide roll in. A sand artist braved stinging grains while completing a sculpture of a sailing ship beyond the high-tide mark. Emily marvelled at the detail.

Moving on, she spotted a bread shop and bought one of her favourite sourdough baguettes, adding a custard-dripping vanilla slice at the last moment. Sifting through Uncle Sebastian's bookcase into the early hours in search of anything Dylanesque proved tiring, especially as nothing of note materialised. She required an energy fix.

As she retraced her steps, swinging a plastic shopping bag, a sudden gust lassoed a toddler's sun hat, sending it tumbling towards the sea wall. Emily thrust out a foot to trap the hat, scooped it up and handed it to the child's mother, who conveyed her gratitude with a distracted smile while juggling the squirming toddler.

"Nice save." A man's voice.

Emily spun around. "Oh, hello." Her tone warm and friendly at seeing Marcus's familiar face. "I almost didn't recognise you without your gardening gear." Marcus wore a pair of khaki shorts, blue and white hooped tee-shirt and trainers. His legs looked tanned and strong, knobbly knees protruding, calf muscles twitching as he stretched. In good shape for sixty-something, which is where the needle alighted on Emily's age predictor.

"My morning walk," explained Marcus. "Forty-five minutes along the sea front and another forty-five back, depending on wind direction. Every day, without fail. Brisk as I can. Keeps me fit, especially as all I do most days is stare at the computer or watch the boats in the bay out of my study window. Everything okay at the bungalow?"

"Yes, lovely. I've started cataloguing Uncle Sebastian's records and books. Not sure I appreciated quite how many he'd collected."

Marcus chuckled. "Books were his life. He loved them. Always said they were precious gifts he could open, enjoying again and again. The sort of gift that keeps on giving. I suppose he's right if you like reading. I know he was devastated after the burglary."

"Burglary?" This was news to Emily. She was sure her mother would have mentioned a break-in.

"Three or four years ago, I can't remember exactly." Marcus sensed Emily's surprise and appeared reluctant to continue.

"Go on," she urged.

A resigned sigh from Marcus before he continued. "Sebastian was in Cambridge at the time which is why I got to know first. I called the police after spotting one of the sliding doors wide open one January morning. I'd gone to check on the place, which I did every other day when he was away. Rain was slicing into the kitchen, leaves and debris everywhere. It was obvious someone had broken in."

"What did they take?" Emily dragged strands of flyaway hair from her face. Marcus ushered her to the road-side of one of the shelters.

"Bit calmer here. What did they take? Well, it must have been someone who knew about books and literature. Or at least knew the value of rare first editions. They stole five or six, all first editions, worth a tidy sum. Anywhere between two and ten grand apparently. They ignored everything else, even his computer and camera. Must have known what they were after."

"What were the books?"

"I don't recall, but I know they weren't insured. I'd told Sebastian to stick his valuable books in the safe but he said he'd bought them to enjoy, not lock them away in some dark place. To him they were like oil paintings. He was sure no-one would find them hidden in his huge collection. He was a bit embarrassed by it all. Somehow the story ended up in the local paper, I don't know how. Sebastian wasn't one for publicity."

"Were the books ever recovered?" Emily was intrigued. She'd regarded Sea View Road as the epicentre of mundanity, where nothing ever happened. Where Uncle Sebastian wiled away his sterile existence. Where the rhubarb crop ripening amounted to excitement. At least in her imagination.

Marcus shook his head. "Not that I know of. Sebastian told me he'd replaced a couple of the cheaper ones and I know he was always on the look-out to replace the rest but he was certain a professional had planned the burglary. Someone who knew about his collection and the value of rare editions, even ones not in mint condition. Mind you, sometimes he'd whisper out of the side of his mouth, 'What they don't know, Marcus, is that they missed the big one'."

"What was the big one?"

"No idea. I don't want to know, but if it's still there I'm sure you'll find it."

Marcus waved, breaking into a gentle jog as he bade farewell, Emily observing his lumpen gait with a quizzical expression as he proceeded along the promenade. *Don't sixty-somethings run funny. Short, over-exaggerated steps as if their shoes are filled with wet cement. Gasping for air like a captured trout.* Emily continued strolling, enjoying the sea air. She passed the café where Al worked and couldn't resist peering in, although her stride accelerated when she spied him carrying a tray, edging to the front of the shop.

Muscles burning as she climbed the steep, twisting road back to the bungalow, her mind whirred with questions around Dylan, records, books, first editions, codes, a cryptic note and a burglary. She needed time to rationalise the events in Sea View Road. Time to find the key to the code in the leather-bound volume, if that's what it was. She only had Al's opinion to consider and she'd known him precisely 24 hours. Didn't even know his surname. That bothered her. She didn't know why, but it did.

On arrival at Uncle Sebastian's she wedged a chunk of brie into the baguette, smeared on apple chutney, brewed a cup of instant coffee and stared at the bookcase as she ate. Her late-night session had eliminated almost a quarter of the books on display. The meticulous nature of Uncle Sebastian's filing made it tempting to skip sections that appeared to have nothing to do with Dylan. But she didn't, instead slipping each book off the shelf, studying the front and back covers and either erasing them from her search or placing them in a stand-by pile for further inspection. That pile amounted to two books, neither filling Emily with confidence.

Meal complete, she set to work. Many young women would have found the task boring. Not Emily. She bathed in the repetitive, rhythmic motion of handling the books, enjoying the different textures, studying, dismissing and replacing each one with care so they formed a Zen-inducing line on the shelf. She contemplated photographing and cataloguing them individually but reasoned it would double the workload. There would be time for that later.

As she worked she listened to the radio, singing along. Four engrossing, if unrewarding, hours flew by. Mid-afternoon surfaced before she took a break, grabbing a fizzy drink from the fridge. She stood by the sliding glass doors, spirits soaring at the deep blue vision of sky and sea as the hot sun streamed in. Two robins were feuding for possession of an apple tree, while in the distance a large industrial-looking boat edged through the harbour entrance. A figure caught her eye in the adjoining garden. The bare-chested figure of a young man. Al.

His shirt flapped in a knot around his waist as he worked his way up the vegetable plot, hoeing out weeds and re-staking plants. He wasn't big-boned, around six feet, slim, thin even, but with well-defined muscles suggesting he took pride in his physicality. His stomach flat as a spade blade, rippling with tension, the hairs on his chest and belly dark and damp with effort. She'd not expected this. She knew he was intelligent with a sharp wit and a nose for numerical puzzles. But as he paused, wiping his forehead with the back of his wrist before bending to lob a clump of weeds into a wheelbarrow, perhaps for the first time in her life she was drawn to a man in a way she could not have anticipated. It was never like this with Blake. She watched Al, entranced, at the same time fighting exciting, yet alien feelings.

Taking a swig of her drink, delighting in the refreshing fizz, she backed away from the window, but as she turned Al caught sight of her. He waved, a jolly gesture accompanied by the warmest of smiles. Emily almost dropped the can. Her cheeks flushed red. A gawky nod proved all she could muster before averting her eyes and scuttling into the study where she slumped on the captain's chair behind the desk to compose herself.

Her gaze alighted on the box containing the book Al had delivered, *The Grapes of Wrath*.

"I wonder," she muttered to herself. "Only one way to find out."

She set the book alongside the leather-bound volume on the desk. Her heart began to thump. *Use the Wrath (wisely).* Those were the words on the compliments slip. The more Emily repeated the phrase, the more it sounded like a clue. Yes, that must be it. The book must be the clue, or the *key* as Al described it, to unlocking the code in the leather-bound journal.

She switched on the angle-poised lamp on the desk, illuminating the numbers in the journal to her left, with *The Grapes of Wrath* to her right.

24-19-7. The first number. If Al was correct, that corresponded to page twenty-four, nineteenth line down, seventh word across. She flicked over pages, tracking her way to the word using her forefinger. *Wonder*. She felt a rush of blood. This was exciting. She repeated the process, carefully selecting each digit, trawling to the relevant position, writing each word on a scrap of paper. After a dozen words or so she picked up the paper, held it to the light and muttered the words out loud:

Wonder right the for never ended whose when building given if can

She stared at the paper for several seconds before returning to the numbers for an hour or more, reversing the pages, lines and words, exploring different combinations. Still no luck. Shaking her head, she screwed up the paper and dropped it in the waste bin.

8

"What's your surname?" Emily held the front door ajar barely wide enough to accommodate her head and the question.

Al filled the doorway. He held up a bottle of cloudy liquid with a green label and a screw top, his eyebrows almost colliding as he pondered the request. "I thought you might enjoy a late afternoon lemonade, cool you down after a busy day."

"What is it?"

"Sicilian lemonade."

"No, not that, your surname."

"Andrews. Alex Andrews. Is this Weymouth's version of the Spanish Inquisition?"

"Thank you. It occurred to me that I'd invited you in, had a meal, spent an evening with you and didn't even know who you are, apart from the guy from the local cafe."

"Well, you know now, although I could have said Andrew Alexandra and you wouldn't have been any wiser."

"I suppose not." Emily stepped aside, allowing Al to enter. As he passed she scented eucalyptus and coconut. Shower gel and shampoo, she surmised. Maybe even a dab of after-shave. They traipsed through to the kitchen and Emily reached into a cupboard, placing two glasses on the worktop. Al poured generous measures of lemonade and they sipped while watching the sky turn red as the sun dipped towards the horizon.

"Good afternoon in the garden?" Emily felt compelled to admit she'd seen Al working, if only to flush away any residual embarrassment.

"A couple of hours, that's all," said Al. "Tidied up a bit. How are you getting on with the cataloguing?"

"Okay."

"What about the search for Dylan? Any luck?"

Emily shook her head. "Came across a couple of books about the history of music but they concentrate on the rise of the great classical composers."

"Sure you wouldn't like a hand?"

Emily's brow furrowed. She wanted to say no, to solve the puzzle by herself. It was rapidly becoming an obsession. A family mission. She'd barely thought of anything else over the past 36 hours. But there were so many books, so many records, while she knew nothing of codes, even less about rock music in the 1960s, and she was looking at someone who did.

"If you like," she said softly with a slight roll of the eyes.

"Don't sound so excited." Al's sarcasm went unheeded.

"I'll show you where I'm up to."

For the next two hours they searched the rest of Uncle Sebastian's collection, Emily continuing from where she'd left off while Al started at the end and worked backwards. The possible pile grew to four books, although that owed more to Al's curiosity in the rise of Motown music than puzzle solving.

Al stepped back to assess how many books remained unchecked. "Time for a break. Only about two hundred to go."

"Let's carry on and get it done." A rasp of frustration in Emily's tone.

"Better to take a short break. We don't want to miss anything. Easy to become word blind looking at all these books. Any beer in the fridge?"

"Help yourself." Emily slid out more books while Al searched for beer. He returned with a bag of crisps and two opened bottles of lager, offering one to Emily as she descended a pair of stepladders she'd been using to locate books on the top shelves. As she reached over her weight transferred and the bottom rung of the ladder wobbled. She almost fell, probably would have done if she hadn't braced herself against Al's shoulder. For a brief moment they clinched, Emily hanging on, sensing powerful muscles, feeling the heat of his body as Al lifted her off the steps with his free arm, returning her to solid ground as a ballroom dancer might set down a partner.

"Easy does it. Most girls take at least two sips before they fall for me." A teasing lilt in Al's voice.

"Well, I'm not most girls and I'd like to get through this lot tonight. So ten minutes only." Emily pushed free of his hold, sounding calm and pragmatic. Cold even. But her cheeks flushed.

They sipped beer and constructed small talk, mostly about music, before Emily decided to reveal what she'd discovered about the book Al delivered the previous day. *The Grapes of Wrath*. A shrewd calculation. If Al were to prove useful, he needed to know all the facts. The book wasn't the only key to solving the leather-bound puzzle. She had already ascertained that much, but it still seemed significant considering Uncle Sebastian appeared to have organised its delivery to arrive weeks after he'd passed away. She reached inside the top drawer of the desk and handed the book to Al.

"What's this?"

"It was in the box you delivered. I think it might have some relevance to our puzzle." Al said nothing but noted the word "*our*". Apparently, he was on the team. Emily's team, although he harboured misgivings, the main one being he didn't see Emily as a team player. He inspected the book from various angles before flicking open the pages.

"What's so interesting?"

Emily reached inside the drawer and handed the compliments slip to Al. His expression hovered between bewilderment and excitement.

"What do you make of this?" he said.

"I was hoping you might have a few ideas."

"If you are reading this I must be gone." Al read the first part of the slip out loud, slowly, letting the words sink in. His eyes darted around the room as if seeking inspiration. "Does he mean gone, as in left Sea View Road, or gone, as in dead."

"I wondered that too. I'm pretty certain he means the second."

"How did he die?"

"Heart attack, I think. At least that's what Dad said the doctors had concluded. It was all a bit hazy, we hadn't been in touch that much recently. Why?"

"Probably nothing. He was in his eighties and heart attacks are common causes of death in the elderly. A heart attack at that age is unlikely to raise any suspicions ..." Al trailed off, as if reluctant to pursue his line of thought.

"What do you mean?"

"If someone wanted to kill an old man and get away with it, a heart attack would do nicely, don't you think?"

"What? Why would anyone want to kill Uncle Sebastian?" Emily slumped into the chair on the opposite side of the desk, her mind and heart hammering, this time for different reasons. Her tone tingled with astonishment.

"I've no idea. Maybe we're jumping to conclusions."

"Maybe you are."

"Maybe the note is so cryptic we're miles off base," said Al, attempting to row back a fraction on his revelation. "But it sounds that either he was seriously ill and knew he had little time left or maybe he knew his life was in danger. The clue might be in the book. *Use the Wrath (wisely)*. That reads like a clue. A book code clue perhaps."

"I've already checked it with the leather volume." Emily had regained her composure, pleased to appear a step ahead of Al.

"And?"

"Nothing. I matched up the numbers with pages, lines and the position of words on lines, in lots of different combinations, as you explained. None of it matches. It read like gobbledygook."

"Mind if I check?"

"You won't find anything." Emily's jaw jutted, a glint of fire in her eyes. She wasn't accustomed to being challenged on the precision of her work where numbers were concerned.

"I'm sure you're right," said Al. "But it doesn't hurt to double check, does it?"

For the next few minutes Al matched the numbers in the leather journal with the words in *The Grapes of Wrath,*

47

registering identical gobbledygook to Emily the evening before. He held up his piece of paper to show her.

She almost said, *I told you so*, but heard her mother's distant advice. *No-one gains from a phrase which rubs someone's face in the dirt for no good reason.* Instead, Emily said, "Well, fancy that."

"Maybe an explanation lies in the leather volume. Let's finish checking the rest of the books." Al jumped up from the captain's chair, Emily detecting genuine eagerness in his desire to share her mission. They worked with renewed vigour over the next couple of hours, pumping books in and out of the shelves to an efficient rhythm until they met at the inevitable rendezvous point.

Emily looked at Al, deflation in her eyes. "That's it. All done. No obvious sign of anything to do with Dylan."

"What about these?" said Al, pointing to the half-dozen books in the possible pile.

They sat at the desk again, double checking each title. After half an hour Al snapped the last one shut. "That's disappointing. I was sure we'd find something useful."

"What now?" asked Emily.

"How about the cd cases?"

"Done that. I looked this afternoon. If anything they're arranged even more tightly than the books. All in alphabetical order by artist. There's no Dylan."

Al drummed his fingers on the desk. "Hmm. Maybe it's got nothing to do with Dylan."

"But you said …"

"I'm not an expert, Emily. Dylan was a theory, that's all. Code breaking's not an exact science."

"Yes, it is, that's the whole point. That's why it's all about numbers, patterns, recurring trends, laws and principles. I've been reading up about it. It's about logic." Her tone shrill, laced with wavers of disappointment.

"Logic will get you from A to B, as a great man once said. Einstein, I think. But imagination will take you everywhere." Al slouched back in the chair, arms forming wing-like shapes behind his head, as if he'd imparted a nugget of vital information.

"What the hell does that mean?"

"It means solving puzzles is not only about science, logic and analysis. Sometimes it has as much to do with art. Codes are exact with definite laws and principles when you find the key, but first you have to discover the entrance. That can be as much about experience and intuition as science."

Emily rolled her eyes. "Dylan doesn't sound too intuitive now, does it?"

"No, I agree, so let's look at the clue again."

"What do you mean?"

"The contents of the leather volume haven't changed. The numbers still point to a book code. And if the book is in this bookcase then we know it has nothing to do with Dylan. So we do know something we didn't know yesterday."

"Not to jump to conclusions about song titles?"

"Bit harsh. It was a perfectly logical suggestion. Maybe the clue, The answer is blowing in the wind, was designed to confuse. Maybe Sebastian wanted to protect the key from the casual observer. Perhaps we, I mean I, fell into the obvious trap. What an idiot." Al's tone was soft and measured. He looked at Emily, expecting reassurance. It never came.

"So if the answer isn't Dylan, what is it?" Emily sounded pragmatic, disappointment wiped clean, mind focused on a fresh path.

"Not sure," said Al. "First, let's eat. I'm starving. It's nearly ten o'clock. I need food to think. I don't class crisps as food."

"I've nothing much in."

"I saw eggs in the fridge and there are tomatoes and cheese. How about an omelette? My mother taught me to cook omelettes. They're a specialty in the Andrews household. Fancy one?"

"Don't mind if I do." Emily's eyes sparkled.

They decamped to the kitchen, Al rummaging in the cupboards for a frying pan and olive oil, while Emily found some soft mushrooms at the back of the fridge, part of Marcus's welcome provisions.

"You wash them, I'll chop tomatoes. How about another beer?" said Al.

Emily pulled two more lagers from the fridge. She snapped off the tops with an opener, sliding a bottle across the worktop towards Al. After she'd washed the mushrooms she leaned back against the wall, sipping cold beer, watching Al work, beating eggs. An intimate domesticity descended on the kitchen, one Emily found strange but relaxing. She felt comfortable in the company of this comparative stranger, who wielded a carving knife with graceful efficiency and easy confidence. More than that, she felt warm and excited.

The eggs hit the hot pan with an inviting sizzle. "Smells good already. How come you learned to cook so young?" asked Emily.

"In Latvia, cooking is an essential art. I'm an only child. I spent many hours with my mother in the kitchen. My father was away working. You soak in the skills at an early age. Cooking was a natural part of my upbringing. My mother taught me to experiment, not to be scared of ditching the recipe book, to be curious about food and people."

"What did you cook?"

"Meat soups and stews mainly, they are big in Latvia. But I also learned to bake cakes, bread and savoury pastries."

"Do you cook in the café?"

Al laughed. "If you call sticking panini in a grill for eight minutes and slipping them inside a greaseproof bag cooking, then yes, I'm a master chef when it comes to fast food, although I don't think my mum would be impressed."

"I'm an only child too, but cooking wasn't on my agenda as a kid." This new territory energised Emily. Rarely did she have the opportunity, audience or inclination to reveal personal stuff. But in Al's company it spilled out naturally, without fishing or coaxing. She told him about her fascination with music. About wearing headphones wherever she went as a teenager. How she could recite lyrics verbatim from a multitude of genres, even if her classmates decided she was odd. About her love of the ocean which saw her standing on the sea wall at Felixstowe on special occasions, along with her father, marvelling at the mammoth cranes dispensing cargo from huge container ships.

"It appealed to my sense of order. I loved seeing thousands of tin boxes stacked high and handsome, like a giant game of jenga, pretending what would happen if a crucial one became inadvertently dislodged. Made me shiver, just thinking about it."

Emily even told him about her childhood passion for noting car registrations, the first time she could remember divulging such information. She'd never told Blake. Their conversations had been shallow and frivolous. As they chatted, a delicious smell, warming and inviting, floated in the ambient air. Al fussed over his creation, ensuring it didn't burn, tossing on a few more herbs. Emily had to agree Al's work of art looked professional as well as tasty.

When it was done they sat either side of the kitchen island, Al halving and dishing up the omelette, only to throw a glance of disdain as Emily immediately reached for the tomato ketchup, proceeding to splatter bloody globules all around her plate. Al contemplated a sarcastic remark about the Valentine Day's massacre, but gritted his teeth instead, wondering what possessed Emily to napalm good food with sugar and vinegar.

"Mmm, lovely," said Emily.

"Seen much of Weymouth yet," said Al, diverting the conversation from food.

Emily recalled meeting Marcus that morning on the promenade and admitted seeing Al in the café.

"Spying on me," said Al.

"Hardly." Emily looked up sharply.

"I'm joking."

"You're always joking."

"No, I'm not. I'm deadly serious about cooking and genuinely keen to discover what this leather volume's all about. Sebastian obviously loved his books. I get the impression he would have guarded them with his life."

"Yes, pity he wasn't around when he was burgled."

"Pardon. What burglary?" Al paused, balancing food on his fork, half-way to its destination.

Emily proceeded to divulge her conversation with Marcus that morning. When she finished Al's tone was earnest.

51

"Let me get this straight. Half a dozen books, all first editions, were stolen, but we don't know which ones?"

"That's what Marcus said."

"This could be the reason we've struck out, Emily. Maybe the book we're searching for, the one that's the key, was stolen. Maybe it has something to do with Dylan after all."

"But Marcus had no idea what the books were."

"No, but if the story was in the local paper, perhaps they were mentioned at the time. Maybe Marcus has just forgotten."

"It was three or four years ago. Marcus wasn't even certain about the date"

"Doesn't matter. All newspapers in the UK are archived. A legal requirement. I shouldn't imagine any local newspapers actually keep their own editions for any length of time. Too costly to store and definitely too expensive to employ someone to scan every page."

"So where are they kept?" Emily's tone signalled respect. She found Al's impressive knowledge on a range of subjects annoying and appealing in equal measure.

"The British Library."

"In London?"

"Not exactly. An edition of every newspaper in print form is kept in Wetherby in Yorkshire. But you can read them in the British Library at St Pancras if you ask nicely. Someone actually roots through a forest of newsprint in a vast warehouse, puts the relevant editions on a lorry and delivers them to London. All free of charge. One of those quaint traditions that could probably only happen in Britain."

"How do you know all this?"

"Because I did work experience at the library in St Pancras for a month years ago before going to university. A bit boring, but I picked up some useful information."

A furrow appeared on Emily's forehead. "How do we ask nicely?"

Al pulled out his mobile phone. "When did Marcus think the burglary happened?"

"As I said, three or four years ago, he couldn't be certain."

"Any clue what time of year?"

"January, he seemed sure about that."

"Great." Al held up one hand to pause the conversation while proceeding to tap and scroll on his phone with the other. After a minute or so, he pronounced, "All done."

"What's all done?"

"I've registered on the British Library website, requesting to read all copies of the Dorset Echo for the month of January three and four years ago."

"It's that simple?"

"Yeah. Monday. British Library reading room. St Pancras. One o'clock. All we need is our ID. That suit you?"

Emily's mind whirred. She didn't understand people who acted on impulse. The only time she'd done so she'd lost her job and her boyfriend. Normally, she weighed actions and consequences, sifted problems for days, weeks sometimes, preferring to live via mathematical theorems and formulae, always with a definitive conclusion. But Al possessed energy, a cavalier nature as well as a natural and persuasive gift for sweeping people to destinations they could never have envisaged. Even Emily.

"Yes, that's good," she said. "We'll take my car."

9

The thought of six hours in a confined space with someone, even as easy-going as Al, had concerned Emily. What if the conversation dried up? What if they broke down? What if she couldn't stand him for so long?

She needn't have worried. The only problem on the drive to London was a traffic jam to allow a flock of sheep to cross a country lane somewhere between Dorchester and Poole. Al chattered about music and the politics of the café while Emily kept hauling the conversation back to the job in hand.

"I do hope it's all worth it and we learn a bit more about Uncle Sebastian," said Emily.

"It will be. If today throws up nothing useful then at least we've eliminated an avenue of investigation. Tied up a loose end. We can concentrate on another direction."

"Like what?"

"No idea, but I'm sure we'll think of something."

When they reached London, Emily felt on familiar ground, having lived in Highgate for much of her life. She identified side roads to dodge the worst of the traffic, knew a metered rank behind King's Cross station to park, allowing them to arrive at the British Library with 10 minutes to spare. They even had time to pause in the piazza in front of the building to peruse the statue of a naked Isaac Newton sitting on a ledge, leaning forward measuring something with a pair of compasses.

"What's that all about?" said Emily, her nose wrinkling in consternation.

"No idea, my work experience didn't stretch to works of art."

They ambled in. A middle-aged librarian with a kind face and serene disposition, forged from half a lifetime assisting the unknowing and unaware, checked their IDs. She supplied them with a reader card and led them through to a reading room containing rows of back-to-back desks serviced by individual strip lights. An ambient odour of wood polish filled the air. Al and Emily sat alongside each other, opposite a sharp-suited man with tightly-coiffured silver hair. Al decided he had the demeanour of a Volvo car salesman. They assessed each other exchanging furtive glances while the librarian disappeared down a corridor. She returned a few minutes later with a colleague, each carrying a box labelled *Dorset Echo January to March*, one dated three years ago, the other four.

"Take your pick." Al motioned for Emily to grab a box. She slid the one with the older label onto her desk top. Al did the same with the other.

"It had to be a daily paper, didn't it?" said Emily.

A rueful smile lit up Al's face. "I think they call that Sod's Law. A weekly paper would have meant looking through four editions. Instead we've got around 25 or 26 papers in each box and the same Sod's Law probably means the story we're searching for is towards the end of January."

For the next two hours, they waded through Dorset news, quickly realising they could exclude sports pages, as well as display and classified advertising spreads. Yet every other page received meticulous attention. There were no clues. The editor may have designed the story in question in bold headlines, complete with eye-catching illustrations, or it could be a news filler, buried at the bottom of a briefs column.

Al was ready for a coffee break when he heard Emily emit a short squeal. Volvo man threw a disapproving look. Al ignored him, glancing sideways to see Emily grasping the paper, dated January 18th, in both hands. She leaned over until her nose almost touched the desk as she digested a story running down the first column of page three. Her hands shook, agitated expression borne of pure excitement.

"I've found it. Al, I've found it. See." Her finger traced the five decks of headline.

Gone
with
the
book
thief

"Let me see." Al snatched the paper, reading the intro out loud.

Police were hunting for a book thief today after five rare editions were stolen from a collection at a house in Sea View Road, Weymouth.

The article described the theft as *professional*, the stolen books estimated to be worth in excess of £20,000. No mention of Uncle Sebastian, although it revealed the owner, a university professor, was away from home at the time.

Al scanned the rest of the story, alighting on the titles and author names of the five stolen books.

The Grapes of Wrath by John Steinbeck
Sons and Lovers by D. H. Lawrence
A Farewell to Arms by Ernest Hemingway
The Mayor of Casterbridge by Thomas Hardy
Gone with the Wind by Margaret Mitchell

Al gasped, gazing at Emily, who was also on her feet. He raised an open palm. "High-five!"

Emily looked perplexed. High-fiving hadn't figured in Emily's upbringing. She was aware of the concept, but had always shied away when her schoolmates indulged in a practice she deemed brash, pointless and unseemly. But as Al's palm dangled, she went for it, palms smashing together in a whip-cracking clap that echoed around the room.

They laughed. Startled heads turned. Volvo man's face a curious shade of purple. "Excuse me. Some of us are trying to study."

Al muttered placatory apologies, making a calming gesture with both hands before reaching for his phone to photograph the article. "That should do it. Only five books, not six as Marcus thought. Let's get out of here."

They bundled the papers back into the boxes and strode to the reception desk, critical glances tracking them all the way.

"Thanks for your help." As they left Al called out to the librarian, prompting a smile of practiced serenity that accompanied them to the exit.

Once outside, Emily blinked back the harsh sunlight, digging in her rucksack for sunglasses while Al guided her to a wooden bench on the side of the piazza. Al studied the article once more on his phone. "Now we know why

Sebastian ordered The Grapes of Wrath. It obviously meant a lot to him."

"All the books must have been precious."

"And I think we might have the answer to our conundrum." Al paused to allow his words to sink in.

"What do you mean?"

He pointed to the last book mentioned in the article: *Gone with the Wind.* "I was wrong about Dylan, but the clue fits with one of the books on the list. Remember the clue in the leather journal?" He didn't wait for a reply. "The answer is blowing in the wind. Emily. Sounds like we've found the book we're searching for."

"You may be right this time, but we still don't have it. It's not in Uncle Sebastian's collection. It's such a famous book and film, I would definitely remember having come across it during the last week. Why would Uncle Sebastian leave a clue to a book he no longer owned? It doesn't make sense."

Al thought for a moment, watching people trek in and out of the library. He knew Emily was right. The point of a numbered book code relies on it corresponding completely with the key, leaving nothing to chance. If the stolen version of *Gone with the Wind* was key to Sebastian's journal then they would need to acquire the correct edition from the right year, one published in the same country and printed to the same exact specifications.

"I have an idea." Al offered a hand to help Emily up from the bench. She declined.

"Go on."

"Let's take a ride across town."

They trudged back along Euston Road, turned left beyond King's Cross where they'd parked the car, all the while Emily listening to Al's plan.

10

Half an hour later they walked into a small, quaint shop in an attractive side street off Chelsea's King's Road. A bell tinkled as they pushed through the door, reminding Al of a scene in a Dickens novel. *The Old Curiosity Shop* came to mind. Stuffy atmosphere. Musty smell. Books lining shelves floor to ceiling. Behind the counter a sign proclaimed:

Carringtons of Chelsea for the discerning reader.

They waited a short time at the counter until a portly man appeared from the rear of the shop. He wore wire-rim round spectacles. Emily thought his bald pate made him look like a Franciscan monk.

He rested his knuckles on the counter. "How can I help?"

"Mr Carrington?" said Al.

"Yes."

"We're looking for a rare first edition for one of your most loyal customers." The man nodded, intrigued.

"Who might that be?"

"Professor Sebastian Stearn of Corpus Christie College, Cambridge University." Al's detailed introduction was designed to impress and Mr Carrington's beam suggested the ruse succeeded.

"Oh yes, we know Professor Stearn very well. Or, should I say, knew. Splendid gentleman. Always treated books like works of art?"

"Knew?" said Al, surprised the shopkeeper had heard of Sebastian's demise.

"Yes, passed away last month. His obituary got a mention in *The Times.*"

Al motioned to Emily. "This is the professor's niece, Emily Stearn. She's helping to administer his estate. We have a couple of questions about his book collection, if you don't mind."

For a moment Mr Carrington sounded flustered before recovering his equilibrium. "I'm sorry. I didn't realise you were family. Commiserations. Like I said, he was a splendid fellow. Only too happy to help. What would you like to know?"

Al cleared his throat, preparing a gentle question about the delivery of *The Grapes of Wrath,* when Emily piped up. "I'd like to know why you sent a book to him two weeks after his death."

Mr Carrington's smile disappeared, replaced by a light cloud of suspicion. He fiddled with his bow tie and Al swiftly intervened. "What Emily means is that we were slightly perplexed to receive The Grapes of Wrath in the post with a compliments slip inside containing a note from Sebastian. I'm sure there's a simple explanation."

"Ah." The shop owner's mouth stayed agape and for a couple of seconds he appeared deep in thought. "I think I know. Let me get this straight." He slid open a wooden drawer underneath the counter, pulled out a hard-back ledger and flicked open the pages. "We do most things on computer these days, but I also like to keep a record of the rare first editions in my special book. I remember my wife telling me the professor had asked for The Grapes of Wrath. She deals with the administration. Must have been a month or two ago. He spoke to her on the telephone and said something about replacing a book he'd lost in a burglary. Had to be the exact same edition. I noted the request down here." Mr Carrington pointed to an indecipherable squiggle.

Emily mouthed to say something but Al deftly cut in. "How long did it take to source?"

"No time."

"Pardon."

"We had one in stock. Steinbeck novels are popular in the first edition world. Quite a lot around. They're not as expensive as some. As I recall it wasn't in mint condition but the professor was more concerned about it being the correct edition. We took a few days, maybe more, to spruce it up and repair some of the damage."

Emily interjected. "What about the compliments slip. It was from Uncle Sebastian himself. Isn't that unusual."

"Not necessarily," said Mr Carrington, guard restored. "The order was taken over the phone, paid for via credit card and the professor had a special request. A personal request."

"Go on." Al and Emily in unison.

"He dictated the message to my wife but stipulated the book hadn't to be posted to his address until after his death."

"What?" Emily looked bewildered.

"More to the point. Why?" said Al.

Mr Carrington extended palms upwards in a gesture of bemusement. "The professor was quite specific. I've learned not to question the customer when it comes to special requests, as long as everything is legal, above board, and within the bounds of decency. He told my wife he'd instructed the undertakers, Cotton & Son of Weymouth, to alert us to his passing. That's what happened."

"Thanks. You've been very helpful." Al nodded, almost bowing his gratitude, at the same time trying to compute Sebastian's reasoning.

He was poised to ask about the price of first editions when Mr Carrington studied his ledger again. He flicked back a page, his forefinger sliding down the entries. "What do you want me to do about this order for Gone with the Wind?"

Al and Emily's eyes flitted between themselves and Mr Carrington.

"When did he order that?" This time Emily sounded warm and friendly.

"Two months ago. Maybe a little more. Probably the same time he ordered The Grapes of Wrath. Been quite a job finding the right version of Gone with the Wind though. He wanted the first printing of the first American edition, containing the original publishing date: May, 1936. Found one eventually via an American collector in Belgravia. Not in great condition, but still had to pay a pretty price for it."

"You mean you've got it here?" said Emily.

"Yes, came in a couple of days ago. My wife was wondering what to do after hearing about the professor passing, but the collector is a good contact and there's never a problem getting rid of quality first editions."

"Can we see it?"

"I suppose so." He consulted a gold watch on a chain peeping from a pocket of his multi-coloured waistcoat. "Yes, I've got time. Not as if I'm rushed off my feet. Never am on a Monday. Wait here, I'll fetch it from the safe."

Mr Carrington waddled behind the bookshelves, through an archway into the back of the premises.

Al nudged Emily, whispering. "This could be the key."

Mr Carrington returned carrying the book in its original dust jacket, balanced on outstretched palms as if protecting a delicate artefact. He placed it on the counter.

"You don't see too many of these. Pity about the little dent in the spine, the staining on the dust cover. There's also slight water damage to some of the pages. Apart from that it's sound."

"How do you know for certain it's an original first edition?" Al's question appealed to Mr Carrington's professional standing. Experts rarely refuse an opportunity to demonstrate their expertise.

Mr Carrington flicked open the book to reveal the title page. He pointed to the date. 1936. "If there's no date the book is probably a book club edition, not an authentic first edition, especially if the date is written in Roman numerals. Those copies are no use to collectors. Virtually valueless."

Al interjected. "Excuse my ignorance, but what's the difference between a book club edition and an original?"

Mr Carrington presented the book, flicking through until alighting on the manuscript's final page. He pointed to the page number.

"One thousand and thirty-seven. Quite a weighty read," said Al.

"Yes, Margaret Mitchell took ten years to finish it. Her only novel, by the way. My point is that book club editions have half that many pages, arranged in double columns, in smaller fonts and they're printed on poor quality paper. A much inferior product."

Mr Carrington turned to the copyright page. "See, again it says published May, 1936. That's another crucial check." He flipped the book on to its back, pointing to faded writing in the right column on the rear panel of the dust jacket where several novels were promoted by the publishing company.

Al bent over, squinting to make out the words. He turned to look at Emily. "Says Gone with the Wind, all written in capitals. It's underneath a mention for another novel, South Riding, by Winifred Holtby."

"How much?" Emily's contribution was blunt, albeit the obvious next question.

Mr Carrington ran his tongue around his lips and sucked his teeth. "A first edition, first printing, like this, in pristine dust jacket signed by the author, with all the required provenance and the right buyer, no change from eighty thousand pounds."

Al let out a sharp whistle, while Emily was keen to chase to the bottom line. "But what about this one, worn, stained, no signature?"

Mr Carrington sighed, head rocking from side to side, assessing the damage and lack of signature. He wasn't to be rushed. "If signed and with a little tender care even this one could fetch twelve grand. As it is, I'd be looking for around four grand."

Al and Emily swapped doubtful glances. "So Professor Stearn hadn't paid up front for this one," said Al.

"No."

"Had he made any special request?"

"No, but any personal requests would probably have been made when paying for it over the phone. That's normal procedure."

"Can I ask one more question, Mr Carrington?" said Al.

"Of course."

"Had Sebastian ordered any other books in recent times? Any other first editions?"

Mr Carrington ran his finger down the ledger entries, flicking over half a dozen pages. "No, I didn't think so. I've gone back twelve months. Those are the only two he has ordered."

"Thank you," said Al, turning to leave, expecting Emily to follow. Instead, she asked a final question.

"Could you put the book to one side for me, Mr Carrington? I'd like to buy it please."

11

Emily studied her father who, in turn, studied Al. Harry's eyes glinted with suspicion and his daughter understood why.

She had turned up at her parents' home with a man they neither knew, nor recognised. Emily didn't make a habit of bringing men home, unless you counted the two occasions she'd entertained David from the sixth form, who recited mathematical theorems on the school bus. No-one counted David. Not even Emily. The only other male suitor had been Blake. It had taken her three months to pluck up enough courage to introduce him.

On top of that, Al hadn't shaved. Dark stubble blended with thick, black eyebrows and slightly unkempt hair to give him the appearance of a dodgy fairground worker. There was something else. Emily was asking for money, another thing she never did.

"Dad, it's for a couple of weeks, that's all. You'll get the cash back in full and there's no risk. It's a sound investment, one that Uncle Sebastian would be proud of."

Harry glanced at his wife, leaning over a coffee table, pouring tea from a China pot into four cups. Eleanor gave him one of her *She could always twist Harry around her little finger* looks.

On the drive from Chelsea, Emily had revealed her simple plan. Knock on Daddy's door, ask for £4,000, take the cash, or most likely cheque, to Carringtons of Chelsea, and return to Weymouth with the first edition copy of *Gone with the Wind*.

"Are you sure your dad will be up for that?" Al harboured reservations.

"Of course he will, he's in the publishing business. He'll know the money's safe."

"But we haven't a clue what's in the journal. That's if the book is the key to the code. We don't even know that for certain yet. Wouldn't it be better to take the journal to Carringtons to check if the code matches the words in the book first?"

"Do you fancy another trek from Weymouth to London?"

"No."

"Neither do I. The book has to be the key."

"We thought that about The Grapes of Wrath and all we came up with was gobbledygook." A cautious lilt infused Al's tone, but Emily's enthusiasm couldn't be dimmed.

"We don't know that for certain. Why would Uncle Sebastian stipulate The Grapes of Wrath should only be delivered after his death? There must be a reason. He was probably going to do the same with Gone with the Wind, but it didn't arrive in time. Another trip to London would waste time and if the book is a match then we'll need it for quite some time." Al couldn't argue with the logic, which is why he was happy to support her and brave the protective stare of a doting father. He was even prepared to advocate on her behalf.

"Mr Stearn, I've seen the journal. It's a beautiful work. Your uncle obviously put a huge amount of time and effort into it. We don't know what it contains, but you must admit it's intriguing." Harry stood up, stretching to his full 6ft 2ins, an imposing figure as he fixed Al with another piercing glare.

"Is the journal going anywhere?" The question was rhetorical but Harry answered it anyway. "I don't think so. Is it time sensitive? I don't think so. Have we a clue what's in it? It would appear not. Do I know you from Adam?"

Harry left the last question dangling. He could have added that another man had betrayed his daughter less than a month ago, but he didn't. Instead, his eyes skewered Al once more. "I could come up with a dozen more reasons why this all sounds a little dubious. For starters, why can't we catalogue the journal with the rest of Sebastian's belongings and decide what to do with it in our own time?"

"You could, of course you could. If you want to do that I'm sure Emily would be happy to wait, but …"

"But what?"

"The first edition at Carringtons is the one Sebastian ordered. It took more than two months to source. That wasn't by accident."

"What do you mean?"

Al allowed the ramifications of his intervention to sink in, before continuing. "Sebastian obviously knew what he wanted. He ordered a particular edition, a rare edition, down to a unique printing, specific to a particular month in 1936. He could have bought a book club printing for pennies, but chose the real thing because he was a classy guy and knew that would be identical to the one that was stolen four years ago. Only the identical book, from what would have been a small printing back then, is relevant."

"So you think this book at Carringtons will allow you to read the journal?"

Al nodded. "I won't lie, Mr Stearn, I can't be certain, but it does seem more than likely that the book holds the key."

On the journey from Chelsea, Al and Emily had agreed not to complicate matters by divulging the delivery of *The Grapes of Wrath*, nor to raise any sinister questions by revealing the note on the compliments slip. Best to focus on one book at a time, Emily reasoned.

Harry put his fist to his chin and rubbed in contemplation. He remained unconvinced.

Emily had listened in silence to Al's eloquence promoting her case, at the same time imploring her mother's support through sideways glances. But Harry still required a nudge in the right direction. Her voice contained a rasp of frustration. "You really can't lose, Dad. Four thousand is a fair price for the book. If you don't believe me, trust Uncle Sebastian. That's what he was prepared to pay. He'd placed the order. I think we should honour it in his memory."

Eleanor smiled. She was lounging on a settee, observing the act playing out in front of her. On a nearby table sat a childhood picture of Emily, hugging a teddy bear tight, her chocolatey face a study in defiant determination. She'd always possessed fire and fight, thought Eleanor. Seemingly happy to most observers, but troubled within, always at odds with the ordinary world, the sort of sinister nuance no caring mother could dismiss. As if a volcano shifted and rumbled deep inside. Eleanor realised her daughter was academically gifted with an obsessive talent for detail, but she had worried for her. Especially these past few weeks. Life could be cruel

66

for those positioned on the touchline of normality. To witness her holding court, composed, assured, in a mental arm twist with her father, was a delight. To see a friend who happened to be a man, if not actually a declared boyfriend, on her arm, watching in admiration, this was all Eleanor had hoped for.

Eleanor said, "Emily has a point, Harry."

"What?" Harry spun around to face his wife.

"Sebastian was meticulous in his work and passionate about his books. If this bookseller has spent time researching and sourcing material on his behalf, I think Sebastian would deem it only right that we honoured the deal. It's what he would have done. There's money in the estate to pay for it and if this bookseller can sell it for four thousand pounds, then why can't we do the same when Emily and this young gentleman have finished with it."

Al's thick eyebrows raised in expectation. Emily's mouth dropped open. For a few seconds, the room fell silent. Harry shook his head, before throwing up his arms. "All right, all right, I know when I'm beaten."

12

A white crescent moon, bright and tilted, as though a blustery wind had dislodged its mooring, glistened across the bay welcoming them back to Sea View Road.

Al glanced at his watch as they turned into the driveway at number seven. Almost 10.30pm. The day had proved exhausting. But as Emily stepped out of the car, she turned to grab a package from the back seat. A smile played on her lips. "Let's find out now, Al."

"It's late, Emily. We've been on the road fifteen hours. Better when we're fresh tomorrow."

"No, I can't wait. We have to know."

Al shook his head in resignation, much like Emily's father earlier that afternoon. Emily on a mission wouldn't rest, couldn't rest, until she had the answer. He traipsed after her into the bungalow.

They had retraced their steps after leaving Highgate, negotiating the late afternoon theatre traffic, arriving at Carringtons shortly before closing time. Mr Carrington's beaming grin signalled his pleasure at seeing them, the shop empty as before. Customers often persuaded Mr Carrington to reserve books and while their intentions appeared honourable, they rarely returned, the relentless rise and fall of everyday existence fraying the initial flush of enthusiasm. Bookshops in affluent Chelsea were not renowned for their bargains, but he had a feeling about this transaction. Something to do with Emily's passion and insistence on writing down her address and contact details.

"We'll be back," she'd said. Three-and-a half hours later they were, Harry's cheque in hand. When Emily walked out of the shop, carrying *The Wind,* as she now referred to the book, her euphoria tinkled like the doorbell in her brain. The mood persisted all the way to Weymouth. She even insisted on paying when they stopped at a motorway services for fish and chips.

But as she strode into Uncle Sebastian's, silvery moonlight composing a mystic vista through the panoramic windows, a sudden fear consumed her. *What if we're wrong? What if the book isn't the key? What if I've wasted everyone's time and Dad's money?* She squeezed her eyes tight, clenching fists, stemming stirrings of panic.

"Everything okay?" said Al.

"Just been a long day. Let's go through to the study."

They sat either side of the desk, Emily taking the captain's chair in front of the leather volume. She passed the package containing *The Wind* to Al.

"Okay," she said. "I'll call out numbers, you look up words."

"Three … three … three."

Al flicked carefully, aware this was by some distance the most expensive and delicate book he'd ever handled, alighting on page three, which turned out to be the first page of the manuscript, following the copyright page. He counted down three lines and ran his forefinger across to the third word. "The," he said, noting the word in biro on a pad of writing paper. Emily's mouth formed a proud pout of anticipation.

"Three … five … two."

Al scrolled down a couple of lines, this time saying "Arresting" as he scribbled the word.

The process continued for several minutes. Emily's heart raced faster as each number projected another word onto Al's pad. After a while, Al held up his hand. "Do you want to hear the first sentence?"

"Go on." A nervous tremor of excitement in Emily's voice.

Al paused for dramatic effect before applying the soft, silky accent of a narrator.

"The arresting call that was to change my life forever came one quiet Sunday afternoon."

Emily closed her eyes, a warm rush gushing in her veins. For a moment she sensed an unusual connection. A communication with a relative she'd dismissed in callow youth as insignificant and boring. She had never truly known him, but in death, in no more than the space of a few days,

Uncle Sebastian had become a source of intense fascination. She yearned to learn more about his mysterious life.

As she mused on that thought, she remembered her conversation with Marcus on the promenade. What had Uncle Sebastian whispered to him about the burglary? *"What they don't know, Marcus, is that they missed the big one."* Emily had taken that to mean one of the first editions, a precious printing worth thousands in the rare book world. But maybe the *big one* didn't refer to a first edition. Maybe Uncle Sebastian meant his journal. Perhaps the most valuable book in his extensive collection was bound in leather and cloaked in numerical secrecy.

"That's a powerful first sentence. Sounds like the intro to an epic novel," said Al.

"What do you think it means?"

"No idea, but it may be fun finding out."

Emily yawned. Exhaustion, sudden and overwhelming, replacing the nervous tension and excitement of a fulfilling day.

"Time for bed," said Al. "We'll get to work on the rest of the journal tomorrow, if that's what you want, of course."

Emily nodded, lifting the journal to gauge its weight. "How long do you think it will take to transcribe the whole book from numbers into words?"

"Weeks. Maybe more. That's if we don't hit any glitches."

"Like what?"

"Don't know, but most cryptographers throw in a few nasty traps to keep any would-be codebreakers honest."

"Are you sure you can afford the time, working in the café."

"I'll make time. I'm only taking morning shifts at the moment, so we could work most afternoons and evenings."

"And I could catalogue everything in the morning."

"It's a deal." Al rose to leave and as Emily followed him down the hallway, a sudden chill descended on her, crawling warily up her spine.

She couldn't remember having enjoyed a day more. Interesting, exciting, invigorating. Al had made it all possible. His knowledge of book codes, help in the library, charm at the bookshop and eloquent support when faced with a grilling

70

from her father. Not to mention his unflappable nature and corny jokes. Yet the chill persisted. A curious defence mechanism perhaps. Where had he come from? How had he parachuted into her life at such an opportune time? Was this all too perfect? Who was Alex Andrews?

He turned as he reached the front door. In a moment of awkward anticipation, she thought he leaned towards her. Their eyes met and a dazzling smile lit up his stubbly cheeks. "Until tomorrow," he said. Then he was gone, silhouette disappearing into the night.

Emily mouthed a faint "Thank you". Al didn't break stride.

13

Emily didn't sleep well, cogitating in the darkness over the details of the road trip to London.

Her dreams circled dark and recurring, filled with shadowy figures whispering, gathered around a bronze of a naked Isaac Newton.

She rose at 6am in need of a bracing walk to the sea front to clear her head before resuming cataloguing chores. On reaching the promenade she leaned against the metal barrier that protected walkers from the drop to the sandy beach below, admiring the sunrise, observing fishing boats in the distance bobbing on the gentle swell.

"You're up early."

She knew that voice. Marcus. Emily spun around. "Oh hello again. I could say the same about you."

"Habit of a lifetime. Always up before the sun shines. Healthy, wealthy and wise, as the saying goes."

"And to snap the sunrise?" Emily noticed a compact Canon camera with stumpy zoom lens dangling from a strap around Marcus's neck. In his hand he carried a pair of binoculars.

"Sometimes. Today I'm after the fishing boats. There's always action when the boats land. Birds swooping, nets drawn, crew working, fish flapping, that type of thing. All make for interesting images."

Marcus trained the binoculars out to sea, twiddling the focus wheel to study the fishing boats. "Enjoy your road trip yesterday?" he muttered.

A quizzical frown clouded Emily's features. "Umm, y-e-s. How do you know about that?"

Marcus continued peering through the binoculars. "You can't do much in Sea View Road without me clocking it. My study's on the third floor overlooking the road. Like a little eyrie up there. Great view across to Portland, as well as your bungalow."

"That's a bit creepy." Emily's tone contained a drop of acid.

Marcus lowered the binoculars, looking flustered. "Oh, I'm sorry, you're right. I didn't think. That sounded strange. All I meant was that I noticed you leaving early yesterday morning with the young man from next door. When you returned I couldn't help see the headlights of your car. I was admiring the moonlight. Wasn't it beautiful last night?"

Emily nodded. "Marcus, do you know much about Al?"

"Pardon."

"The guy from next door."

Marcus shrugged. "I've nodded to him a couple of times in the street. Seems pleasant enough. Always has a smile, although I suppose there's no knowing if that's genuine. Jim and Jean must have thought so. Told me they'd found the perfect person to look after the house while they're away. I'm sure they must have taken up references. But can't say I've ever spoken to him. Why, what did you want to know?"

"Nothing, really." Emily trailed off, staring out to sea for a few moments before continuing. "He seems a nice man. Anyway, I must get back, I've got a pile of cataloguing to do. I'll leave you to take your pictures."

Fifteen minutes later she was back in Sea View Road, staring at Marcus's third floor attic window. His description was accurate. A crow's nest came to mind, attractive apex jutting into the roof providing an ideal vantage point. She walked past the bungalow. Time to explore the rest of the road, ascending gently over 200 yards as it tapered to the point of the cul-de-sac. The Victorian properties at the end comprised two imposing three-storey semi-detached houses, undergoing conversion into luxury apartments, the upper floors enjoying magnificent views. Not that the occupants would be moving in anytime soon. Rubble littered the site, intricate scaffolding scaling the walls on front and sides. A sign with camera motif and guard dog's snarling head warned off intruders:

Trespassers will be prosecuted. This site is protected by CCTV.

Emily wandered back down the gradient, mind now free of night-time fuzziness. She studied houses on each side, already having stored information from little vignettes over the past few days. She knew the man at number 16 walked to the end of his driveway at eight each morning wearing bedroom slippers and a bath robe that billowed at an indecent angle, smoked a cigarette leaning on his garden gate, flicking the stub when he'd finished into the undergrowth. Bush fire in the making.

The young couple at 13 tore down the street a few minutes later, tyres squealing, the woman applying make-up in the passenger seat, late again for their daily commute, while the curtains at number 14 twitched when anything moved. Emily had caught a faint glimpse of the lady twitcher one evening and predicted a nonagenarian.

When she reached number seven Emily devoured orange juice, muesli and croissant, before launching into a session in the study, instituting a system to utilise cardboard boxes in the garage. Her plan involved sorting books into genres. Academic, fiction, non-fiction and miscellaneous with any suggesting special value filtered in a separate pile. A job for a librarian. Emily was a scientist. An obvious flaw, but what Emily lacked in literary knowledge she compensated for with a forensic approach. Every volume catalogued, each title page photographed.

Over the next few hours, the only interruption came when her mum texted, enquiring whether everything had gone to plan at the bookshop the evening before. In all the excitement Emily had forgotten to keep her parents informed. *Sorry, Mum*, she wrote back. *The Wind has landed in Weymouth. Tell Dad the key works. Thanks. Emily.*

The doorbell rang at the same moment the grandmother clock, leaning against the study wall, chimed one o'clock. Emily finished the note she was writing, stepped over a pile of crime novels, hoping it was Al.

"How do you fancy a panino?' Al held up a brown paper bag and a bottle of Sicilian lemonade.

Emily chuckled. "You're like a delivery man."

"What?"

"Every time I open the front door you're standing there with food and drink in your hand."

"Are you complaining?"

74

"No, what sort of panino?"

"Cheese. Cheddar, I think."

She took the paper bag from him. Still warm. As was, somewhere deep and vague, the growing friendship with this enigmatic stranger who she'd met by chance at an unplanned crossroads in her life. They went through to the kitchen and enjoyed lunch, Al relating the goings-on in the café, charming manner raising the humdrum conversation a notch or two.

After 20 minutes, Emily brought lunch to a sudden halt. "Let's get busy. No time to waste."

They assumed work positions at the study desk, Emily occupying the captain's chair as before while Al sat opposite. Al pulled a small laptop computer from his rucksack. "Thought it would be better to record Sebastian's journal on this rather than noting every word in longhand. Wouldn't like to get to the end and not be able to read my own writing. I can email it to you."

Emily nodded. "Agreed. Good idea. Another thing. I don't want to hear every word as we go along. We'll read each session at the end of the day."

"Yes boss. Like a bedtime story, you mean."

"Well, if it's about history and Uncle Sebastian's academic world, it might send us to sleep."

"Did Emily Stearn just make a joke?" Al's tone was gently mocking.

A coy smile lit up Emily's face as she called out the numbers. "Twenty-four, nineteen, seven."

For the next hour they worked back and forth, Emily calling the digits, Al identifying the words, tapping them into his keyboard, falling into an efficient, satisfying rhythm.

Al let out a whistle at one of the numbers. "Page one thousand and twenty-eight? I can see why Sebastian chose The Wind. Epic. Lots of words to go at. Must read it one day."

He noted the word on the laptop as Emily called out the next number. "Page three hundred and sixty-five, line twenty-four, eighth word."

"That's odd."

"What?"

"It doesn't make sense."

"What doesn't?"

Al checked again, sliding his finger down the page and across the line to find the allotted word. "Are you sure that's the right number?"

Emily inhaled a sharp breath, isolating the number with one of her fingers, repeating the digits.

"Sure?" said Al.

"Of course I'm sure. Stop asking if I'm sure. I wouldn't have said the same number if I wasn't sure."

Al's eyebrows raised. He almost said, *Who rattled your cage, Miss Perfect?* but stopped himself in time and was instantly grateful for his restraint. "We have a problem. The word *when* is followed by the word *why,* and trust me it doesn't make sense."

Emily glared at the journal, looking for clues. "Could Uncle Sebastian have made an error? One wrong number would throw it out."

"That could be it," said Al. "Read out the next numbers." Emily did so but Al's brow furrowed once more. "No, that doesn't make sense either. Can I look?" He stretched an arm across the desk motioning for the journal. A tricky pause followed. Al and Emily's relationship hung in the foot-or-so void between them. Stick or twist. For an instant Emily smouldered, but, without a word, she slid the journal towards Al.

It took several minutes for Al to become attuned to the forest of numbers, a few more before Emily noticed his manner change, blue eyes darting, laughter lines dancing.

"Emily, where's the copy of The Grapes of Wrath?"

"Why?"

"Because that's the key too."

Emily reached in the top right-hand drawer of the desk and lifted out the book Al had delivered the week before. Al walked around to Emily's side of the desk.

He pointed a forefinger at the errant number. "Look Emily, this doesn't denote a word."

"Pardon."

"It corresponds to a letter. Not in The Wind, but if I'm right, a letter in The Grapes of Wrath."

"How do you know?"

He reached over Emily's shoulder and she could sense his body heat, feel the texture of his cotton shirt. "See this squiggle before the number. I think it's an opening bracket and if you look here." He pointed to the end of the next line of numbers. Another squiggle, this time appearing more like a round bracket. "If I'm right that's the closing bracket. There are eight sets of numbers between the brackets, denoting an eight-letter word."

"Why are you sure they're letters?"

"Look here. One of the last numbers in this three-number sequence is nineteen, another is twenty-four. There aren't nineteen or twenty-four words on any of the lines in The Wind or the The Grapes of Wrath. It must represent a letter on a line, not a word."

Emily gazed up at Al, exuding a mixture of wonder and excitement. "I like the logic, grab The Grapes. Let's check it out." Five minutes later the numbers had spelled *Trooping,* another check confirming the word made sense with its place in the context of the journal.

"How did you know the squiggles were brackets?" Emily's question triggered Al's smile.

"Something bothered me about the compliments slip that came with The Grapes of Wrath. Remember, it said, Use The Wrath (wisely). Cryptographers don't leave anything to chance. There's a reason, a clue, in anything they commit to record. Sebastian strikes me as that sort of guy. The brackets around wisely had to mean something, had to be part of the clue."

Emily remained perplexed. "But why go to the trouble of encoding letters when you could continue with words?"

"That's the point, Emily. Sebastian couldn't encode it all with words. Not using The Wind anyway. I'd guess The Wind doesn't contain the word Trooping on any of its one thousand and thirty-seven pages. The same goes for The Grapes, or most books for that matter, so he had to resort to letter coding in places, even though it's much more laborious. And using a second book makes it more complex. That would appeal to Sebastian, too. We'll find lots of brackets on the pages ahead for names and places as well as unusual words. Probably explains why the journal is so thick. Must have taken him years, literally, to compile."

Emily sighed. "This is going to take us forever. It's like mining with a knife and fork. Chip by chip, not getting very far."

Al sauntered through to the kitchen, returning with two cans of soft drinks. He slid one across the desktop. "Think we'll need to get some more beers in."

They worked into the evening, halting for half an hour while Al threw together a vegetable stir fry in a sticky caramelised sauce, cooked in an authentic Chinese wok he discovered at the back of one of Sebastian's cupboards.

"Any jokes about woks?" said Emily as they ate, watching the sun go down.

"Bit too silly. They're either puns on work, or walk, or rock. Not very cerebral. I have to draw the line somewhere."

"I hadn't noticed." Emily chuckled, raising her fork to denote her gratitude as she shovelled in another mouthful. "By the way, this is delicious. I can't wait to hear the first slab of the journal."

"Me too," said Al, eager tone feigning expectancy, although in reality he'd pieced together enough words already while tapping them into the laptop to realise why Sebastian had invested thousands of hours of effort into encoding his journal.

At 10 o'clock they called a halt, retiring to the lounge, Emily sitting in a comfy chair, legs jack-knifed beneath her, Al reading out loud, as Uncle Sebastian introduced them to a world more sinister than they could ever have imagined.

14

The arresting call that was to change my life forever came one quiet Sunday afternoon. June 14th, 1981.

I have tried to shake the memory loose down the years but it defies distraction. I was listening to the radio at the time, catching up on news from the day before when someone had fired six shots at The Queen as she rode her ceremonial horse at the Trooping of the Colour. The shots turned out to be blanks. Not that The Queen knew. For a moment as her horse stuttered she probably thought her reign had come to a violent and senseless end. According to the news, the shooter wanted to be famous, like the man who assassinated John Lennon the year before. That's what struck me most. Of all the reasons for killing someone, and I concede there are many, that surely has to be among the most unattractive. While musing on that thought, the telephone rang.

"Can you tell me your name?" said the caller.

"Pardon. Who is this?" I thought it might be a prankster. I'd received several nuisance phone calls over recent months. Most silent, some swearing. Probably children, a student with a grudge perhaps. The odd one took exception to a low mark or robust criticism, however constructive.

"Professor Stearn, operational name please, if you would be so kind." The man's voice was polite, BBC-refined, but firm and persuasive. The word *operational* left no doubt.

"Whisper," I said, so softly that he asked me to repeat, which I duly did, only louder, although by now the thunder in my ears and hammering in my chest drowned out the word. I realised one day this call might come. There came days I yearned for it to arrive, though not for some while and certainly not since I had turned 40 a couple of years before.

"Thank you, that will do nicely. Designated location. Twenty-hundred hours."

The phone clicked off, although I remember grasping the receiver for many more seconds, trying and failing to control my shaking hands. I wondered if The Queen had felt like this, vulnerable, afraid, yet strangely invigorated, when she'd heard the shots the day before. I couldn't eat, nervous stomach churning for the rest of the day. Excitement built as the hours passed. When the time came to leave my university study apartment I was ready.

I could hardly remember why I'd chosen the designated location. It was so long ago, except what better place for a university type to melt into the city's ambience than watching the punts slide by on a summer's evening from the vantage point of a bridge over the River Cam. Clare Bridge to be precise. Cambridge's oldest and most striking, with its famous balustrade and globe-like stonework. The night was warm, the air still and light almost spookily bright. The fellows' garden was filled with gaiety and youth, champagne corks popping, waves of laughter rippling. A celebration of some kind, perhaps a degree ceremony or a wedding reception. I knew not what. As I walked along the approach to the bridge, I remember thinking John le Carré would never have picked this spot. He'd have chosen the shadows of Senate House Passage for a secret rendezvous.

Leaning against the balustrade, facing King's Chapel, I waited for my watch hand to strike eight o'clock. A few seconds before it did, a big man, suit straining at the biceps, wearing a bowler hat, so many university staff did back then, bustled across the bridge. He stooped to tie his bootlace. "Professor Stearn, would you follow me, please," he hissed.

I neither knew, nor recognised, the man.

"Whisper, follow me." The voice stern, laden with authority, the sort I suspected wasn't accustomed to being defied.

On hearing the codename, I fell in behind at a loping pace heading towards Clare College Old Court. When the man reached the stone archway, leading to the college's inner square, he pushed open a heavy wooden door to his right and ushered me through, checking to make sure no one was following. He stopped at the bottom of a spiral stone staircase.

"Arms out," he ordered, proceeding to pat me down. I told him he could keep as many pens as he could find, but he didn't laugh.

"Is this really necessary?" I said. A withering look, although he seemed satisfied. Shivering against a chill draft, I followed as he climbed the stairs. When we reached the top step the man prompted me to climb through an open sash window onto a narrow ledge, a low wall protecting against the drop.

Struggling through, grazing my head on the window frame, I emerged on a ledge that formed part of the leaded roof. A man lounged against the chimney brickwork, charcoal suit, flat black cap pulled down masking fine features. He was sucking so deeply on a cigarette that his cheeks appeared hollow. Age difficult to gauge. Late-thirties, my best guess. The man I came to know as Porter. I never knew his real name.

"Ah, Whisper, at last," said Porter. "You're probably wondering why you're here."

"Yes."

"Time to serve your country, Whisper, put all that training to good use."

"What did you have in mind?" A silly question, I knew. My training had a single purpose. One aim. Accepted with eager enthusiasm in those years of physical verve, idealistic vigour and youthful ignorance.

To kill people.

15

Emily sat forward on the edge of the settee, hands covering her face, strands of hair dangling, rubbing her brow. "I didn't expect that. Did you?"

Al shook his head. "I only met Sebastian once for five minutes. Not long enough to form a considered opinion. But there was something about him. Hard to explain. Some people have an aura about them. As if they've done great things. Faced dangers. Climbed mountains. Jumped out of aeroplanes. You know what I'm saying. Things other people only dream about. Sebastian could be one of those. Or it may all be a work of fiction."

Emily's head jerked up. "What are you saying? He might have made all this up."

"Well, it doesn't read like a diary. It reads like a novel."

"Uncle Sebastian was a writer. He'd written half a dozen books. If he's telling his life story, a memoir of a special part of his existence, then I think that's how he'd do it." Emily surprised herself at how protective she felt towards the uncle she barely knew. Shocked as she was by the journal's initial revelations, she also felt a jolt of relief that the journal wasn't a stuffy, dry, historical dissertation. A sense of pride, too, that by cracking the code she and Al had spared it from being consigned to the back of a dusty bookshelf to spend eternity unfathomable and unread.

Al nodded. "You're probably right. Let's not jump to conclusions, that's all I'm saying."

"So you don't think we should tell anybody?"

"Not yet. Not until we've read more."

A sudden thought struck Emily. "But if Uncle Sebastian was involved in something secret, to do with killing people, then you might be right, Al. Maybe he didn't die of a heart attack, after all."

"That's exactly what I was thinking."

"Shit! I think we should tell the police."

It was the first time Al had heard Emily swear. No abbreviations this time. Somehow, it sounded awkward, as if the word had stumbled from her lips wearing shoes two sizes too big. Little did he know that there was plenty more where that came from if required. "Up to you, he's your uncle. But we've got absolutely no proof other than a book full of numbers and squiggles, and a story that has a beginning but no middle, or ending, yet."

"I'm going to start asking some questions."

"I'm going to bed. Don't have bad dreams." Al picked up his bag and headed for the front door."

"See you tomorrow. Same time?"

Al turned. "One it is. Your turn to provide lunch."

Emily's sleep once again proved troubled. No nightmares this time. Instead, hard thinking to piece together everything she knew about Uncle Sebastian. How could she know so little about one of her few relatives? Why did her parents not visit him more often? Did they know about his past? Was it a family secret, consigned to a dark crevice. Buried, never to be mentioned for fear of opening grievous wounds?

The alarm she'd set for seven stirred her from a muzzy place, the ringing harsh, bruising. She slammed her palm on the cut-off button, grabbed her dressing gown, brain foggy, bare feet cold on the wooden floor. She needed fresh air. Sliding the bolt on the front door, she craned her head outside, took a few steps and felt dampness on her cheeks. Refreshing rain, falling softly. Diagonally opposite at number 14, she noticed curtains twitch and instinctively drew tight the neck of her gown. *I wonder.*

After showering and toying with a bowl of muesli, she resumed trawling through the books in the study, but quickly surrendered, her mind refusing to concentrate on mundanities, brain stuck in obsessive mode. The only subject, Uncle Sebastian and events surrounding his death. His journal, his secret, the apparent fact that he trained to kill people.

She had an idea. Sitting at the desk, she flicked though the desk calendar, working out the day Uncle Sebastian died. She knew police had informed her father on March 17th. St Patrick's Day. The feast meant nothing special to her family, but it was at least an aide-memoire. A Wednesday, according to the calendar. The cleaner had found him, the doctor determining death occurred at least 24 hours before. So Tuesday, March 16th, was most likely. Or even Monday the 15th if he died late in the evening. Emily noted the dates on a pad. The funeral had occurred two weeks later and she'd arrived in Sea View Road almost a fortnight after that. Six weeks had now passed since Uncle Sebastian's death. What were the chances of anyone remembering anything?

Obsession doesn't recognise such logic. Emily grabbed her raincoat and a small umbrella from a rack in the porch. She headed to Marcus's house. The doorbell chimed several times before he answered. He looked dishevelled, thinning hair uncombed, shirt tucked clumsily into corduroy trousers. Emily apologised for disturbing him.

"Don't worry. I'm alone. Mary's gone to see our daughter. I have the day to myself."

"Could I ask a few questions about Uncle Sebastian?"

"Of course, but come in out of the rain, Dear, you'll get soaked."

Emily stepped inside and immediately realised Marcus and his wife didn't keep a tidy house. Piles of old newspapers littered the hallway, coats hung haphazard on an old-fashioned rack. Wallpaper curled and peeled from a damp patch while a musty aroma permeated the air.

"Let's go through to the lounge," said Marcus.

"If you don't mind, could you show me your study? I'd love to see the view from up there."

"It's quite a climb."

"No problem. I'm fit, all that walking I've been doing."

Marcus led the way up three flights of stairs, the top steps narrowing sharply. When they reached the study Emily lowered her head to enter. The room was tiny. A small desk in front of the window housed a telescope and compact laptop computer. Photographs of birds, fishing boats and seascapes decorated the walls. A swivel chair nestled in the desk foot-well, an uninviting wooden chair up against another wall.

Emily sat on the hard seat while Marcus eased into the swivel chair. "What did you want to ask?"

"First, how well did you know Uncle Sebastian?"

"As I said, I knew his mother first when she lived over the road. While I met Sebastian then, I got to know him better twenty years ago."

"Did he tell you about his life outside the university?"

"Not really. He'd get a bit nostalgic after a drink. Or at least I thought that's what it was. It was difficult to tell with Sebastian. I once asked him why he'd never got married."

"What did he say?"

"Said there was someone once, but it wasn't meant to be. He always laughed it off, but you could see sadness in his eyes as if recalling tender times. Whenever I probed a little further he always clammed up. Ever so politely, of course. That was Sebastian, the perfect gentleman. Only saw him get prickly once and that was my fault."

"Why?"

"I said he should have had kids because the world needed more fine men like him around. I don't think it was the kids' remark. I think he took exception to me calling him a fine man. 'What do you know?' he said. 'You know nothing about me'."

Emily strained forward to steal a clearer view of the road. Marcus hadn't exaggerated. A perfect vantage spot, high enough to see over the houses in front and beyond as far as the communications beacons on Portland. There was also an ideal angle to view the bungalow, every aspect of Uncle Sebastian's plot laid bare. If only he'd been home when Uncle Sebastian died, he may have seen something.

Emily sighed. No point musing over that. "Thanks Marcus, I suppose I'm trying to forge a relationship with an uncle I didn't really know, but wish I had. His books and music are so inspiring."

"I understand. He was a special friend. Pity he can't tell me off for saying that now. We spent quite a bit of time together since I retired."

"When was that?"

"Only eighteen months ago. I managed the pharmacy on the High Street for thirty years."

"I didn't realise. Do you miss it?"

Marcus tilted his head, as if in deep thought. "I do, actually. I trained as a chemist and went straight into pharmacy, so it's all I've known. But a national chain took over the shop and the bosses wanted to introduce eyesight and hearing testing, as well as vaccinations. I was too old to get my head around all that new stuff."

They admired the seascape for a few more minutes, Marcus pointing out the misty sheen of Chesil Beach in the distance and dramatic waves crashing against the Portland headland.

"Thanks for showing me the view, Marcus. It's beautiful even on a murky day. I can see why you like it here." Emily picked up her bag and they negotiated the stairs, Emily bidding farewell as she flicked the button on her umbrella. The rain sliced in heavier, little puddles forming in potholes. She set off for the bungalow but stopped mid-road, turning left, a whim taking her to number 14 instead. In the motion of rapping on the door knocker she wondered what she was doing. *This isn't me. Banging on a stranger's door? Me. Emily Stearn. If only Mum could see me now.*

Emily knocked twice and when no answer came she made to return to the bungalow. She'd taken a couple of steps when she heard the metallic scrape of the sliding bolt. The door opened six inches.

"Yes, what do you want?" A frail shrillness to an otherwise hoarse woman's voice, suggesting advanced age, or perhaps illness.

Emily spun around. "Sorry to bother you, I'm Emily from number seven across the road. I wondered if I could have a word."

"You're the girl in the dressing gown," said the woman, face ashen and heavily lined.

"That's right. Sorry, I don't usually walk out before I'm properly dressed. I needed a bit of air this morning. Can I come in?"

"Is it about the lorries?"

"No."

"Are you from the council about the bins?"

"No."

The woman moved jerkily away from the door. "All right, you'd better come in. But be careful. William and Kate are here."

Emily eased open the door revealing the reason for the woman's awkward motion. She clung to a Zimmer frame. Her knuckles were white, skeletal arms full of purple veins and age-related bruises. Turning in the narrow hallway required a four-point procedure.

"Come on then." The woman's silver hair glinted under the hall light as she picked up speed leading Emily down the passageway to the kitchen. "Oh, Kate's finished. William, have you had enough?" Two cats, one tortoiseshell, the other black and white, sat by bowls, one licking its lips while the other looked appropriately regal. Emily could hear purring and may have been tempted to stroke them but for the acid stench of stale urine inviting her to gag.

Emily and the old lady sat opposite each other at the kitchen table. "I'm Katharine, by the way. That's Katharine with a K, like Katharine Hepburn. You know Katharine Hepburn, don't you?"

"Um, not really."

"*The African Queen, Guess Who's Coming to Dinner?* You must have heard of … oh never mind. I'm just an old woman who looks after cats. Ninety-two. That's how old, if you're wondering."

"Do you live by yourself?" asked Emily, flush of congratulation in her tone.

"No, with Kate and William."

Emily smiled, wondering, not for the first time, if this was a good idea.

"I was a JP, you know."

"JP?" Her blank expression set Katharine's head shaking again.

"Justice of the Peace. Youngsters these days. A magistrate. Someone who sits in court. Protects the public from offenders, thieves and the like."

Emily's talents didn't stretch to small talk, or any type of chit-chat, other than ones with maths at their central core. She understood that and half-wished she'd waited to approach

87

Katharine in the company of Al. He always knew what to say, how to coax a conversation along. Directness was Emily's forte.

"Katharine, I'm investigating the death of my uncle, Sebastian Stearn."

"Ah, the professor. Nice man. I saw the funeral car." Another head shake.

"He died six weeks ago, on March the sixteenth. I wondered if you could remember anything unusual around that time. Any odd visitors or vehicles, anything out of the ordinary."

Katharine's head lolled back, her laugh revealing a patchy row of stained teeth. "I've told you, I'm ninety-two. I can't remember what I had for breakfast."

"Oh."

"Good job I write everything down."

Katharine looked fragile and wasn't averse to milking the freedom of eccentric expression that age confers, but Emily detected the mischievous rays of a bright intellect burning behind shrewd eyes.

Reaching for the frame, Katharine rose unsteadily from her seat, affecting another turning manoeuvre. She edged along the kitchen worktop, heading for a desk-like structure where she slid back a drawer and lifted out a small, black diary, before Zimmering back to the table via the same route.

"If anything moved or parked illegally in Sea View Road it will be in here. When did you say it was?"

"March the sixteenth."

"Oh yes, the day before St Patrick's Day. My surname is O'Toole. Sweet Jesus, we used to celebrate when my husband was alive. Not enough Guinness in Weymouth. Had to make do with whisky some years." She chuckled at the memory as she flicked through the diary, each day filled with copious entries. No wonder those curtains twitched so often, thought Emily. A bony finger traced its way through March until Katharine alighted on the 16th.

"Busy day."

"Can I see?" Emily rose from her chair to peer over Katharine's shoulder.

On the left side of the entry appeared a list of registration plate numbers belonging to lorries that Katharine had noted visiting the building site at the end of the cul-de-sac. Katharine tapped an irritated finger on the listings. "All spewing toxic fumes, as well as mud and muck on the street. I've sent all the plate numbers to our local councillor, not that he'll do anything. Big companies, back-handers, the ordinary resident's got no chance."

Emily leaned over, her interest triggered by the right-hand side of the entry. This was familiar territory. Half a dozen more registration numbers, this time with additional notes in Katharine's shaky hand-writing. One number, in particular, PG18 XBT, leapt off the page, mainly because the note alongside it read: *Large white van parked outside Professor Stearn's house. Partially blocking pavement. 9am to 11am.*

Emily's heart began to race. She reached in her bag for her phone. "Katharine, would you mind if I took a picture of this page?"

Katharine shrugged, which Emily considered consent. She snapped off a couple of photos.

"Do I get commission?" said Katharine.

Emily smiled. "Tell me, Katharine, do you remember anything about the white van outside the professor's house that day? Any writing on it? Did you see who was driving?"

Katharine turned up her palms and shrugged. "The road's full of white vans most days. Plasterers. Painters. Plumbers. Everybody seems to be having work done."

"Never mind." Emily flicked over the diary page to check the 17th. Sure enough, there was a flurry of entries, including a note of several vehicles, an ambulance and a police car, parked outside Uncle Sebastian's.

"You've been very helpful Katharine. Nice meeting you."

"Oh dear, I never even offered you a cup of tea. Would you like …"

"Perhaps another time. Don't get up. I can see myself out." Emily scooped up her bag, taking care to step over the cat bowls. As she walked down the hallway she heard Katharine say, "Now, what did you think, Kate? What a nice young lady."

The rain had eased. Instead of returning to the bungalow Emily walked down the hill to the town, sifting through what she'd learned, although it didn't take long to conclude the morning yielded nothing definite. More questions than answers. She headed for the food hall. Al had challenged her to provide lunch. It would be rude not to accept.

Two hours later Al was tucking into a spread that made his cheese panini appear inadequate. Quiche, empanadas, smoked salmon pastries. Even mini-cheesecake slices. He stuffed in a third helping. "I could get used to this."

"Don't. It's strictly a one-off." Emily started to clear the debris while recounting her visit to Katharine. Al listened, engrossed, especially when learning Katharine had made a note of the vehicles outside number seven on the day Sebastian died.

"That white van is worth checking out," said Al.

"How do we do that?"

"Leave it with me. I have a friend in the licensing agency. He may not be able to give us names and addresses, but he'd know if it was a trade vehicle and what sort of company owned it."

"Right, let's get started," said Emily. They wandered through to the study, eager to decode Uncle Sebastian's next instalment.

16

Porter stubbed out his cigarette on the chimney stack, flicking the remnant over the side of the building. We watched it plummet four floors, landing in one of the rose beds.

"I presume you heard the news yesterday," Porter said.

"What news?"

"The Queen."

I nodded. A few isolated souls may have been unaware of the shots fired, but the news had dominated the world's media outlets. It would continue to do so for the best part of a week. Police had apprehended the culprit, who wouldn't see the light of freedom for years. Quite why it was being discussed on the roof of a famous Cambridge college escaped me.

Porter paused for a couple of seconds, before continuing. "That changed everything."

"How?" I wasn't following this strand of thought. I wanted to scream. *Just tell me what you want me to do.*

"We can't have people taking liberties with The Queen and the Royal Family. Don't you agree?"

"Yes."

"The problem is that some of the people with their sights on the Royal Family are a little more capable, not to say a good deal more powerful, than the young idiot who fired six blanks yesterday because he wanted to be famous. I can't tell you too much more, but we have identified a real and present danger." Porter lifted both hands, painting quote marks in the air with his fingers around the last phrase.

"A danger to The Queen?"

Porter fixed me with a steady gaze. I understood his game. I'd done much the same with students before pushing them through final examinations. Porter was weighing me up. Did I possess the mental and physical aptitude? Would I wilt under pressure? Could I give my best when nothing less was required? Did I have the ruthless streak that separates those who achieve from those who merely participate? You can tell that in a man's eyes, or so I was told. By the way he holds your gaze. Full of purpose and discipline.

"Not exactly," said Porter.

"Who then?"

He ignored my question. "The powers-that-be have identified you as the best, the only, operative for this particular job. We understand your first mission has come somewhat late in the day, but this job demands experience and knowledge. Requires a man of standing. A man who can walk with the rich and powerful, talk history with vigour and detail. You can do that, can't you?"

I neither confirmed, nor denied. History had been my passion ever since my days as a Cambridge undergraduate, green and innocent. I'd devoured books. Always lighting a candle for the exploited and downtrodden. From Muslims at the hands of Meccans at the time of prophet Muhammed, to Christians fed to the lions in Ancient Rome, to the horrors of Auschwitz, and the centuries of Rohingya persecution in Burma. I could still talk a good fight, but my 40th birthday had been and gone. Something happens to a man after 40. My father told me that. It's true. Not just worse hangovers either, although I'm quite happy to confirm that is a fact.

"I'm sure you haven't brought me here merely because I can walk and talk. Can you get to the point?" Porter was beginning to annoy me. My stomach had settled, nervous tension dissipated, a sudden implant of adrenalin begun to kick in.

"Colonel Igor Kalenkov."

"Pardon."

Porter repeated the name, asking if it meant anything to me.

"Not a thing," I said.

"Kalenkov is by some distance the biggest current threat to western democracy, but I'm not surprised you haven't heard of him. This is 1981. There are many ways enemies threaten our way of life. Some by fostering oppression, corruption, division and segregation. Kalenkov prefers the old-fashioned ways of terror and murder."

"Who is Kalenkov?"

Porter sensed he'd captured my attention. I could feel it. He was right. The man in the bowler hat clicked his fingers. He was standing guard by the open sash window, motioning for silence. We paused for a while, still and statuesque as the chimneys around us, listening to the animated chatter of a group of students echoing as they climbed the staircase before pouring into one of the Old Court bedrooms leading off it. The bowler hat nodded that it was safe to continue.

"Where were we? Ah, yes, Kalenkov. Tell me, Professor, do you recall a man named Henry Winter?"

I shook my head.

"No reason you should. Henry died twenty years ago on a London Tube train while on his way home to have dinner with his wife. Ostensibly a heart attack. That's what the death certificate said, what his wife was told. Still believes it today. Didn't merit a line in the local paper. But it wasn't a heart attack."

"What was it?"

"Poison, professor. Propelled from an improvised device at short distance. On a crowded train. The sort of poison that dissipates swiftly leaving no trace. Except everything leaves a trace, a residue of some kind, if you look hard enough. Henry Winter wasn't his real name."

"What was his real name?"

"Sergey Kuznetsov. A former colonel in the KGB. A man instrumental in saving the lives of many British agents."

It still wasn't obvious where Porter's train of thought was heading. Double agents were commonplace in the Cold War on both sides. Ideology. Blackmail. Money. Agents switched sides for all sorts of reasons, most accepting, if caught, traitors would pay the ultimate price.

"That's very sad. I'm sorry for Mrs Winter, but doesn't that sort of thing go with the territory. Tit for tat. The perils of a double agent."

Porter pulled a cigarette packet from the inside pocket of his jacket. He flipped the lid and offered me one. I shook my head. He lit a cigarette, took a long, deep drag, exhaling an extended plume of smoke. I could hear the faint strains of

93

Stand and Deliver by Adam and the Ants playing in a distant college bedroom.

"Correct, Professor. Tit for tat. An acceptable mechanism, as long as there are as many tits as tats. The problem is that when it comes to *tats* Kalenkov is the most ruthless and deadly operative. Twenty-four confirmed kills to date since poor Henry Winter met his maker, probably double that number with those we don't know about. Now, Kalenkov is the driving force behind the Soviet policy of killing anyone or anything that threatens their ideology."

"How can I help?"

Porter grinned, but his thin lips radiated no warmth. "We'd like you to help dispose of him."

"What?" I sounded astonished. For good reason. I *was* astonished. "What are you saying? Just pop over to Moscow and eliminate a professional hit-man who has been killing for the past twenty years while I've been teaching history."

"Don't be modest, Professor. You were chosen for great things all those years ago."

"But that was then. I was young and stupid. Knew nothing. It seemed like an adventure, but I was glad I was never called upon. I'm a different person now. I can't, I won't kill anyone."

"But you still love your country?"

"Yes."

"And you still support the Royal Family."

"Yes, but what have they got to do with it?"

Porter stubbed out his cigarette, this time grinding it into the lead flashing beneath his feet. His voice hushed, assuming an even graver tone. "Kalenkov is out of control. As far as we know, he doesn't actually get his hands bloody these days. Not since he developed a heart condition that required aortic root surgery two years ago. But he's the driving force behind almost every killing ordered in that part of the world. He has assumed authority and resurrected the philosophy of the Thirteenth Directorate."

"What on Earth's that?" Porter was reeling me in. I could sense it more keenly with every sentence. I still had no intention of taking the mission but somewhere deep inside I needed to know.

"The Thirteenth Directorate was the department responsible for what the Soviets called executive action, or wet affairs." He paused to let the phrase sink in. "Wet, Professor. In other words, anything messy that involved spilling blood. Murders. Kidnapping. The department ordered the killing of Henry Winter back in nineteen sixty-one. The Thirteenth no longer exists in name. It has been re-titled and re-designated several times. Nowadays, it concentrates on sabotaging our computer systems and vital infrastructure. But Kalenkov is on a one-man mission to keep the Thirteenth legacy alive."

"You mean kill people," I said. Porter nodded slowly. I had to know. "You said earlier you'd identified a real and present danger."

"Does July the twenty-ninth mean anything to you?"

I pondered for a moment. One would think a history professor would be good with dates, but nothing registered. I shrugged. "No, should it?"

"It's the day Prince Charles is scheduled to marry Lady Diana Spencer at St Paul's Cathedral."

"Okay." My mind was racing to compute the relevance.

"We have compelling intelligence to believe a squad under Kalenkov's control is planning to murder the happy couple, or at least one of them, either at the cathedral or on the balcony at Buckingham Palace. Probably mid-kiss to intensify the impact."

I could feel my mouth morphing into an ugly leer to disguise the grin on my face. I almost laughed. This was preposterous. I half-expected Porter to guffaw and shout 'Fooled you!' as if acting out some surreal party game. But Porter wasn't laughing. Far from it. His jaw jutted, eyes cold. Deadly serious. My stomach ached as crushing reality dawned.

Porter would not have revealed this information if I had the option of saying no.

17

Pensioners jammed the cafe, a hum of silver-haired conversation reverberating around the white-tiled walls, all taking advantage of Happy Hour.

Not an alcoholic drink in sight. The owners had sandwiched their daily promotion at Tasty Treat between the hours of noon and 1pm. All meals half price. A shrewd ploy to ignite the spring trade. Not that everyone seemed happy as Emily waited by the entrance for Al to clock off for the day.

"The food here's awful," she heard one old man moan to another as they headed for the exit.

"And expensive," said his mate.

Emily made a mental note to tell Al. He'd appreciate the grumpy feedback. She watched the two men, one stumbling along with the aid of a cane, shuffle down the promenade and when she turned around Al was heading her way, having swapped his café uniform for jeans and a round-necked jumper.

They had toiled past midnight, Uncle Sebastian keeping them up until 2pm, discussing and digesting his latest revelations. Emily was struggling to come to terms with the enormity of what she and Al were discovering. If everything they read in the journal were true, then this was high-grade information. Official Secrets Act intelligence. They should probably be reporting it right now at the nearest police station, or to some foreign office mandarin in Whitehall. But Al and Emily had caught the wave, bought into the first hypnotic ripples of Uncle Sebastian's story. They were determined to surf to wherever it took them. As Al reasoned, no-one's going to get hurt.

Al had promised to raise Emily's lunchtime treat by taking her to The Handmade Pie House before they began any more transcribing. "Okay, ready for a pie? Their steak and Guinness are to die for."

"Can we stop talking about death, please?" said Emily.

"Fair point, in the circumstances."

It took them five minutes to stroll to the pie shop, located in a side street off the promenade. On the way Emily recounted the conversation she'd overheard with the grumpy old men.

"Damn cheek," said Al. "They're getting good food for next to nothing. That's the problem with pensioners. Give them a good deal and pretty soon they see it as an entitlement."

Al proceeded to tell a string of corny jokes about pensioners and Emily groaned. "I don't know how you remember them all."

"It's a gift," said Al, assuming a coy smile, bumping playfully into Emily so that he had to steady her by draping his arm around her shoulder. To his surprise, she didn't shrug him off. They reached the pie shop, taking a table for two in a dark alcove at the back of the only room. Eight tables in all. Small, compact, half a dozen other diners, a short queue at the takeaway counter. Al ordered his Guinness pie, Emily opting for cheese and onion.

While they were waiting for their food, Al's ringtone trilled. "Hi Paul. How are you?" The call lasted no more than a minute, Al making several disappointed murmurs.

"No joy on the white van outside Uncle Sebastian's, I'm afraid."

"Pity," said Emily, although she detected a touch of equivocation in Al's tone.

"Well, it didn't sound like any joy. All Paul could find out was that it was a hire vehicle. I suppose that means it probably wasn't a trades person."

"No, but if it was hired then we might be able to find out who was driving it. Did you get the name of the company?"

"Hudson's of Dorchester. Never heard of it. Must be a small private firm."

Steaming pies arrived, Al's swimming in thick gravy, dark as tar, Emily's pale and naked, lettuce leaf and tomato slices providing a hint of modesty.

Al cast a disapproving frown in Emily's direction.

"What? That's the way I like my pie. I don't like pies drowning in gravy. Makes the pastry all soggy."

"Each to his, or her, own." They tucked in and were half-way through their meal when a commotion outside attracted their attention.

A woman burst in. Frantic shrill in her voice. "Can anyone help? An old man's fallen. Anyone know first aid?"

Without a glance to Emily, Al leapt out of his chair. Five strides and he was out of the door, clearing the three steps at the entrance in a single bound. A man lay prone on the pavement, ashen face, lips blue, unconscious. His walking stick lay askew a few feet away. Another man, around the same age, late-seventies, full Captain Birdseye white beard, was attending to him. Attempts at resuscitation appeared to amount to, "Come on Jack, wake up," while tapping him softly on the cheek.

The old man appeared in danger. This was no fall.

"What happened?" Al grabbed the man's hand. Limp, cold, no discernible pulse. No intelligible answer from his pal. All the signs of cardiac arrest. Speed essential. Al laid the man's head back to open the airway and felt in his mouth to ensure no obstruction. He began pumping his chest, deep thrusts, urgent rhythm. Emily had followed him out.

"Ring 999," gasped Al. Emily reached for her phone.

"Can I help?" A lad, around 18, astride a bicycle, rucksack on his back, concerned look on his face.

"Do you know the pier hut, around the corner?" Al continued pumping.

"Yep."

"There's a defibrillator on the wall."

"What?" The lad looked blank.

"Yellow case. On the wall. Fetch it, please. Now."

The lad stood on his pedals and veered off, accelerating away. Emily described their location to the ambulance service while the thoughtful owner of the pie shop supplied a chair for the old man's pal, who was trembling in shock. A small crowd gathered.

Al stopped pumping. He realised the man needed air. Knew how to give it, too, but clamping his mouth around a stranger's in a perilous moment, with vomit present, no knowledge of what illness the man might have contracted or where his mouth had been, required commitment. Al took a deep breath, pinched the man's nose and plunged in, watching the man's chest rise from the corner of his eye as he administered two breaths. The cyclist returned, steering with one hand, clinging on to the defibrillator with the other.

"Thanks," said Al. "Open it. Come on, Jack, stay with us." Defibrillator unpacked, Al ripped open the old man's shirt, placing electrode pads on his chest.

The machine took over. An automated, robotic voice, analysing the heart rhythm, walking through the procedure. "Preparing shock, move away from the patient."

The man's chest jerked and Al returned to pumping. Still no sign of life. A siren sounded in the distance. Al pumped some more. A couple of minutes later the ambulance arrived. Paramedics took over.

Al stood up, legs trembling with a mix of adrenalin and exhaustion. He scanned the gathering, searching for Emily. He spotted her sitting on a chair by the wall of the pie shop, sipping a glass of water, face white as chalk, the waitress hovering over her. "Hey, you okay?"

Emily nodded. Al wasn't convinced. He glanced at the waitress.

"I think she had a funny turn," she said.

"Thanks for looking after her."

"I'll be all right. Come on, let's go," protested Emily, weakly rising to her feet, voice frail yet determined.

Al took the glass from her, drained the water, swilling it around in his mouth before spitting the taste of vomit into the gutter and handing the glass to the waitress. "That's better," he gasped, wiping his mouth with a tissue. He draped an arm around Emily and led her away, anxious glance behind eliciting a grateful thumbs-up from one of the paramedics. The stricken man's hand twitched. *Thank God.* They made their way to the promenade and sat on the nearest bench looking out to sea.

"Sorry Al, I feel like an idiot. You were trying to save that guy's life and all I could do was nearly faint."

"Rubbish, you called the ambulance. It came in record time. You must have done something right."

Emily shook her head. "I don't think so. But how did you know to do all that stuff? You reacted as if you did that sort of thing every day of the week. Calm. In control. You were brilliant."

"I took a first aid course at University a few years ago, that's all. Learned how to use a defibrillator. Not much to it, believe me. The machines these days do everything for you. Let's forget the journal today, let's …"

Before he could finish the sentence, Emily interrupted. "No, I want to continue. We need to find out what happened to Uncle Sebastian as soon as possible. I like reading out the numbers. There's something soothing about seeing all those rows of figures and listening to your jokes now and then."

"Sure?"

Emily nodded. She started to utter something, but snatched it back, instead sucking in a deep breath. She licked her lips and tried again. "Al, what happened today wasn't the first time. When lots of things are happening. I mean, stressful stuff, like you trying to save that old guy's life, but sometimes just ordinary things happening at the same time, it's as if my brain shuts down. I can't cope. I panic. I sort of feel …" She couldn't find the word.

"Overwhelmed," suggested Al.

"Exactly. I've always been like that. I don't like it, but it's who I am." Emily recalled her childhood and numerous occasions when she'd cancelled parties, sleepovers, holiday weekends, because she couldn't face the pressure of interaction. An ache gnawed in the pit of her stomach. The friends she'd lost. Opportunities she'd missed.

"Don't worry about it. It's what makes you special." Al's tone soft and soothing.

It didn't seem special. Not to Emily, who had recoiled at the thought of intimacy with another person for much of her adult life. Not because she didn't crave friendship and approval. She did. But because intimacy meant conforming to confusing rituals, managing expectations, all impregnated with the possibility of misunderstanding and the probability of disappointment. She had let her guard down with Blake. The proof that intimacy meant heartache and betrayal now resided in the photo archive in her phone.

"Let's go back to the bungalow." Emily sounded weary. "By the way, Al, those two old guys were the grumpy ones I was telling you about. You don't think it was the café food that did for him, do you?"

Al feigned concern, licking his lips, before chortling. "Probably wouldn't be the first time a cheese omelette had caused a heart attack."

18

The road was long, winding and familiar as it cut a swathe deep into the Brechfa Forest, each corner revealing another vista of Welsh remoteness.

I knew I was close when I reached the village of Gwernogle, a haphazard collection of isolated stone houses, having seen better times. The sort of village where a bicycle passing constitutes rush hour. A couple of miles further on, an unsigned path jags into the trees. I took it, caressing the car over the rockiest of ground, shielding my eyes against the sunlight strobing through the trunks, until the building loomed into sight. I called it Secretarium, which is Latin for hiding place, although as far as I know it has no official name, no address, no map reference. No confirmation anywhere that it exists.

Secretarium resembled an enormous hide, wood panelled within a concrete frame, eco-friendly, grassy roof blending with nature. The green feel was scarred by a 12-foot high steel-spiked grey fence, topped with razor wire, surrounding the site. Outside, birds chirped. A stream trickled. Life appeared lazy and carefree. Inside, agents from MI5 and MI6 practised the dark arts of their profession. Learned how to deceive, survive, manipulate. And kill. I knew because I'd first come here 20 years before.

How did an ordinary history teacher come to the attention of the British intelligence service? The Eagle pub in Cambridge is the simple answer, the place where James Watson and Francis Crick discovered the DNA double helix in the 1950s.

The Eagle was a magnet for students enjoying, among other things, rock 'n roll from America. One summer's night in 1961, *That'll Be the Day* was blaring out on the juke box as I and a group of friends lamented the death of Buddy Holly a couple of years before. As usual, I'd sunk too many beers and left the pub alone around 11pm. Strolling along King's Parade, I became aware of a man in the shadows across the road, brimmed hat pulled down hiding his eyes, overcoat collar standing to attention despite the mild night. He resembled a lazy cliche from a Humphrey Bogart film, except that back in the sixties such stereotypes crammed Cambridge.

Imagination racing, I felt uneasy, quickening the pace, but the man matched my stride. When I turned out of sight into the cobbled Senate House Passage I started to jog. A drunken jog. I was fit and handy with my fists and feet in those days, but I didn't court trouble. Slipping behind the brick buttress of one of the tall buildings, I hugged the wall and held my breath, waiting for him to pass.

"Don't move." A voice out of the blackness to my right. Close. Clipped and controlling. I heard the heavy shuffle of other men. Perhaps three more. Someone shone a torchlight in my eyes. I shielded my face, a lurch of fear knotting my stomach. Through my fingers I saw the blurry silhouette of the man in the overcoat as he put a hand on my shoulder. A firm but gentle hand that administered a reassuring rub.

"Mister Stearn. We've been admiring your progress these past two years. You're a model student. A-grades, blues in tennis and rowing, black belt in karate, fluent in Russian. A healthy interest in politics and the world."

I needed a pee. Urgently. Fear mixed with beer. "What do you want?" I said.

"I like that. Direct. Straight to the point. No prevarication."

"No, I really need to pee."

"Feel free. Go ahead."

The man took a step backwards as I turned towards the wall.

Mid-stream, he continued, "Tell me, Mister Stearn, how would you like to help your country? To make a difference. Do things only available to the chosen few."

It could have been the alcohol, or the fact I'd been evaluating my existence as I prepared to enter my final year. Or maybe the influence of Buddy Holly and the pub discussion on the futility of talent snuffed out too young. It could have been that while I had excelled academically and at sports at university, I'd always felt something was missing. When the man in the overcoat revealed how I could help my country I didn't feel apprehensive or confused. Didn't need

103

time to think. As the torchlight illuminated the stream of urine trickling down the cobbled street, elation matched my relief.

"Count me in," I said. I never knew the name of the man in the overcoat. Saw him only once more when, months later, I visited Secretarium for the first time, driven by people I'd never met in the back of a blacked-out van. To a young student yearning to embrace manhood the clandestine nature of the exercise felt invigorating. I don't intend revealing the details of what I did or learned at Secretarium. The oath of secrecy reverberates beyond the grave. Suffice to say, for the next decade I visited for a fortnight every year, by now trusted with directions, honing my skills, and always left hoping that sometime soon I would receive the call to serve. In the department, I was known as a *Waiter*. An operative waiting for a mission. Invisible on foreign intelligence radar. Dark and unsullied by previous ops. Unknown to the enemy.

The call never came, not until that day on the roof at Clare College, long after my discharge from the service's *waiting* list.

On reaching Secretarium in June 1981, I showed my passport to a security guard at the front gate. It took a few minutes to complete the necessary checks. There were furtive conversations into telephones before the guard waved me through and another aide escorted me to the operations room.

"We meet again, on terra firma this time." Porter nodded across the table. No handshake or pleasantries. Nobody else present. "I'll not waste any more time, Whisper. I'm sure you want to know exactly what we have in mind for you." He used my codename, one of the sacred rules at Secretarium to safeguard operatives' identities, even from each other.

I nodded. I'd agreed to help partly because I knew the department would make life difficult for me if I didn't. They couldn't tolerate individuals running around with highly classified information and would go to extraordinary lengths to shut down the lives and careers of operatives who'd failed to comply with their wishes after being entrusted with information much less sensitive than I possessed. One banished with new name, passport, but no overt protection to a remote farm in Tasmania. Another, having disappeared overnight, rumoured to be serving in a mundane capacity at a North Pole meteorological compound. I shivered at the thought. I was better than that. At 42, no wife, no children, I needed to stamp my footprint on the world. That realisation clinched my acceptance.

Porter looked older than my memory of him on the college roof. Probably the hair. Dark, curly, but scruffy grey patches that hadn't been evident under the cap he'd worn. His manner was business-like, although a frayed edge in his tone betrayed a hidden tension, as if the daily churn of responsibility weighed heavy.

"The plan is very simple. We need a facilitator. Someone who can manoeuvre Kalenkov into position for us to get a shot at him."

"How do you propose I do that?"

"Whisper, you are one of the world authorities on Russian history."

"I'm not following you."

"Listen and you will. In three weeks' time, the weekend of July the eighth, Moscow is to host an annual history symposium, the chosen subject being great Russian leaders. The Moscow History Society have invited speakers from all over the world."

I nodded. "I'm aware of that. I've already said I won't be able to attend."

Porter sharpened his chin with a crooked finger. "But you will, Whisper. You must. We have accepted the invitation on your behalf, all on Cambridge University correspondence, with apologies for any confusion. We need you to give the best lecture you have ever presented on Ivan the Great and Ivan the Terrible."

"Why?" I could feel my face grimacing with incredulity. My book, *The Two Ivans,* one of five I'd published, had sold thousands in academic quarters. Translated into 20 different languages, including Russian, for obvious reasons. I was proud of it. But how the knowledge I'd gained from painstaking research and debate into two Russian rulers could help trap one of the world's most prolific assassins escaped me.

"Kalenkov is a student of history," explained Porter. "He has a particular interest in the two Ivans. He is rarely seen in public but intelligence suggests he intends to attend the conference. He has done so on occasion in the past. Your presence, as a lecturer on his favourite subject, would make that attendance almost certain."

"And?" There must be more, I reasoned.

"As an eminent professor, your lecture, again almost certainly, would be held in the main pavilion hall at the Sokolniki Exhibition Centre in Sokolniki Park. Kalenkov would be among the guests of honour, along with General Secretary Leonid Brezhnev. The main pavilion is an old hall with plenty of ceiling space, boxes and high structures affording opportunities for a resourceful operative."

"You mean a sniper."

"Whisper, you're ahead of me."

"So I'm the bait, the cheese in the trap." I spat out the phrase, my thoughts whirling and colliding. Relief that no-one was asking me to pull the trigger mixed with a griping sense of dishonour that Porter intended exploiting my academic reputation for such malevolence.

"I'd not thought of it like that," said Porter. "But yes, bait sums it up nicely. A juicy morsel thrown in front of someone who can't resist the taste of blood."

Porter could sense distaste in my furrowed frown. "Don't look like that, Whisper. The best part of the plan is that no one will ever suspect you were involved. All you need do is spend a week in Moscow in a top hotel, eat good food, drink fine wine, go sightseeing like most ordinary British tourists, talk about your favourite subject, act naturally, and let events unfold. What we call a soft mission. We'll even throw in a tour guide."

He made it sound easy. A package tour with all the extras. Maybe it would be. My experience didn't extend to activities relying on timing and co-ordination by third parties in a foreign city, especially one housing the seat of power in a totalitarian state. But my gut told me such activities rarely went to plan.

"I'll say goodbye now, Whisper, and leave you in the capable hands of mission control."

"One question." I held up a single finger. It was the last chance to address a conundrum gnawing at my comprehension. "Why would a Russian security department want to kill members of the British Royal Family? I don't see how it works for them. What do the Russians gain?"

"Fair question and one I wouldn't normally answer. Operatives execute, Whisper. They don't analyse, as well you know. But, I'll make an exception this once." Porter thought for a few seconds before assuming his gravest tone. "I can't get inside Kalenkov's head, but the days are gone when his department concentrated on hunting down treacherous individuals simply for retribution. The aim now is to influence the bigger picture."

"As in?"

"As in sabotage, spreading insurrection to weaken those around them. The Russians wouldn't admit responsibility for killing Charles or Diana, of course they wouldn't. They'd most likely blame it on some splinter organisation of the Welsh Nationalists. Sons of Glyndwr? An arm of the Welsh Socialist Republican Army? Who knows? Anyone with a beef against the English. Divide and weaken. That's what the Cold War's all about. Tanks, planes and submarines are still important and will be for some time to come. But there's a new game afoot. Subtler, more insidious, based on generating internal conflict so no-one realises what the Russians are really up to. It's called the grey zone. It's a bigger threat to democracy than any missile."

I wasn't convinced, but Porter tapped on the door and two aides in black track suits entered to escort me to my quarters. I won't lie, I enjoyed the next fortnight. Running at dawn through wild flower meadows, scattering rabbits on tracks that meandered through the forest. Honing my strength and fitness in the gym. Learning the topography of Moscow's streets and underground rail network. Familiarising myself with a range of weapons as well as details of the mission, although no-one identified the trigger operative. I also worked on my lecture with a verve and enthusiasm I hadn't experienced in years.

On my final morning at Secretarium a brown envelope appeared under my door. Return business class tickets from Heathrow to Moscow, reservations at a city centre hotel, and a contact number to be memorised and destroyed.

19

It was the first time Emily had visited Dorchester.

Impressions were favourable. Clean pavements. Period buildings. A warm and comforting quaintness, despite Emily hating the idea of driving around new places. She found a spot to park, heading for the Corn Exchange. Hudson's was close by and she pushed open the door right on opening time.

"Can I help?" said the woman behind the counter, fishing a tea bag out of the day's opening cuppa.

"Hope so. I wondered if you could help me to find a man."

"Think you'll need Tinder for that, darlin'." The woman chuckled at her quip. Emily looked bemused, but smiled anyway.

"A gentleman was doing some work for us over in Weymouth and he left behind some valuables. I'm trying to return them to him."

"What's that to do with us?"

Emily experienced a breath of panic. She'd hatched the plan with Al the evening before after they'd read the latest instalment of Uncle Sebastian's journal. Emily was now even more convinced something sinister lay behind his sudden demise. She had endured another disturbed sleep, dreaming of dark secrets, snipers and Russian agents. She needed to clear her head. As Dorchester lay a mere seven miles to the north of Weymouth, a face-to-face visit to Hudson's seemed preferable to a phone call. In her dream, the white van parked outside Uncle Sebastian's the night he died held the clue.

"The gentleman hired a white van from you six weeks ago to do work at my house in Weymouth. I'm pretty sure it was just for the day."

"What's his name?"

"I'm sorry, I can't remember. He did say, but it sounded foreign and now escapes me."

"Why's it taken six weeks for you to get in touch if the things he left are valuable?" The woman looked down her nose, suspicion lining her brow.

Emily's heart pounded. Unaccustomed to being cross examined, she sucked in a deep breath and remembered the story Al had concocted. "He left them in a bag in a corner of the garage and like most people I hardly ever put the car away these days. I only came across the bag yesterday. He's probably wondering which house he left it in."

"What day was it?"

"Tuesday, March the Sixteenth."

The woman hooked the tea bag with a spoon, flicking it into a waste basket as she edged over to a geriatric desktop computer on the corner of the counter. She fired up the cumbersome machine, yawning as the reluctant screen chugged into life. "We scan a customer's driving licence at the time of booking, but names and vehicles should be recorded on the order page."

A few gasps and sighs later. "Three white vans out that day, all twenty-four hours only."

"Could you tell me the hirer's names please?"

"We're not supposed to. Data protection and all that."

Emily's features crumpled into a look of hurt innocence. "I'm only trying to do someone a good turn."

The woman glanced out of the window to make sure no customers were approaching before spinning the computer until it faced Emily. "You've got ten seconds. And don't tell anyone. Okay?" Emily nodded. It took a moment for her eyes to adjust to the flickering screen, but fortunately the dates and names stood out clearly.

Emily flipped her phone from her handbag and made to take a picture of the screen, but the woman thrust out a palm, shaking it in agitation. She slid a pad and pencil towards Emily, hissing, "No pictures. You'll get me sacked."

Emily cringed in apology as she searched for the relevant details. Three names stood out. Mr. D. Smith. Jamie van Wyck. Dimitor Puszkin. Her finger traced a horizontal line along each name to match up with the relevant licence number. The first two didn't tally. Not even close. The third one, PG18 XBT. *That's it. Well done Katharine.* Emily noted the name, Puszkin, and the Dorchester address, although she scribbled so fast she wasn't confident anyone would manage to read it, including herself. She'd barely finished before the woman spun the screen around and seconds later a colleague emerged from a door marked *Staff only*.

"Thank you," said Emily.

"No problem. Hope you find the right man." The woman gave a cheery wave as she left.

Emily couldn't wait to tell Al. A man with a foreign name, East European by the sound of it, drove the mysterious white van. This could be the vital clue. She toyed with the idea of phoning Al, but he'd be busy frying sausages in the middle of Tasty Treat's breakfast rush. She even contemplated jabbing the address into the satnav and driving to Mr Puszkin's. What would she do? Knock on his door and ask him what he was doing in Sea View Road on March 16th. *Oh, by the way, are you a KGB agent and did you have anything to do with Uncle Sebastian's death?* Even with adrenalin rushing, Emily could see the folly in such an approach. Instead, she gunned the accelerator, deciding individual interrogations perhaps were not her forte. Best to rest on her success that morning.

Fifteen minutes later she was busy again in Sea View Road, researching Puszkin in the Yellow Pages and local trades directory. No listings. She pottered around the bungalow, tidying, unwilling to immerse herself in any job requiring undivided attention while the same persistent thoughts drummed in her mind. The journal. The white van. The inescapable conclusion that Uncle Sebastian's sudden death hid a sinister secret.

By the time Al arrived she had worked herself into a blizzard of confusion.

"What if we can't find this Puszkin guy? What if that's not his name? What if he had a false driving licence? What if there were more of them? What if they're no longer in the country? How are we going to find out who killed Uncle Sebastian then?" Emily's voice was shrill. She had become obsessed with imponderables.

Al strolled over to the sink. "What you need is a glass of water."

"I don't need water, Al. Thank you. I need answers." Her tone sharp, laced with sarcasm.

"I think you do, Emily."

Al proceeded to fill the glass until it was half-full, turning around so he faced Emily before raising the glass over his head.

"What are you doing?" Irritation in Emily's tone.

"It's all about keeping things in perspective, Emily."

"I suppose you're going to spout that old chestnut about my glass being half empty."

Al gifted one of his dazzling smiles. "Actually I'm not. Come on, humour me, how heavy is this glass of water?"

"No idea, six ounces?" Emily's eyes rolled.

Al swirled the water with the glass still above his head. "Actually, the weight is irrelevant. If I hold it for a minute or so, it's fairly light. If I held it like this for a couple of hours, I guarantee my arm would be aching. If I held it through the afternoon until we'd finished work on the journal tonight, then I'd no longer be able to feel my arm. It would be paralysed and most likely the water would have spilled all over the floor. The weight wouldn't have changed, but the longer I hold it the heavier it feels."

Emily's shoulders relaxed. Her eyes closed. She took a deep breath. "I think I know where this is going."

Al lowered the glass and took a sip. "This water represents your worries and concerns, and you've had a few recently. Your uncle dying, decoding the journal, that angst with the old man yesterday and today chasing white van man. If you think about them all for a little while you can stay calm. Nothing happens. A bit more and it gets painful, you start to fret. Think of them all day long and you begin to feel numb. Your brain freezes and you won't be able to do anything else until you drop them."

Al tipped up the glass and drained it in one, provoking a paroxysm of coughing as the water located the wrong passageway. Fluid dripped from his mouth, squeezed in large droplets out of his eyes. He bent over, choking, hands on knees, battling to suck oxygen into bruised lungs.

When he looked up, Emily was laughing as never before. Not in Al's brief experience anyway. Her shoulders shook, head nodding as she gasped through a fit of snorts. "Who's paralysed now, Dr Freud?"

Al chuckled, still fighting for breath. "Don't make me laugh. I'm expiring here. Weymouth water's dangerous. Should come with a health warning."

They chuckled and panted until the transient hysteria eased. Emily was first to break the calm. "Thank you, Al. That's exactly what I needed."

"Me too. You can't beat a bit of psychobabble."

They worked for the next couple of hours, radio playing in the background, Al maintaining the light tone with his endless supply of amusing stories. There was also an uplifting one. Apparently, the old man's mate from the day before had called into the café that morning with a thank-you card and a bottle of fine wine.

"Told me Jack was stable and expected to make a full recovery in Dorset County Hospital," said Al. "Nice of him to drop by, I thought"

"How did he know you worked in the café?"

"He didn't. People don't tend to recognise you out of uniform. Actually, he said he remembered seeing you in the café and saw us walking off together. Thought he'd take a punt, pop into the café, and there I was."

"That's nice."

Al perceived tension in Emily's shoulders easing. Strain no longer creasing the corner of her eyes, the overwhelming pressure of earlier lifting.

"How about we visit Mr Puszkin?"

Emily looked up, surprised Al had brought up the subject. "I thought you said it was best to drop it, not think about all that for a while."

Al put down his pad. "Emily, we've not known each other that long, but I'd risk a week of my paltry wages that the moment I walked out of here your mind would be all over what you discovered this morning. Am I right?"

Emily didn't need to speak. A coy smile answered for her.

"Okay, let's go. It's the only way you'll get any sleep tonight."

Half an hour later they turned into Chapel Road on the fringe of a run-down estate, at odds with the quaint ambience of Dorchester's centre. The address Emily had scribbled led them to a big grey stone building, imposing in its pomp but now a mishmash of one-bedroom flats.

Up two flights of stairs to number eight, off a dingy landing, dimly lit, paint peeling from the bannister. Al knocked three times. No answer. He tried again. A door creaked in the next apartment along the corridor. A woman, around 30, spiky bottle-blonde hair, craned her neck. "No-one lives there at the moment. Not for weeks, maybe months."

"We're looking for a guy called Puszkin. Did he live here?" Al strolled towards the neighbour's flat, the woman backing behind the door, leaving it a few inches ajar.

"Never knew his name. Didn't speak much English. But this house is full of foreigners, Romanians, Poles, you name it. If it's any use, he was a plasterer. Skimmed that wall." The woman eased the door open enough to point towards the opposite wall, still bare plaster. "It was supposed to be painted or wallpapered by now, but try getting the landlord to do anything."

"Any ideas where Puszkin went?" The woman shook her head.

"Could you let us know if he returns, or if anyone else knows where he went?" said Al.

The woman shrugged, then nodded. Al dug in his pocket, locating a scrap of paper. Emily supplied a pen and Al wrote down his name, phone number and an aide memoire, *Looking for Puszkin. Flat 8*. He handed it to the woman. "Thanks, you've been a big help."

On the way back to the car, Emily offered an opinion. "Seems like that was a waste of time and petrol."

"Maybe. But you never know. This Puszkin guy, if that's his real name, may show up. And that woman might ring. Then again, it might be somebody else using a false driving licence. Happens all the time, especially with hire firms. Anyway, nothing ventured, and all that."

20

The flight into Sheremetyevo Airport was uneventful. I watched *The Elephant Man* on a grainy screen, marvelling at John Hurt's portrayal while doodling a few thoughts to augment my lecture. It wasn't a chore. I knew *The Two Ivans* as well as any historian alive. I'd grown to admire and respect them both in different ways, although in the case of *The Terrible* it was difficult to like someone who killed his eldest son and heir, and his unborn child, during one of his rages.

At the arrivals gate I spied a smart, if sullen, gentleman in a black suit holding a sign. *Prof. Sebastian Stearn*. He spoke no English, other than muttering something guttural I translated as, *Welcome to Moscow, I'm your driver*, although the hard consonants sounded harsh and metallic, rather than welcoming. Like the discharge of a Kalashnikov.

After an hour's drive through depressing outskirts, strewn with decrepit high-rise blocks, concrete crumbling as if mirroring the Soviet regime, the car dropped me off at the Four Seasons Hotel. I'd stayed here once before when the University picked up the bill. Impressive views of the Kremlin, a short walk from Red Square, rectangular stone pillars at the main entrance affording the building a grand, if stumpy, appearance.

"Professor Stearn, welcome back," said the desk clerk in fractured English, having done his homework. He handed me the key to Room 303, motioning for a bell boy. The room was big, a plush suite, the Kremlin's spearing towers silhouetted against the dying sun through the panoramic window. I unpacked, stomach queasy, mind foggy as it processed the job in hand. A recurring nightmare had troubled my sleep these past few nights. I'd open my lecture file in front of 2,000 people packed into a grand hall, only to find every page blank. Opening my mouth to speak, no words would come. I'd stand there frozen in time, sinister eyes boring into my soul. A thunderous bang would jerk me awake, sweat pouring down my back, heart pounding. I'd yearn for my old life. Safe in mundanity.

I forced my brain to concentrate on practicalities. How was I going to spend the next five days before the key lecture? I'd agreed to a couple of seminars in a questions and answers format, but they would amount to little more than an hour each.

The room telephone rang. "Hello, Professor Stearn. This is Anastasia. I'm your tour guide." The voice soft, accent mixed, English perfect. "I'm down in the bar if you would like to join me for a welcome drink." She could have been a travel rep on a package holiday to Majorca, but I appreciated the diversion.

"Ten minutes?" I said.

"Perfect."

I freshened up, changed shirts and 10 minutes later walked into the bar. Quiet. Three or four couples dotted in corners sipping cocktails, nibbling light snacks. A group of businessmen indulged in whispered conversation at one end of the bar while generic background crooning, Sinatra, I think, filtered through a hidden speaker. At the other end of the bar a woman with auburn hair, tied in the tidiest of buns held together with a tortoiseshell comb, sat on a stool, flicking through a folder on her lap. A fountain of bubbles detonated in a tall glass in front of her, as if poured recently. She looked up. I noticed a flash of shapely legs as she slid off the stool with an easy grace and walked towards me. She was beautiful, or had been at one time. As I looked into her sparkling eyes I began to sense the awkwardness I always felt around women to whom I was attracted.

She wore an air of efficiency, enhanced by her two-piece suit and high-heels that made her stand tall, although her frame was slight, features delicate. Around 40, I decided, although she could have been a couple of years either way. A badge on her lapel proclaimed, *Moscow Tours Guide*, over a logo of the Kremlin. Silver sheen accentuated rosebud lips as she spoke.

"Professor Stearn?"

"Yes."

"I'm Anastasia, but please call me Anna, everyone does."
We shook hands.

"Okay."

"Would you like a drink, on the tour company of course?"

"Whisky sour would do fine."

She fired out a hail of Russian and the bartender nodded. We retired to a table furthest from the other drinkers, indulging in small talk about my flight for a couple of minutes until my drink landed. She opened her file, proceeding to inform me of my itinerary.

"Tomorrow, we visit the new Memorial Museum of Cosmonautics. It opened earlier this year and is dedicated to space. I think you'll particularly enjoy the Gagarin exhibition. Most interesting and very famous, of course." I sensed she expected a reaction and I smiled obligingly, although space wasn't my thing. She continued, speaking louder than required, as if happy for others to hear. "Wednesday is your first seminar. Starts at eleven o'clock and a car will be outside the foyer at ten. Thursday we visit St Basil's Cathedral and Lenin's Mausoleum. Friday is your second seminar, again starts at eleven. In the afternoon the Pushkin State Museum of Fine Arts. Saturday is the most important. Your lecture, Professor. One o'clock. I know many dignitaries are looking forward to it."

The bartender wandered by, collecting used ashtrays off nearby tables, dropping off a small bowl of nuts on ours. Anna waited for him to return to the bar and disappear into the back room.

"I do hope the itinerary suits. Everything is going to plan ... Whisper." She fixed me with those sparkling eyes. I barely caught what she'd said. When it registered my training kicked in. Body language neutral. Breathing steady. Blank expression. But my heart was thumping. When Porter said he would supply a tour guide I hadn't expected she would also be my contact. Nor had I bargained for a beautiful woman who I'd known precisely 10 minutes and yet who stirred something inside I hadn't experienced in years.

I raised my voice a touch as the barman returned. "Thank you Anna. That all sounds very efficient. I look forward to a few days seeing the history and sampling the artistic delights of Moscow."

"Forgive me, Professor, you must be tired after your trip." Anna gathered her files, stood up, and I drained my glass. "Until tomorrow," she said.

We shook hands and I studied the easy sway of her hips, the natural poise of her deportment, as she strolled through the bar, along the foyer, into the Moscow night.

21

"Mum, you know I hate surprises."

Emily had opened the front door expecting to see the postman. Her parents were on the doorstep, Dad languishing a metre behind, smiling in expectation of the usual mother and daughter banter.

"Oh, thanks, Emily. Nice to see you too. We've driven two-and-a half hours, you know," said Eleanor.

"Why didn't you call?"

"It would have spoiled the surprise."

"I hate ... never mind, come in." Emily led them through to the lounge, although on the way Harry craned his head around the study door. Tidy piles of books, records and cds littered the floor.

"Looks like an aerial view of Tower Hamlets. Someone's been working hard," he said.

"That's what I'm here for."

"How's it going?"

"A bit slow. Lots to do."

"How's the journal working out? Made any sense of it?"

"Erm, yes. It all makes sense. Al cracked the code."

"And?"

"What do you mean?"

"Was it worth forking out four thousand pounds for? Any juicy bits?"

Emily chuckled. Nervous.

Harry looked perplexed. "Do we get to hear any of it?"

"All in good time, Dad. It's not easy decoding everything. We're working on it every day but it's slow going. It's a memoir of part of Uncle Sebastian's life. It could be fiction for all we know." Emily didn't want to share the story. Not yet. Too many imponderables. Too many loose ends, although she believed every page was true and accurate. In life, she'd spoken no more than a few inconsequential sentences to Uncle Sebastian, but in death she had bought into his voice. She understood his revelations could be construed as fiction, but the tone of his memoir appeared authentic. No glorifying in adventure. Instead, an honest fragility she found more beguiling with each reading. The possibility also remained that his past adventure had precipitated his sudden death. Again, a stretch, but it was too soon, too confused and cumbersome, to explain. The evidence amounted to no more than a feeling, as well as the unexplained sighting of a white van by an eccentric 92-year-old.

"You said *we*." Eleanor picked up on the pronoun.

"Pardon."

"You said, '*We* are working on it'."

"Me and Al, of course. It's faster that way." A catch of frustration in Emily's voice.

"Are you two serious?"

"Serious? How old-fashioned, Mum. Yes, we're serious about getting the journal decoded, if that's what you mean."

"It's not what I meant."

Harry sensed a squall brewing. Smoothing conversation between mother and daughter had become one of his essential life skills. He usually knew when to intervene. "Okay," he said. "We'll look forward to hearing Sebastian's story when you're ready."

The tension eased, Emily offering to make tea. "Why are you here? Apart from to give me a surprise."

Harry explained he needed to visit a local estate agent to discuss the value of the bungalow for probate purposes. He was considering keeping the property as a holiday bolthole. "So Mum and I can come down for weekends after I've had a busy week in London. You'd go a long way to rival these views. I'm also thinking of buying a little sailing boat. Nothing fancy, something to paddle around in. I'll probably need to get the agency to look after the bungalow during the week. Make sure there are no leaks, keep the garden tidy, that sort of thing."

"Doesn't Marcus do that?"

"He's been keeping an eye on the place, but it's not fair to impose on him any longer. He was a good friend to Sebastian."

"I find him a bit creepy." Emily's directness provoked a troubled frown on her mother's face.

"Why?"

"No one reason. Just seems to pop up all the time … like a stalker."

"That's a horrible thing to say. He does live here in the same road. Hardly surprising if you bump into him now and then."

"I know, but he watches the place all the time from his study and he's got binoculars in there. I've seen them."

Harry lifted a pair of binoculars in a case from a kitchen cupboard. "Sebastian had a pair too, Emily. That's what you do when you live by the sea with views like this." Harry swept his arm in a wide arc, mirroring the expansive panorama of another sunshine morning.

"Maybe you're right." Emily poured tea, handed out the cups, even supplied a selection of biscuits, and changed the subject. "Did Uncle Sebastian travel a lot?"

"Only when he was younger," said Harry. "Mostly in Europe, although I remember him going to New York once or twice to give lectures."

"What about Russia?"

"Yes, I have a vague memory of him going there when his publishers asked him to promote one of his books. Moscow, I think."

"Did he say anything about it?"

"Not that I recall. But Sebastian wouldn't. He wasn't boastful. Exactly the opposite. Always down to Earth. Why?"

"No reason. Trying to build a picture of his life, that's all."

"You've changed your tune," said Eleanor, crunching a ginger biscuit. Emily threw her a dark look. "No, I'm glad to hear it. I didn't think you were too impressed at the funeral."

Harry and Eleanor stayed an hour, during which Harry took an inventory of the furniture items and white goods for probate valuations, while Eleanor attacked the kitchen floor with a mop.

"You don't need to do that, Mum."

"Might as well make myself useful while your dad's auditing."

They chatted while she worked, Emily probing for information about Uncle Sebastian, mainly why he'd never married. Nothing, or at least nothing useful, was forthcoming, although the conversation remained convivial. When Harry and Eleanor were ready to leave, Emily accompanied them to the car and Harry seized the opportunity to study the bungalow's infrastructure, roof tiles and chimney pots in particular. He walked up the street, comparing them from different angles, eyes assimilating the sweep of the cul-de-sac.

"That big house on the end is quite a project, isn't it?" he said, staring at the red-brick building with its forest of scaffolding.

"Yeah, apartments. Lots of them, fancy prices too."

"You can tell that with all the cameras. Look at those two big beasts pointing our way. Big brother's watching you, Emily." He pointed out twin cameras, slung under the roof soffits like a pair of alien eyes, lenses reflecting the morning sun.

Harry and Eleanor departed and Emily made a mental note. She'd had an idea.

Al arrived later than usual. A fat fryer had caught fire at the café and a 17-year-old assistant had thrown a dishcloth over it in an attempt to stem the flames.

"She'd seen it done on television," explained Al. "Except she forgot the rag must be wet first and you're supposed to drape it over the pan and let go of it. She kept hold, the rag caught fire, the next thing she's running around the shop with a rag dripping fiery fat over all the tables."

"Anyone hurt?" said Emily.

"Fortunately, no. But it made a mess of the kitchen and because of the smoke we had to chuck most of the fresh sandwiches. It was all hands on deck for an hour. Anyway. I'm here now. What have you been up to?"

Emily told Al about her parents' visit, her father's plans for the bungalow, and the security cameras he'd spotted atop the red-brick building. Intrigued at the mention of cameras, Al walked to the front door, Emily following.

Al gazed at the end of the cul-de-sac. "That's interesting. I wonder if they work or whether they're for show, as a deterrent. Most cameras would be trained on the actual site, not down the road."

"Let's go and look." Emily was eager.

As they ambled up the road a big lorry rumbled by, carrying a cumbersome load of roof supports. It braked at the bottom of the cul-de-sac, performing a laborious six-point turn, sending its parking sensors into audio meltdown. Four men wearing hard-hats and yellow high-viz jackets emerged from the bowels of the building to assist unloading. Al held back. Not the optimum time to ask questions. The men went about their work while Al pointed out half a dozen more cameras clinging to vantage points.

They were about to return to the bungalow when another worker, this time in a red jacket and hard-hat, carrying a clipboard, walked towards them. He wore a shirt and tie. Not tradesman gear. His manner polite but inquisitive. "Can I help? Are you interested in one of the apartments?"

Al's initial thought clocked him as an estate agent, running an eye over a future investment, spotting a couple he might snare to land a commission. "Not exactly. We're from the bungalow down the street. More interested in the cameras actually."

"Why?" A note of suspicion in the man's question. Residents, especially Katharine, had already complained about the lorries, the mud on the road, the noise and security lights illuminating the site all night.

"We wondered whether they worked around the clock. Actually, we wondered whether they worked, full stop."

The man's shoulders relaxed, a smile playing on his lips. "I can assure you these are all working, 24-hour surveillance. I'm the site manager. Some of them are for site safety, making sure contract workers comply with regulations on hard hats, goggles, face masks, that sort of thing. Others are to deter anyone who might want to drive up at night, sometimes even during the day, to steal tools, equipment, diggers, cement mixers, you name it. You'd be surprised what goes missing from building sites."

"What about those?" Al pointed to the two large cameras trained down the street.

"They video every vehicle arriving on site. Means we have date, time and record of every delivery. Because there's only one way in, any thieves would be caught. I think the phrase is, red-handed."

"How long are the recordings kept?"

"Pete." One of the workmen shouted from the back of the lorry and the man broke away from Al and Emily to discuss the delivery. An animated conversation followed, after which Pete fished his mobile phone from his pocket and started to walk back towards the building.

Emily looked at Al, determined glint in her eyes. She started to stride after Pete, but Al put his arm out to halt her progress. "No, I'll go." He jogged past the lorry, catching up with Pete before he slipped inside the security barriers protecting the site. "Pete, one more question, please."

Pete spun around. "Sorry, it's not a good time. The delivery's all wrong and if we don't get it right we'll have men idle on site all afternoon."

"Please, one minute."

"Okay." Pete sighed.

"Would the cameras trained down the street have footage from six weeks ago?"

"Almost certainly."

"Is there any way we could get hold of it?"

"That's two questions."

"Sorry, it's important."

"Why do you want it?" Pete sounded intrigued.

"A white van visited our bungalow one morning six weeks ago and we need to find its driver. It's a complicated story, but it would be an enormous help."

Pete dug in his pocket and pulled out a wallet. Slipping the clipboard under an arm he rifled through the compartments, extracting a business card, handing it to Al. "ACE Security, that's who we use here. They provide all the security and cameras. The recordings are all stored on memory cards, I think for a year."

"So six weeks should be no problem."

"No, but you'll need to write or phone, telling them the date and time. Finding the right card should be easy. The only

124

problem you'll have is data protection. Everyone's hot on that these days. For all they know you could be snooping on a cheating husband or wife, or planning a burglary. They wouldn't want to get mixed up in anything like that. Not unless there's been a crime and the police asked for it. Now, I really must go."

Al offered his hand and they shook. "Thanks Pete, you've been a big help."

22

I rose early next morning and went for a run by the banks of the Moskva River, passing the opulent spires of the Kremlin, trying to reconcile the unthinking mundanity of pounding one foot in front of the other with the surreal thoughts whirling through my mind.

Giving a lecture was second nature. I had presented thousands over the last 20 years. If we all have a talent, I'd come to recognise that selling the past to the present was mine. This lecture was no different, apart from the prospect of a lethal and explosive event interrupting at any moment. No training could entirely erase that expectation, but the mind games I had undergone with the department's psychological experts at Secretarium helped.

I showered, dressed, managed a decent breakfast of eggs on a toasted muffin, arriving outside the front of the hotel a few minutes before 10am. A Moscow taxi pulled up, Anna waving from the back seat. I clambered in.

"Good run?" she said.

"How did you …?" I didn't finish the sentence. She knew I'd been jogging. Of course she did. Someone was monitoring my every move, probably both British and Russian security services. I was the meat in a sandwich of covert intelligence. A sobering thought. I composed myself. "Yes, I try to get out first thing whenever I'm away. Gets the blood pumping. Sets me up for the day."

We swapped small talk as the car crawled north out of the city centre, Anna ensuring the hotel was to my liking. Pointing out landmarks. Tour guide chat. The sort of neutral conversation employed when others may be listening. I assumed the taxi was a commercial cab and the driver hadn't been checked. That would explain it.

The taxi steered into the car park alongside the Museum of Cosmonautics and Anna arranged for the driver to return in three hours. We strolled down the driveway, adorned in a blaze of spring colour, admiring the late-flowering white and golden daffodils, tulips and azalea. At the entrance to the museum stood a space capsule. I was struck by the size, tiny, squat, as if shrunk by the stamp of a malevolent giant in one of those ubiquitous children's cartoons.

"You wouldn't get me in one of those," I said.

"No. Too dangerous?"

I flattened my palm against the top of my head. "No, literally, you wouldn't get me in. I'm over six foot. Every time I breathed in, I'd bang my head on the roof."

Anna laughed. "Come on. Let's go inside, I'll show you around."

For the next two hours that's exactly what she did. We visited the Gagarin exhibition and studied the capsule used by Yuri Gagarin when he became the first human to orbit the Earth 20 years earlier. One orbit only, I learned. The flight lasting 108 minutes from launch to landing. Anna recited a plethora of other details, grid references, orbital parameters, space co-ordinates, but most of them went over my head, much like Vostok 1.

When you've seen one capsule, you've seen them all. That's what I was thinking. I didn't say it, not wanting to appear rude as Anna proved a conscientious guide, her manner easy, laugh infectious. A procession of tourists, having spied Anna's *Tour Guide* lapel badge, even tagged behind at one stage, soaking in the free commentary. We moved on to view Moon fragments behind a sign explaining American president Richard Nixon presented them to Soviet citizens in June 1970. From there, on to a portfolio of space photographs, the ones taken of Earth by far the most spectacular. Swirls of vivid blue and white, the perfect aspect of mankind's illuminated sphere against black infinity strangely humbling. After two hours I was all spaced out. I thought I'd got away with it when I masked a yawn with a hand and a little cough, but Anna missed nothing.

"Okay, I think that's enough. You've had your spacewalk. Let's enjoy some sunshine," she said.

I found her accent enchanting. Not the rough, Slavic, heavy grunt of some Russians. Anna's voice benefited from delicate modulation, a touch nasal, hoarse even, but with a pleasing lilt.

We ambled out through the café and Anna stopped to buy sandwiches. "Cheese fine?" I nodded and once outside she headed for a wooden bench seat by a fountain, the aspect open, constant trickling water supplying convenient sound proofing. At least that's why I decided she'd chosen the spot.

"Did you enjoy the tour?" she said.

"Oh yes, very interesting."

"Liar." Her tongue curled around the accusation, the word trailing out, long and sensual.

"What?" I spluttered, feeling cheese crumbs trying to escape from the side of my mouth.

"I can tell when a man is bored. All your questions were simple. Polite, but simple. A man with fire and passion in his subject asks complicated questions. Ones that sparkle with curiosity."

I put my cheese sandwich back in the cardboard container balanced on my lap and took a sip of water from the bottle Anna had also supplied. She had a point. "Well, my mind wasn't entirely on space," I admitted.

"It's important that everything is normal." Her voice lowered, a steely edge in her tone.

"Don't you think I realise that. It's why I went for a run this morning, as I always do. It's actually not normal for me to walk around a museum in the middle of the day." I sensed the irritated hiss in my voice and took a calming breath.

"But it looks perfectly normal, Professor. Perception is everything."

I took a bite from my sandwich. Tangy and smooth. Anna did the same with hers. We sat chewing for around a minute before I broke the silence. "I've not done extensive research on this, Anna, but in my opinion there are few meals that can't be improved by the addition of cheese. Even Russian cheese."

Anna nodded. "That, Professor, is profound."

"I thought that too."

"But the same goes for photographs." I must have looked perplexed because Anna proceeded to explain. "They are improved by cheese also. Did you know the reason people say *cheese* when taking a photograph is because it's guaranteed to make your mouth and teeth assume the position of a smile?"

"Of course I know that. Everyone who speaks English knows that."

"But do you know how that tradition began?" I shook my head, half-wishing I'd asked for a ham sandwich.

"Well, there is a Russian connection. It is thought it was first spoken of by an American ambassador to the Soviet Union. A man named Joseph E. Davies. He wrote a book entitled *Mission to Moscow* and a film of the same name came out in 1943."

"Never heard of it."

"Aha." Anna raised a hand to indicate there was more. "While Mr Davies was having his picture taken on the film set, he revealed his secret for taking a good picture. Always say *cheese*. He said a politician had given him the advice. Didn't say who, but everyone reckons it was American president Franklin D. Roosevelt. The world has been doing so ever since."

It might have been the backdrop of the warm sun, the scent of beautiful flowers and the sound of the trickling fountain, but at that moment I found the animation in Anna's face as she told her inconsequential story beguiling.

"So what do people say in Russia?"

"Seer," said Anna. "That's Russian for cheese and by happy coincidence it also forms a smile-like shape on the face. To be honest, people here in Russia also say *cheese*. Like Moon dust, Russians are not all averse to receiving gifts from America."

Anna was clever. She had detected my nervous tension earlier that morning, assumed the persona of a diligent tour guide, added a sprinkle of feminine guile, and here I was laughing in public like a man without a care in the world. As planned. I bit into the sandwich once more. This time, as I chewed, Anna's voice was soft, eyes smiley, despite the chilling nature of her message.

"Kalenkov has confirmed his attendance. He will be sitting alongside Brezhnev in the front row of the hall, immediately before the lectern from where you will be giving your lecture."

I nodded, immediately transported from soft cheese stories to hard reality.

"All you need to do is act naturally."

"What about when it happens in front of me? What do you suggest I do naturally then?"

I was testing her. I didn't like myself for it, but curious to hear her reaction. I had practised every possible scenario at Secretarium. *How to respond naturally to a traumatic event.* That was the title of the role play. The procedure was clear. Don't run away. Don't hit the floor. Don't rush to help. Initially, don't do anything, except freeze. Look shocked. Numb. Detached. People react in different ways to catastrophic events, but the first instinct is to survive. The brain takes seconds to work out how to do that. Survival favours those most effective at utilising those brief moments.

A fiery glint replaced Anna's smile. "Professor, don't play with me. If you didn't know how to act natural in such circumstances, you wouldn't be here." In an instant, the sunny disposition returned and she laughed out loud. "What a beautiful day."

Our taxi driver returned. I spent the rest of the afternoon at the hotel, preparing for my first seminar the next day, listening to Vivaldi on my Sony Walkman. Unusually, I struggled to absorb the seminar notes. I couldn't stop thinking of Anna, wondering about a woman who could make cheese a source of intelligent conversation, who gleaned genuine excitement from squashed lumps of metal and fragments of Moon dust. Who could criticise without causing offence and speak in lyrical fashion on all manner of topics. A woman who appeared to straddle the worlds of light and darkness as a leaf dances on the shifting wind.

I found myself mouthing Keats. "*I almost wish we were butterflies and lived but three summer days, three such days with you I could fill with more delight than fifty common years could ever contain.*"

I was useless with relationships. Always had been. Bad days. Good days. Arguments. Misunderstandings. Like clearing a path through thorny brambles. I'd known Anna precisely 24 hours. Knew nothing about her, except that she was the conduit keeping me informed, guiding my way, supplying protection. In return, all she required was my trust.

Concentrate on the job in hand, I told myself. *There's nothing like an old fool.*

23

She gazed at the painting of Uncle Sebastian on the kitchen wall, the one with the piercing eyes that followed her around the room. A strange feeling came upon her. A tense discomfort.

Al had finished reciting the journal's latest instalment minutes before and they had adjourned to the kitchen for a late beer. Something was troubling Emily. She couldn't put her finger on it but it kept creeping into her mind, noisy yet indistinct, like scratching in the eaves. *Doubt? Sadness? Regret?*

She wasn't sure she'd fully experienced any of those emotions, yet tension is how she imagined regret. Regret that she'd been mean towards her mum at the funeral. Regret that she'd been disrespectful to Uncle Sebastian's memory. For the first time, Uncle Sebastian was talking to her in the journal. That's what it felt like. Revealing his innermost thoughts. His reluctance. His fears. His feelings towards a woman he barely knew. With each reading the man she'd dismissed as sad and boring was transforming into a character of such yearning complexity it made her heart race.

Al was first to voice his opinion, popping a couple of beer tops with a gentle hiss. "I hardly dare think what's going to happen when he gives his lecture. Must have taken nerve to get embroiled in something like that in Moscow in the middle of the Cold War. I feel nervous for him."

Emily's gaze remained glued to the painting. "Don't you think he has kind eyes? Piercing, but kind, as if he's looking out for us."

"I'd never thought of that, but now you mention it, I see how they follow you." Al walked back and forth, arching his head backwards, manufacturing the illusion of movement.

Emily dragged her attention away from the painting, fixing her eyes on Al. "That's why we have to look out for him, Al. We must get that CCTV footage and find that white van driver. If something dreadful happened in Moscow, then

Uncle Sebastian's death could have been the Russians taking revenge. That's what they do."

"In spy novels maybe."

Emily put her beer bottle down. "No, Al, not only in spy novels. What about Alexander Litvinenko, a Russian defector poisoned in Britain in 2006 when someone put a radioactive substance in his tea? What about Georgi Markov, killed by a poisoned umbrella tip in London in 1978?" Her voice gained in animation as she warmed to her theme. "What about the Novichok poisoning in Salisbury in 2018 when Sergei Skripal, a double agent, and his daughter, almost died, and a member of the public did after picking up a stray bottle. Then there's Alexei Navalny, the Russian opposition leader, who almost died of poisoning in 2020. I could go on, Al. That's what the Russians do. In real life."

Al's eyes widened, nonplussed at the eloquence and overt fire in Emily's monologue. "You've been doing your research. But let's not get too far ahead of ourselves. I'll grant the white van is a bit of a mystery, but there may well be a harmless explanation. I think we should get on to this ACE Security place and see where it takes us. I'll do that tomorrow."

A nod of determination from Emily, eyes dancing with zeal and purpose. "I'll start asking around. Someone might have seen something unusual, had their reservations, but been too timid to report them."

"House-to-house enquiries, you mean."

"Something like that."

"Okay, but be careful. You don't want to scare anyone or come across as odd."

Emily's brow furrowed. "Odd? Why would people think I was odd?" Al smiled, unsure if that was Emily's little joke, but not brave enough to ask. They finished their beers and agreed to meet up as usual the next day.

***

Al slipped out of Tasty Treat mid-morning. He rarely took advantage of his half-hour break each shift, but he needed to make the phone call. Ambling down the promenade, he chose one of the shelters on the shaded road side, out of the sea breeze, punching in the number on the business card Pete had given him.

"ACE Security. How can I help?" The receptionist owned the sort of voice that sang rather than spoke. Bright and cheerful. A good sign, thought Al, proceeding to explain the reason for his call.

"Hmm, not sure we can help. Not without the consent of the building company. Hold on a minute. I'll check." Five minutes later, seconds before Al would have decided he'd been stood up, the woman's voice sang again. "Thanks for waiting. Sorry to keep you, but I've spoken to the manager. As I thought, you need to take it up with the building company."

"But the site boss told me to ring you."

"I'm sorry, the building company, that's what the manager told me." Exasperated, Al rang off.

Arriving at the bungalow two hours later, he expected to hear a breakdown of Emily's house-to-house enquiries. Instead, she met him at the front door, coat in hand, explaining she'd had second thoughts. Best if they made their enquiries together. He said nothing, but took it as a compliment. First call was to Katharine.

"Hello Dear, what a nice surprise. Oh, good, you've brought your young man to see me too. What a lovely smile." Katharine seemed genuinely pleased to see Emily as she negotiated the turning procedure at her front door.

Al threw Emily a smug look, stepping in past William and Kate on their way out as he did so.

"Oh, they are naughty," said Katharine. "First chance they get, they're off. Like my first husband. Come in. You'll have a cup of tea, won't you?"

Al, nose battling the first wave of cat urine, shook his head, but Emily nodded. "Of course, we'd love one. I'll make it Katharine. Sit yourself down."

While Emily made tea, Katharine treated Al to a potted history of her life story. Scurrying into Tube tunnels when bombs dropped on London during the Second World War, marrying twice, an American serviceman followed by an Irish geography teacher. Sitting on the bench as a magistrate. She would have continued, but Al interrupted.

"Katharine, we're trying to find out a bit more about Emily's Uncle Sebastian. How well did you know him?"

"I knew he was kind. The postman told me he always gave him a bonus at Christmas. Once he came across and shovelled snow from my driveway, asked if I needed any shopping doing. I didn't, but it was nice of him to care."

"Was that it?"

"Well, we weren't seeing each other or anything, if that's what you mean."

Al stifled a chuckle. "No, I didn't mean that."

Emily served up the teas.

"There are biscuits in the cupboard." Katharine pointed behind her.

"No thanks. Can you remember anything else about him?" said Emily. She took a notebook from her bag to jot down any relevant facts.

"No, I don't … actually, yes, he did come over to check on me when I had my funny turn a few years ago. The doctors had a name for it. A medical name. I can't remember now, but it was a little stroke. Sat with me for more than an hour. I told him I was all right but he insisted. Showed me a photograph of his lady."

"Really?" Emily glanced at Al, intrigued.

"Maybe it was his wife, maybe she'd died, I can't remember now."

"He never married, Katharine." Al eased a palm downwards, semaphore for Emily to lower her tone. Her eagerness didn't travel well.

"Well, I don't know who she was, but she was pretty."

Al interjected. "I bet the boys thought you were pretty too."

Katharine preened. "Not like this lady. She looked like a film star. Long hair. Lovely smile."

"Were they together on the photograph?"

"No, only the lady. Riding a bicycle. Or at least standing there astride a bicycle."

Emily jumped in again. "Was the photo in a frame? Was it colour or black and white?"

Katharine looked flustered. "I'm not sure. He took it from his wallet, I think. It was only small, but I could tell she meant a lot to him."

"How?" said Emily.

"I just could. Women know these things. A woman shares secrets with her closest friend. A man is more likely to share secrets with strangers, or acquaintances, or sometimes a strange woman from across the road he hardly knows."

That was deep, thought Al. Katharine had all but lost the use of her legs, struggled to hear, eyes refused at times to focus, and she talked to cats, but the wisdom of ages appeared intact. "Very wise," he said.

"Well, there's one advantage to being old." Her rheumy eyes twinkled.

"What's that?"

"Good judgment, the sort that comes from life experience. And at 92 I've had more than most."

"Yeah, but where does experience come from?" Al was almost flirting.

Katharine chuckled. "That comes from poor judgment." Al and Emily both laughed, nodding in youthful agreement as they drained their tea.

Al was about to suggest it was time they left when a thought occurred. "Tell me Katharine, who did Sebastian see most around here? Who knew him best?"

Her reply was instant. "Marcus. I used to see him heading across to visit the professor all the time. Never the other way around. I think Marcus must have liked the view from the bungalow. They seemed like good friends."

Emily wondered. She knew the view from Marcus's study rivalled anything from the bungalow. If anything, the extra height made the panorama even more expansive. "Did Mary, Marcus's wife, ever join them?"

"A few years back I'd watch her pottering across the road with their teenaged daughter. She used to practise on the professor's piano. But can't say I've seen Mary for months. She has a dodgy hip, never gets out much. Keeps herself to herself. Always has done."

136

Al rose from his seat. They shook hands, Katharine holding on firmer and longer than she needed to. "Katharine, it has been a pleasure to meet you. We'll see ourselves out."

"Keep me in touch with your investigations, young man, won't you?"

"You'll be the first to hear."

The front door clicked shut. As they trundled down the path Emily turned to Al. "Do you think …?"

Al interrupted. "I know what you're going to say. Who knows? The lady in the photo could be Anna from Moscow, or she could be Angela from Manchester. We'll probably never know."

Emily stopped mid-path, mulling her thoughts. "I'll speak to Dad. He has Uncle Sebastian's personal effects. He must have his wallet. The photo might still be in there."

"Good idea. Anyway, where to now?"

They went next door to number 16, the dressing gown and slippers man. Fortunately, he answered the door fully dressed, but kept them on the doorstep, denying any knowledge of the mysterious white van and proved less than helpful when asked about Uncle Sebastian. "Never saw or heard from him. But then I keep myself to myself. Most people do around here."

They bypassed the young couple's house at number 13 as there was no car in the driveway. No one answered the doorbell at number 11, the house next to Al. Emily turned towards the bungalow, but Al stopped. "You go on. I'll nip up to the site and have a word with Pete."

"Okay."

Al broke into a jog, spying Pete half-way up the scaffolding, in animated conversation with two tradesmen. When Al arrived at the perimeter fence he waited until Pete broke away from his chat and then whistled, a shrill single note, as if hailing a cab. Pete turned and Al beckoned him, sensing a frown fix on the manager's features. At least Pete waved to indicate he was on his way.

"People accuse builders of whistling at the public, don't they? Not usually the other way round," said Pete, as he emerged from the bowels of the building, approaching the other side of the fence from Al.

"Sorry. I didn't want to miss you."

"Any luck with the cameras?"

Al shook his head. "ACE told me to come back to you. You own the footage so they'd need your permission. I wondered if you might be able to help. It's important to my girlfriend." It was the first time Al had described Emily in that way. He was surprised how easily it tripped off the tongue considering their relationship was unlike any he'd experienced.

"Why is it so important?"

"Emily's trying to understand the final hours of her uncle's life. They'd not been that close, even though she comes from a small family. She regrets that. It's troubling her. She's looking for closure. Maybe she'll spot him on camera." Al milked the truth, but convinced himself it was in a good cause.

"I thought you were looking for a white van driver." Pete's brow knitted. He looked dubious.

"We are, but only because she thinks the van might solve a puzzle. Chances are it was a simple delivery somewhere on the street. Nothing to do with her uncle. If so, she can move on."

Pete sighed. He could do without the hassle, more pressing matters on his mind. The building job had slipped months behind schedule. A late delivery penalty would mean forfeiting his bonus. No Caribbean cruise for the family next year. Al, however, seemed amiable. He reminded Pete of his younger self. Polite, yet confident and eager. If he could enable his girlfriend a little comfort at a dark time in her life, then where was the harm in that?

"Okay, remind me of the date?"

"March the sixteenth."

"I'll request the memory card. We sometimes have to do that to check on deliveries. Don't know how long it will take, a few days, a week at most, but I'll drop it into your bungalow when it arrives. Just between you and me, right."

"Of course," said Al.

"What's the number?"

"Sorry."

"Of the bungalow."

"Number seven. Thanks Pete. I owe you one. If there's anything I can do."

Pete noted the number on his clipboard, turned, but before sauntering towards the building spun around again and shouted. "Mud on the road."

"Pardon," said Al.

"Stop the bloody residents complaining about mud on the road."

24

I arrived at the Sokolniki Centre alone, in good time, courtesy of a taxi Anna ordered.

An organiser accompanied me to one of the small halls where a poster at the entrance bore my name and the seminar's title, *Empress or Temptress?* I had chosen to speak and field questions on Catherine the Great, one of my specialist subjects guaranteed to entice a capacity audience. Never failed.

There was something bewitching about the lady who ruled Russia for three decades in the 18th Century, extending its power, turning the nation into one of the world's major political players. She appealed to anyone with a pulse. Students in particular. Her allure probably lay in the myths describing her as a nymphomaniac and a voyeur. My lectures always cut through the myths. Dismissed the sex, in favour of analysing the power axis of the lovers Catherine took after overthrowing her only husband, Czar Peter III, in a coup d'etat, installing them in prime positions in Russian government.

I estimated around 150 seats. With 20 minutes to go, the hall, floor sloping upwards away from the stage, was already filling. By 11am standing room only. I relished the cut and thrust of lively historical debate, especially as organisers had invested in a state-of-the-art audio loop system allowing an interpreter to relate my words to the audience in real time via headphones. My Russian was passable, fluent in ordinary conversation, but inadequate at times to cope with the pace and demanding nuance of a technical debate.

Flurries of applause greeted my opening remarks. Knowing looks and the odd wink swapped between a bunch of middle-aged men to my left as I mentioned Sergei Saltykov, Catherine's lover during her marriage. Talk turned to Stanislaus Poniatowski, with whom she bore a daughter, and who was later installed as king of Poland. More knowing looks.

Sensing an enthusiastic connection, I switched from the lectern, sliding onto a seat centre stage. I slipped on headphones, inviting questions. As the first one arrived, a commotion at the entrance attracted my attention. Six soldiers, bearing rifles, clattered in, taking up stations either side of the door. A few seconds later three officers entered. Heads turned, a murmur of anticipation reverberated around the hall.

At first I struggled to identify them, the bright spotlight compromising my vision while the back of the hall was dark. But as the officers strode forward, their green parade uniforms and service caps complete with crowns and black visors, became visible.

An usher escorted them to the front of the hall while another swiftly vacated three seats in the front row. As they took their places my heart thumped. I knew these men. I'd plastered pictures of them, along with half a dozen other high-ranking Soviets, on my bedroom wall at Secretarium. Last thing I thought of at night. First thing I saw in the morning. The crowd settled, two ushers making calming signals with their outstretched palms. The room fell silent. An usher nodded, as if affording me permission to continue. I ignored him.

Instead, my eyes fixed on the officers, my brain computing what I knew about them, although my training kicked in to ensure no adverse body language. I couldn't help it. The three wise monkeys of Japanese maxim came to mind. See no evil. Hear no evil. Speak no evil.

On the left of the trio, flicking dandruff from his shoulder pads, was Maksim Sokolov, a veteran force in Russian military strategy. In the middle sat Yuri Drozdov, in charge of Department S in Moscow, responsible for the placement and deployment of foreign spies. He was also the man who led KGB forces that stormed the Afghan presidential palace in 1979 to pave the way for the Soviet invasion of Afghanistan. According to Secretarium, Drozdov was busy creating a new KGB special forces unit called Vympel.

But the man on the right caused sweat to trickle even more freely down the middle of my back. Colonel Igor Kalenkov. Younger, sterner than the others, chiselled features, dark hair, piercing eyes boring into mine. How had Porter described him on the roof in Cambridge? *The biggest current threat to Western democracy*. He'd added, *Out of control*, for good measure. I fought to prevent my mind overloading, concentrating on the subject of the seminar.

A man in the middle of the audience snapped the tension by standing to ask a question. The translation crackled in my headphones. "Catherine ruled for 34 years, until 1796. Why do you think no woman has ruled Russia since?" Heads turned towards the three officers, sniggers rippling through the audience. A loaded question, requiring a nuanced response. I sucked in a deep breath.

My tone was measured. "Women, irrespective of their party affiliations, must contend with all sorts of accusations and pressures if they are to wield political power. This is true of great women down the sweep of history. Cleopatra was derided as a sexual deviant, Ann Boleyn falsely accused of affairs with a string of courtiers, including incest with her brother. Catherine de Medici portrayed as nurturing a harem of ladies-in-waiting to seduce noblemen and act as prostitutes for her young sons. The notion of sex is used against women in power. Probably by jealous men. It is hardly surprising that women might think twice before running the gauntlet of men's imaginations."

As a round of polite applause rippled across the hall, from my peripheral vision I watched Kalenkov absorb my answer, only to yank off his headphones. He rose to his feet, standing tall, a commanding figure in dress uniform. He spoke in perfect English.

"Professor, your prime minister in the UK is the most powerful woman in the world right now. Mrs Thatcher wears a skirt, but in every way she tries to be a man. You do not see her promoting women. Instead, she surrounds herself with sycophants in grey suits, men who would dance to her tune. They call her the best man in the cabinet. Is it not the truth that women in power do their gender a disservice?"

A deep murmur, like the tuning groans of a double bass, resonated around the hall. I wondered how to play it, before responding. "Catherine must have filled Russian men with insecurities beyond measure."

"Why do you say that, Professor?" Kalenkov folded his arms, apparently eager to hear my riposte.

"Because her son, Emperor Paul the First, who Catherine had tried to prevent inheriting the throne, passed a law forbidding any woman from ascending the Russian crown in the future. What could he have been so afraid of?" Applause, this time generous and enthusiastic.

A thin smile played on Kalenkov's lips. I thought he might counter with another retort but he didn't, sitting down, crossing his legs, fiddling with the strap on his jackboot. A short while later he departed, along with the other officers. The questions continued to fire in and I warmed to the challenge, enjoying the thrust and parry of debate more than I could remember.

The session overran and when the moderator called an end to proceedings he motioned for me to follow an usher. I grabbed my jacket, heading back stage to my waiting taxi. The engine was running, but a man stood by the bonnet, smoking a cigarette, flanked by two rifle-bearing troops. Kalenkov. *How could he know?* That was my first thought. I began to palpitate. I forced myself to calm, breathing deep, face stony. *No, he couldn't know. If he knew I'd have been on the way to a Kremlin dungeon an hour ago instead of discussing the reign of Catherine the Great and the role of women leaders in general.*

Kalenkov took a long drag on his cigarette as I approached. "Professor, I congratulate you. A most interesting seminar. I'm not sure I agree with every philosophy you advocate but then agreeing all the time is boring, don't you think?"

"So long as we agree to disagree," I said, not entirely sure what I meant.

Kalenkov smirked. "I knew you would be interesting, Professor. I have read your books."

"Any in particular?"

"The Two Ivans. They are men close to my heart. How to rule as a great autocrat. A subject that goes to the core of Russian history."

"My lecture on Saturday is on exactly that topic." We were conversing like two old friends on university campus, wondering what to do and where to go at the weekend.

"Yes, I shall be there. The General Secretary, too. We are honoured to have such an eminent student of Russian history at our nation's conference."

We shook hands. For an instant, as I felt the twist of bony fingers, I contemplated what evil they had wrought. *Touch no evil.* My mind shuddered with my own version of the Japanese wise monkey maxim, but my lips smiled. Kalenkov and his guards clambered into a large black 4x4. The taxi ferried me back to my hotel.

I picked up the key from reception and headed for my room. The *Do not disturb* sign was in place, as I had left it, the maid having serviced the room before I departed for the seminar. I didn't relish hotel staff snooping through my room even though nothing more incriminating than old history essays filled my suitcase.

I glanced at the bedside cupboard and froze. My fine silver neck chain, a present from my mother, no longer conformed to the shape of a figure three where I'd left it on the surface by the table lamp. An old trick, but effective when deliberating the presence of an imposter. I opened the top drawer to discover a clumsy hand had displaced the thin strand of blue wool I'd left on top of my diary. The same person had probably rifled through the rest of my belongings too. Perhaps a disreputable staff member on the look-out for an easy touch. Guests often leave cash lying around. Or it could be … I didn't dare think. My mind scurried down dark alleys, none of them ending with an apology from an embarrassed hotel manager. But who would be interested in a boring, middle-aged history professor?

I decided to take lunch in the cocktail bar. Nothing fancy. A burger with fries and salad garnish, a cold beer to chase it down. I had almost finished when I spotted Anna through the double doors, bustling through reception. A radiant smile as fresh as a raindrop for the desk clerk, a breezy chat with the concierge, her blue suit and tour guide badge allowing her to blend with the environment. I wondered how long that guise must have taken to perfect. How many hours of normalcy, how many foot-plodding miles around the numerous hotels and landmarks of Moscow must be baked into her cover story.

She parked herself and her ever-present clipboard on a plush leather armchair in a sedate corner of the foyer. When I approached she jumped up and assumed the sunny demeanour that acts as currency in the travel business. *Acts.* A good description. The more I saw Anna, the more I appreciated her talent. She was a sublime actress.

"Are you having a lovely day, Professor?" The tenor and pitch of her voice sweet and tuneful. Reminded me of a skylark's call.

"Yes, Anna, the seminar went smoothly. In fact, exceeded expectations. It was quite a success. A full house no less."

"Excellent, what would you like to do with the rest of the afternoon?"

"Nothing too strenuous. A walk in a park. Take in some fresh air, soak up Moscow's rare sunshine."

"I know just the place, Professor."

Half an hour later we were strolling in Neskuchny Garden, the oldest park in Moscow Views of the Moskva River, birds singing, squirrels running freely in the trees. A green hideaway.

I sucked in clean air. "That's better. I needed that. It was quite a morning."

Anna scanned the immediate fields and woods, head swivelling, steady stare searching for prying eyes or the glint of binoculars. She'd chosen the quietest section of the park. Away from the tennis courts and football field, from where we could hear distant shouts and cheers, as well as the occasional whistle. No-one within 50 metres.

"Why? What was so exciting?" she asked.

"I met him."

"Who?"

"Kalenkov. Shook hands with him. Or he shook my hand, to be precise. He came to the seminar with two other officers. We exchanged views on Catherine the Great. He stayed behind afterwards to tell me how much he enjoyed it."

Anna absorbed the information. When she spoke I sensed a mix of relief and excitement in her tone. "That's great. Means he's much more likely to turn up on Saturday."

"Said he was looking forward to it."

"Brilliant."

"There's another thing."

"What?"

"Someone's been rummaging through my hotel room."

25

The dramatic vista of King's College chapel hove into view.

"Pull in there." Al pointed to a space by a parking meter and Emily steered in. She'd only seen the chapel on television before. *Carols from King's at Christmas*. The building appeared even more impressive in real life, luminescent stone making it seem the sun was shining although the grey cloud cover hung thick enough to feel a few drops of rain.

After listening to the latest instalment of the journal, Emily had persuaded Al to take a day off from the café to accompany her to Cambridge. He'd had to swap his easy midweek shift for a busy Saturday but he realised Emily simmered with pent-up tension. She felt Uncle Sebastian's danger. It rivalled her own desire to find the white van man. Al asked her what she wanted from the Cambridge trip.

"Explanation. Evidence. Something tangible to prove what we're reading is true," she'd said.

"Don't think you're going to get that."

It didn't matter. Emily remained determined to visit the site where Uncle Sebastian's story began. They fed the meter, walked to Clare College gates and paid the admission fee to a chatty lady in a reception hut, who informed them the fellows' gardens, Old Court college chapel, hall and quadrangle were open, but student accommodation and study blocks off limits. They ambled onto Clare Bridge.

"What a fantastic place," said Emily. "This must be where Uncle Sebastian waited for his clandestine meeting. The exact spot, I'm sure, just as he described it."

They stopped, leaning on the balustrade, Emily's fingers caressing one of the stone orbs, smooth to the touch, watching a couple of punts in the distance.

"If it is, then that's where his meeting with Porter must have been." Al pointed to the college roof, lofty brick chimneys reaching for the grey sky, dormer windows set into slate, a view that probably hadn't changed for centuries. They proceeded through Old Court's arched entrance, spying a heavy wooden door on their right. A sign proclaimed *Students only*. Al glanced over his shoulder, pushing the door open at the same time. Moments later they were climbing a cold stone staircase.

"This is it, this is it, Al," Emily's intended whisper equalling her anticipation as her voice echoed around the walls. Al put a finger to his lips. They reached the top, facing them a sash window leading on to the lead guttering, matching the description in the journal. Al tried to lever the window open. Stuck fast. Emily clenched her fists, shaking them in excitement as she spied Clare Bridge below, imagining Porter watching Uncle Sebastian from his vantage point all those years before.

Al's voice contained a heavy note of caution. "This doesn't prove anything, Emily."

"I know that, but everything's exactly as Uncle Sebastian described it. Let's not be negative."

"I don't want you to be disappointed, that's all."

Emily ignored his remark, too intent on her next plan. She descended the staircase in double time, Al hurrying to catch up. A few minutes later she'd discovered the whereabouts of Corpus Christie College and they were heading along King's Parade, past King's College on the right. They marched straight into Corpus Christie porter's lodge, an array of post boxes and scores of keys dangling from metal hooks. No one at the counter. Emily pressed the bell.

A short man in a dark suit, wearing black-framed spectacles too thick and austere for his pallid complexion, appeared from a back room. "I'm James. Can I help you?"

"We'd like to see my uncle's room."

"Pardon."

"My Uncle Sebastian, he was a professor here."

"I haven't been here that long. Did he have a surname?"

Al took over. "Sebastian Stearn. A professor of history, James. Spent most of his life in Cambridge. Most of it studying or lecturing in this college."

"Professor Stearn. Delightful gentleman. I met him a few times. Passed away a number of weeks ago. I read about him in the college newsletter. I'm sorry."

148

"That's right. He had a study here."

James heaved a large diary from underneath the counter, letting it land with a hollow thud. He flicked through the pages. "Let's see. Yes, here it is. A study apartment no less. But I'm afraid the college has re-allocated the room."

"Already?" Emily's disappointed tone contained too much fire.

James peered over the top of his glasses, an admonishing glint in his eyes. "College accommodation is at a premium, Miss."

Al intervened. "Has the new occupant moved in yet? If not, I wonder, would it be possible to see where Uncle Sebastian spent most of his days? It would mean a lot to Emily."

A few minutes later, after trekking through a maze of corridors, they alighted on a room hewn from another century. Oak panelling, grainy wood hacked in Tudor times, heavy furniture, leaded windows and the polished smell of pine. James left them alone for five minutes. Emily gazed out of the window overlooking the pristine lawns. Students sauntered between the buildings, carrying bags and books, some wearing black gowns that billowed in the wind. Emily thought they resembled crows.

"An education of crows," she said, pleased with her improvised collective noun. Al seemed dubious.

"Surely, it's a murder of crows?"

Emily ignored him. "What a life he must have lived here. It's like stepping into another world."

"Yes, one of serious privilege."

"Sounds as if you don't approve."

"It's not that. Good luck to the students. Lots of them go on to become the scientists, doctors, great minds, entrepreneurs, all countries need. You can almost feel the brain power. I wish more people could get that opportunity. Sebastian was a lucky man to spend most of his life in a place like this."

Al slid open the solid drawers of the big desk. He did the same with the tall dresser and checked the furniture in the adjoining bedroom. All empty.

"Where did you go to college?" Emily suddenly realised she knew nothing of Al's education. He was due to start a postgraduate course in Bristol, studying maths like herself, but that was in the future. What about his past? How could she not know that after all the hours they'd spent together?

"Edinburgh," said Al. "My dad had lots of connections in Scotland. It seemed the obvious place. The course was decent, some of Dad's family were around and the social life had a good vibe. I'd been to the Christmas market off Princes Street a few times. Got drunk one year on Gluhwein. I felt comfortable there, loved the old stone buildings. It all seemed, I don't know … historic."

"What about your mother?"

"What about her?"

"What did she think about you going there? She's Latvian, didn't you say?"

Before he could answer, James returned, informing them he had to return to the porter's lodge and would accompany them back through the maze. When they reached the exit, he bade farewell and they thanked him for his time. They headed for the steps, but Emily spun around. "James, sorry, I forgot to ask."

"What?"

"What happened to Uncle Sebastian's personal belongings?"

"They would have been cleared out several weeks ago."

"Where are they now?"

He returned to the counter, once more flicking through the desktop diary, Emily waiting by the door.

"As I thought, we've packed them in cases. They're under lock and key in the University property department."

"Can we see them?"

"I'm afraid we'd need a letter of authentication from the executor of Professor Stearn's will to release them."

"My father's the executor."

"Then I suggest you speak to him."

They returned along King's Parade, listening for a while to one of the omnipresent buskers making a decent stab at Lada Gaga's *Shallow*. "Fancy a bite to eat?" said Al. Emily nodded, Al linking her arm to veer right into a side street.

Al pointed to the pub sign, a picture of an eagle swooping over water, talons poised to make a kill. "Remember The Eagle, where Sebastian says he was the night he was recruited as …" Al trailed off.

"Go on, you can say it."

"As a spy, I was going to say. But he didn't do much spying, if any, that we've discovered, apart from one mission. So far that involves giving a lecture. He's hardly in the league of Blunt and Burgess."

"Who?"

"Students at Cambridge who ended up spying for Russia. Traitors. Probably recruited in this pub too, for all we know."

"Uncle Sebastian would never have done that."

"No. But we've not finished the journal yet."

"He wouldn't. I know it. Uncle Sebastian was a good man." They entered the pub, darker and dingier than they'd expected, bench seats, stone floor, a rowdy bunch of students drinking on one side of the bar, several couples eating snacks on the other. A sharp scent of vinegar and spice mixed with the sweet odour of stale beer. They ordered sandwiches with salad, a bowl of chips to share and two glasses of lemonade. Al excused himself to use the toilet. When he returned Emily was busy sending a text message to her father while a man wearing a flat peaked cap over shoulder-length brown hair, an odd combination, was sitting with a young woman opposite him at the next table. Holding hands, seemingly oblivious to anything or anyone but themselves. As the man leaned over the table the sleeve of his cotton shirt rode up his forearm, revealing a small tattoo, resembling a spider, above his wrist. A strange choice, thought Al, who had developed a distaste, bordering on fear, for spiders from an early age. He turned away, thinking no more of it.

While eating their meal, they chatted for half an hour, mostly about the white van on Sea View Road the day Sebastian died.

"If Pete comes up with the memory card then we'll know for sure what the driver was doing and what time the van came and went," said Al. "Real evidence. At the moment we're basing everything on Katharine's notebook and while she's pretty impressive for 92, I wouldn't trust her in court, m'lud."

"From what I've seen I'd trust Katharine more than most folk in Sea View Road."

"You've only met Katharine, the dressing gown guy, Marcus and me."

"I suppose three out of four's not bad," said Emily, wiping her fingers on a serviette, scrunching it into a ball.

"Who's the odd one out you don't trust?"

"I've not decided yet."

Al wasn't used to Emily being playful. He'd decided she wasn't the playful type. Kind and considerate. Her banquet gesture clinched that. Determined. Without doubt. Probably the most focused woman he'd ever met. Obsessive even. Weird? A tad. He mused on the issue for a few seconds. Yes, he liked playful.

"By the way, I've texted Dad about Uncle Sebastian's belongings," said Emily. "I've asked him to write to the college and told him we'll pick them up when they release them. That okay with you?"

"I guess so." It didn't sound like Al had a choice.

26

"Ivan Vasilyevich, the first Czar of Russia, deemed the cathedral so magnificent that he blinded the architect so no one could replicate its design."

With that chilling thought, Anna snapped her guide book shut. We were standing in Red Square, gazing at the multi-coloured swirling spires that make St Basil's Cathedral one of Russia's premier tourist attractions. I even snapped a couple of photographs with the cheap, throwaway tourist camera the technicians at Secretarium had issued. No use posing as a tourist without a camera, especially as the sun bathed the square in a warm, mid-morning glow.

I'd endured a tormented night. Every footstep in the hotel corridor jolting me from a semi-conscious state in which I imagined the metallic creak of a key turning in the lock, shadowy figures filching valuables from my suitcase. Never far away, the face of Kalenkov. Thin lips, steely smile mocking my attempts at sleep.

I sighed. "Myth and legend."

"Pardon," said Anna.

"That's what the guide books peddle. Gory myths to keep the tourists amused. The blinding story is a case in point. No evidence to back it up, but let's throw it out there because that's what the masses prefer to hear. I'm a historian, Anna. Not a poet. We don't deal in imagination. We deal in facts."

"Okay, I was only reading the book."

"Sorry, perverting history is a bete-noire of mine. Some people like to reduce history to a game show with bad comedians telling tall tales."

We spent an hour traipsing around the cathedral that Soviet rulers transformed into a state historical museum in 1928, allowing me to cast off the lethargy from my sleepless night. We moved on to Lenin's Mausoleum, literally a stone's throw across the square for a man possessing a powerful arm. It meant joining the queue of tourists but the atmosphere seemed agreeable, at least as welcoming as it could be with guards toting machine guns patrolling the area.

We'd queued for half an hour and were within 10 metres of the entrance when an official emerged to reveal a power cut had thrown the mausoleum into darkness. No predictions on when it might be fixed. Communism didn't have the answer for everything, after all.

"I dare say I can live without seeing a dead Soviet leader," I said. We broke from the queue, heading towards the banks of the Moskva River. I'd no intention of returning to the hotel, having informed Anna as we queued that I needed time to clear my head.

We strolled for a mile, admiring the architectural man-made majesty of the Kremlin on one side against the constantly changing hue of river nature on the other, our conversation stilted and generic. As we reached the bend in the river Anna had a thought. "Let's hire a couple of bicycles. It would be fun. We could see more of the city."

As a *tour guide* who took her role seriously Anna knew where to hire city bikes and soon we were pedalling through the streets of Moscow on sit-up-and-beg machines, creaking and groaning at every turn, wind in our hair, petrol fumes scratching the back of our throats. Lives in the hands of Moscow's maniacal motorists. It was a crazy idea, but for the first time in weeks I felt neck muscles relax, laughing at Anna's comical attempts to steer her oversized cycle. This was not how I'd envisaged a foreign mission. I'd imagined secret trysts, smoky bars, shadowy figures, meticulous surveillance, not careering around in broad daylight from one landmark to another for all Moscow to see.

After a while, Anna pointed to steps leading to a waterway and her cry was laced with laughter, "Stop! Let's go down here." I pulled in to the kerb.

"This is the canal linking the Moskva and Volga rivers," she explained. "Some beautiful greenery around it. Flat for around one hundred and twenty kilometres."

"Gets my vote then."

We carried the bikes down the steps and continued riding until we came to a layby off the concrete path, leading to a grassy area with picnic tables. Dismounting, we leaned the bicycles against the wooden bench seat and sat at one of the tables. Anna dug in her back pack, producing a white paper bag containing a couple of syrniki, cottage cheese scones, dusted with icing sugar. A Russian delicacy.

"You came prepared," I said, again impressed with Anna's attention to detail.

"Always know where your next meal's coming from. That's what my mother taught me. I got the sweet variety, rather than the savoury. Hope that's okay."

"More than okay. An unexpected treat." I bit into the scone. Soft and crumbly, drier than the moist, currant scones my mother used to bake, but still delicious.

"Professor."

"Call me Sebastian."

"I think I'll stick with Professor, if you don't mind. Reminds us where we need to be."

"Okay." I licked my fingers.

"This is your first mission, I think."

I nodded.

"Why has it taken so long?"

I'd never thought about it like that. Maybe I was wrong, but I detected a negative twist to her question. But why had it taken so long? Why had 20 years passed since my first visit to Secretarium, without once being contacted for active service? As each year passed I'd told myself I was becoming more valuable. Building my academic career. Immersing myself in the world of the ordinary. Assuming the characteristics of the perfect sleeper. Was I fooling myself? Had the department viewed me as a liability all these years, until now, when a mission presented itself that required minimal risk? All the department were asking me to do was present a lecture, something I'd done hundreds of times, as well as play the tourist with an attractive woman. Albeit one I knew nothing about.

"I don't know, I've been waiting and available," I said.

"I know you will be perfect."

"Tell me, Anna, what's your story? Why are you here? Do you have children?"

155

Her smile vanished. We both knew this conversation was off-piste. First law of the operative. No personal details. No extraneous chit-chat. Stay in character for the duration of the mission. Before I asked the last of those questions I sensed she was about to ram the bolt on our conversation. But something registered. A nerve touched. A soft smile once more lit her features. She nodded.

"Lena. She's ten years old. I wish I had a picture to show you. She's full of mischief, but so beautiful."

"Is her father looking after her?"

Anna shook her head, eyes lowering as if burdened by the weight of dark thoughts. "Her father never saw her. He died when I was five months pregnant."

"That's awful. I'm sorry, Anna. I shouldn't have asked."

She shrugged. "It's fine. It's right that I should talk about him. He was a brave, principled man. I would never deny his memory."

Brave. Principled. Those weren't ordinary words, especially when delivered in a grave, whispered tone. They were words suggesting something other than a natural death. I couldn't help myself. I had to ask.

"Anna, what happened? How did he die? He must have been young."

"Thirty-three. A wonderful mind. A researcher in the bio-medical chemistry department at Lomonosov University."

"Researching what?"

She fiddled with the strap of her backpack. Her left eye twitched and her bottom lip trembled. The pain obvious. I thought she might cry. She didn't, but once more I handed her an exit. "Never mind. It doesn't matter."

"Yes it does matter. It will always matter." Her strident tone came as a jolt.

"Of course, I didn't mean ..." She cut me off.

"Rudi was the kindest, sweetest man. His work involved vaccine technology to combat viruses. Sometime in the future, he used to say, the entire planet will be gripped by a disease that will kill millions indiscriminately. A raging pandemic. Worse than war, worse than a nuclear strike. The only defence will be science and we have to be ready."

156

"That sounds a noble profession."

"It was. It is. But then they started to put pressure on him to turn his research into ways to kill, rather than to protect people."

"What do you mean? Like germ warfare."

"That's exactly what I mean. Not on the battlefield though. In the big cities and huge conurbations. What better way to strangle the economies of the West than to introduce a pandemic, a killer disease that cripples your enemies' way of life. Brings down Wall Street. Paralyses transport systems. A killer disease that only you have the knowledge to eradicate."

"Who are *they*?"

She looked around as if checking for observers. I'd noticed her doing that before. In the hotel and at the Cosmonautics museum. I thought she was interested in her surroundings. But it was more than that. A habit. The jerking head like a feeding bird wary of predators. An unconscious affectation, triggered by tension and fuelled by her current role.

"*They* are the faceless murderers inside the Kremlin. The ones who came to the university and persuaded Rudi to go one step further. To explore genetic mutations and virus variants. At first he thought they wanted to protect the Russian people. But pretty soon it was obvious what they were really after."

"What did he do?"

Her face set concrete firm, eyes cold. Words spat out with venom left festering for years. "Refused. Point blank. Said he'd have nothing to do with any research designed for a malevolent purpose. But they wouldn't let him go. They kept returning. Persisted in threatening him. He'd lose his job, his house, lose his living. And we had a baby on the way."

I didn't dare ask the obvious question. For a moment I thought Anna would leave the story hanging there, in limbo, somewhere between the Moskva and the Volga, but she didn't. The dam had breached. The emotional cascade too intense, too urgent to stem.

"When he still refused, they killed him, Professor. Rudi had never been seriously ill in his life but suddenly he caught a mystery disease and died in agony, even though he fought it for two weeks. A death you wouldn't wish on a dog. They said it was his negligence. That was the worst thing of all. They blamed him for his own death, saying he'd put other lives at risk with incompetent genetic research. That I cannot forgive. Ever. I don't know exactly how they did it, but I know they killed him."

She sucked in a deep breath. I sensed relief as well as a trace of embarrassment. I wanted to know if that was why she had become an operative and how the process had transpired, but the moment had passed. Her radiant smile returned. She busied herself collecting the scone wrappings, stuffing them into her backpack.

"Come on, let's get going." The sing-song tone once more modulating her voice.

I fished in my pocket, pulled out the tourist camera, and pointed the lens. "Hold on. Say Seer."

"You mean *cheese*," laughed Anna, emphasising the English translation as she stood astride her bicycle, long tresses billowing in the breeze against the backdrop of a clear blue sky. It may not have conformed with Secretarium protocol. There may have been more significant pictures to take in Moscow that summer's day, but right then I couldn't think of a subject more deserving. Or more beautiful.

27

Emily flicked through her notebook, jabbing the page with her finger when she found the appropriate scribble.

"See, Al, it's here. Indisputable."

Al leaned over Emily's shoulder at the study desk as she used her nail to underscore the notes she'd taken in Katharine's kitchen a couple of days before.

Emily read out loud. "She looked like a film star. Long hair. Lovely smile … riding a bicycle. Or at least standing there astride a bicycle. That's what Katharine said." Emily gazed at Al, triumphant glint in her eyes.

"Sounds like Anna, I'll give you that."

"It has to be, Al. The photo Uncle Sebastian showed Katharine must be the one he took on the bicycle ride in Moscow all those years ago. But it's not in Uncle Sebastian's wallet. I asked Dad to look and there weren't any photos."

"Maybe it's in the cases in Cambridge."

"Let's hope so."

Al walked around the desk and sat back in the chair opposite Emily, deliberating. "I'd say it was more evidence that the journal is accurate. I suppose there's still a chance that Sebastian was fantasising about an old flame to Katharine, but why do that to a relative stranger? More likely the story is factual."

"Truth is stranger than fiction."

"It would appear so, Emily. I'm already thinking Sebastian was one hell of a guy."

"Me too."

The Cambridge trip had generated tangible evidence to support the geography of the journal. The staircase at Clare College, the sash window leading onto the lead flashing roof. It had also affected something more personal. In the mind of Al at least. He enjoyed Emily's company. Not merely the thrill of unravelling the conundrum wrapped in the journal. He respected her passion, focus, the way she drove their transcribing sessions with considered zeal. He was the analytical problem solver, the one adept at communication and constructing logical arguments, but she was the master of time management. He was the life of the party, the loquacious joke teller, the smooth operator, but she got things done. He couldn't believe it, but he was actually assessing their relationship as if it were a mathematical equation. Time plus energy equals logic plus social grace, all multiplied by a common purpose.

It didn't matter to Al that Emily could appear awkward in company. He gained energy from social situations. She didn't. But in his company she seemed entirely comfortable. More than that. She appeared happy and invigorated.

Which was why, as they reached the front door after another post-midnight finish, Al turned to Emily and, totally unplanned, did what came naturally. He bent forward making to kiss her. Not a full-frontal lunge, more a gentle bow. He sensed the heat of her body, his face skimmed her hair, scented the sweet musk of her perfume, their lips brushed, the faintest touch. He felt a sharp dig in his ribs as she pushed him away.

"Sorry." Al stumbled back. He shook his head. Bemused.

"It's not you. It's me. Please, can you go." Emily's head bowed, avoiding eye contact. Voice tremulous. Hands shaking. Mind confused.

"Of course. But why?" An awkward silence. Al shuffled out, the door banging shut behind him.

He wandered around to his own house, striving to unscramble a myriad of thoughts. Had he misread the last couple of weeks? Had the increasing warmth and intimacy between them derived solely from a common desire to unlock the secrets of the journal? Was their friendship based on nothing more than pragmatism? Surely not. Al was no stranger to relationships. His easy manner, sharp intellect and good looks had attracted girls aplenty at university. Mostly casual relationships, apart from Rosie, an undergraduate in languages. Their relationship had lasted almost two years, ending only when she moved on to a year-long course in Madrid while he stayed in Edinburgh.

160

Their parting was bruising but Al being Al had deflected the hurt by throwing himself into a fresh social whirl. That was his way. Always had been. *Live for today because tomorrow might never come.* When he reached home he sat nursing a beer on the decking, observing the twinkling lights of boats bobbing in the harbour, his mind fixed on the kiss, or the near-kiss as he preferred to think of it. *Like a near-miss between two jets,* he mused. *Although, shouldn't that be a near-hit? After all, if they don't crash then surely it is a miss, not a near-miss. No harm done. Maybe our near-kiss was the same.*

He thought of Rosie and a conversation they'd once shared about her younger sister, who registered on the autism spectrum.

"So much love and affection to give," Rosie had told him. "But she didn't know how to flirt. She couldn't read the signals of romance. Happy and comfortable being friendly with a boy, but struggled taking a relationship to the next stage."

Al's mind went back to the night he'd cooked Emily an omelette and she'd revealed how she used to recite lyrics verbatim, counted tin boxes at Felixstowe and recorded car registrations in her notebook. He'd gauged them endearing traits, a young girl's idiosyncratic behaviour. Perhaps it was more complicated. Maybe Emily's obsessions existed on the same spectrum as Rosie's sister. Al drained his beer, brushed his teeth, flopping into bed as the phone rang. Emily.

"Al." He looked at his watch. Almost 1am.

"Hi."

"I'm not good with hugs." Voice croaky.

"Pardon." Silence. "Emily?"

"I mean it was a surprise. When people surprise me I don't know what to do. I get confused. My mum always told me that. I don't know what people are thinking. I didn't know that's what you were thinking. It's too soon after ..." Her voice trailed off.

"After what?"

"Nothing. Really, it's nothing ..." Emily wanted to tell Al about Blake's betrayal but the words wouldn't come.

161

Al's tone was caring and compassionate. "I wasn't thinking anything, Emily. I was just saying goodnight because I like you. I like you a lot."

"Oh. I didn't know."

Al's mind was racing. He thought back to Rosie's sister. The signals. That was it. Emily hadn't picked up on any of the signals. His jokes. His help. His attentiveness. All had sailed over her head. He had never witnessed Emily indulge in any show of affection. Admittedly, he hadn't known her long but there were no hugs or kisses for her parents, not in Highgate on their visit or, from what he'd gleaned, when Harry and Eleanor had turned up in Weymouth. Maybe, Al thought, she struggled to express and understand emotions.

"Don't worry about it, Emily."

"Is everything okay then?"

"Yes, of course."

"Sure?"

"Yes, I'm sure I'm sure."

"Okay then."

Emily hung up, returning to a mess of tangled thoughts. Why had she never learned to like or love someone? Why had she settled for Blake, her one extended relationship? Why did she move in with him? She knew he didn't love her. He made her laugh but he didn't look after her or cherish her company. Not like the leading men in the scores of romantic films she'd watched. Why couldn't she tell Al about him?

Her thoughts drifted, as always, to her teenaged date with a boy from the same class, only to discover mid-date that he was doing it for a dare. "Go out with the nerd," his classmates had taunted him. "Go out with the girl who can't cry." She could still feel the burn of embarrassment and hurt on discovering the truth. The scars had never healed. Ever since, when people asked about a special friend, she always answered, "I have my maths. That is special to me."

Al was different from Blake. She sensed that, even if she didn't know how to categorise him. Naturally gifted in many ways. Understanding. Sympathetic. Socially adept, even if his jokes were corny. Why hadn't she kissed him? She fell asleep, mind in turmoil, anxious at what thoughts morning would bring.

***

The sun woke Emily a shade after 6am, a rogue shaft of light scything through the gap she'd left when drawing the curtains, arrowing in on her face. An air of foreboding still rumbled within her. Time for a bracing stroll.

When she reached the promenade, waves were washing the sand, their relentless rhythm reaching almost to the sea wall. A couple of anglers stood side by side, rods pointing to the sky, casting long lines. She skirted around them, increasing pace until she came across a man leaning against the metal barrier, peering through a pair of binoculars. Marcus.

She tried to slide around without him noticing, but Marcus didn't seem to miss anything. "My Dear, how nice to see you. Up early again, I see."

"This lovely sunshine. Gets you out of bed whether you like it or not."

"See you've been burning the midnight oil with your young man."

Emily nodded, but looked suspicious. The statement was correct and she knew Marcus couldn't help but notice the lights burning late at number seven from the vantage point of his study, yet still the comment seemed loaded with perverse innuendo.

"By the way, I emailed Jim and Jean about your young man after you asked about him." The phrase, *young man*, grated, especially considering the events of the night before.

"And?"

"They said he was by far the best candidate for the house-sitting role and they were pleased to be able to help him in his time of need."

"Time of need?" A perplexed frown worried Emily's features.

"Apparently his mother died in a car crash three months ago. Hit head-on by a lorry on the motorway. Terrible business. Didn't you know?"

"Thanks Marcus." Emily hurried away without answering, a screeching, clanking, disconnected cacophony in her brain as

163

she endeavoured to compute what she'd learned. Al had kept his mother's death a secret. He'd mentioned her a couple of times, but only in passing, without a trace of emotion. Did he not think it relevant? Or was he too consumed with grief to talk about her? As Emily climbed the hill back to the bungalow the questions continued to detonate. *Should I tell him I know? Should I sympathise? Should I bring up the near-kiss? Why is life so complicated?*

28

I admit I was nervous. It had been a long time since I'd looked forward to a first date. I hated the unpredictability, small talk and pretence surrounding such occasions. This was different. A night out in Moscow with a remarkable woman. Anna. A woman I'd known for a few days only but who stirred something inside that I hadn't felt for half a lifetime.

I brushed my jacket, checked my hair, set my silver chain in a distinctive shape on the bedside table. After a final glance in the mirror I headed for the foyer.

It had been a frantic Friday, starting with an atmospheric run along the river, mist still rising, sun promising to burst upon another shimmering day. I left for the second seminar at Sokolniki at around 10am. I'd chosen the Romanov dynasty as the subject. A weighty topic considering the House of Romanov was the reigning imperial force in Russia from 1613 to 1917. I decided to concentrate on the fall of the House, the dramatic finale, brought about by the February revolution in 1917, resulting in the abdication of Nicholas II.

Countless books and films have recited the story culminating in July 1918 when Bolsheviks executed Nicholas and all the Romanovs held prisoner inside the Ipatiev House in Yekaterinburg. Yet the brutality of their slayings remains a subject of fascination, likewise the theory that some of the younger family members escaped. I knew from experience with students that the treatment of the Romanovs provokes lively debate, shining a light on the savagery of Russian politics. The seminar was no different, overrunning by almost half an hour, the badinage on the floor of the hall becoming heated at times, to the point where I wondered if the moderator might intervene. He didn't. I was back at the Four Seasons mid-afternoon, ready for a trawl around the Pushkin State Museum of Fine Arts.

I headed with Anna for the room containing Ancient Egypt artefacts, renowned as one of the museum's finest collections. We spent an agreeable hour browsing, before I asked to return to the hotel. I felt uneasy, agitation causing my stomach to cramp. I knew why. The anticipation of tomorrow's lecture had begun to chisel away at my equilibrium, tipping my emotional balance one way and then the other. Big lectures always provoked nerves, but not like this. In the taxi returning to the Four Seasons I tried to remember the training. Suck in deep breaths to calm the panic. Stem the unease. Anna didn't say anything, but she noticed, laying a comforting hand on top of mine in the back of the cab, pressing gently.

When we reached the hotel the panic passed. Anna made great play of discussing the day in front of the desk clerk, her manner frothy and matter-of-fact. "How about sampling the delights of Moscow this weekend, Professor? There are some wonderful restaurants. I could show you one, if you like. You cannot go home without a Russian gourmet treat. I know just the place. How about tonight?"

I can't concentrate. My heart's racing. I don't think I could eat anything. I can't get the image of a bullet blasting the brains of Kalenkov tomorrow afternoon out of my head. That's what I wanted to say. What I actually said was, "How could I say no?" The desk clerk smiled.

Three hours later I met Anna in the foyer. She'd changed out of her regimented blue working suit into a flowing red dress, newly washed hair cascading in waves down her shoulders, plunging neckline framing a striking oval pendant hanging from a gold chain.

"You scrub up all right." It wasn't a chat-up line to be proud of, nor did it do Anna justice. In my mind's eye, I can still see her now standing in that foyer. Laughing. Sing-song voice filling the dark corners with musical chatter. Light and warm. She looked and sounded feminine. I could smell her perfume, fragrant and sophisticated. When she linked my arm, she said, "Okay. Rimsky's here we come."

"What's special about Rimsky's?"

"You'll find out, Professor. We're off to Patriki, one of the more delightful areas of Moscow, to a Russian restaurant on Malaya Bronnaya street. I don't think you'll be disappointed." As we passed the desk clerk he smiled and nodded. I couldn't be sure, but I think he winked also.

What can I tell you about the rest of the evening? In short, in all my days I can't remember hearing clearer, seeing brighter, laughing louder, feeling happier, or existing in such perfect alignment with another human being.

Rimsky's was small and unpretentious. Decorated with softly-lit standard lamps and book cases, a huge dresser filling most of one wall. A dozen white wooden tables, surrounded by chairs with brightly embroidered cushioned seats, added to the homely ambience, while unobtrusive music played in the background. There were four other couples dining and a party of six, allowing us an intimate alcove to ourselves, although we were swiftly joined by the resident cat. Black as tar with a tiny blob of white on his head, as if he'd walked under a painter's ladder. Anna tickled under his chin and he curled up on a spare chair.

On Anna's recommendation I chose homemade beef stew, while she ordered chopped salmon with cucumber and sour cream. The food was delicious, the waiters attentive, not intrusive, but this enchanting night wasn't about food. Or the surroundings.

We talked non-stop about an eclectic mix of subjects. About books and films, Anna revealing she couldn't wait to take her daughter to see Andrew Lloyd Webber's new musical, *Cats,* if she ever travelled to London. About space exploration, current affairs, the troubles in Northern Ireland in particular. About John McEnroe, who, days before, had launched his infamous "You cannot be serious!" tirade of abuse at a Wimbledon tennis umpire.

To my surprise and amusement, Anna defended McEnroe. "Those umpires are a little old-fashioned. How do you say in English … fuzzy duzzy."

I chuckled. "Fuddy duddy, you mean, although I prefer your description. You needn't worry. Pretty soon, tennis umpires and men in general will be obsolete."

"Why do you say that?"

"Lots of reasons. For a start, three years ago the first test-tube baby was born. I remember the name, Louise Brown. Now some scientists even talk about being able to clone mammals from adult cells in the not-too-distant future. No male participation whatsoever. We're on our way out. The descent of man."

"That's science fiction."

"Maybe, but with all the advances in computers and technology, manufacturers using robots to assemble cars, machinery putting workers out of jobs, computers predicted to become smarter than the average human, who's to say what might be possible in ten, twenty, forty years? Little helicopters without pilots might be delivering the shopping to your door."

Anna laughed. "Do you know what I think, Professor?"

I smiled as she rested her chin on interlocked hands, gazed into my eyes, changing the subject.

"Go on," I said.

"I think you're a man who has been unlucky in love. I can hear it in your words, see it in your face. You have a noble face. Honest. Golden hair. Trustworthy. You seem strong, but just because there are no tears rolling down your cheeks doesn't mean that your heart doesn't weep. Too often people with good and gentle hearts are unlucky. I think, Professor, you're one of those people."

I considered a quick quip. *You make your own luck.* Instead I stayed silent, the reality of Anna's words screeching in my brain. If onlys and what ifs. If only I'd plucked up courage to put aside my awkwardness to ask out Alice, a third year history colleague at Cambridge, whose dissertations I adored and whose company and carrot cake I enjoyed. If only I'd been blessed in matters of the heart with the same confidence I displayed at sports, earning blues in tennis and rowing. And what if I'd rejected the request to help my country all those years ago? My annual visits to Secretarium needed to be hidden from family, friends and colleagues, including any girlfriends. In my confused youth I'd extended the same secrecy to the rest of my existence. I'd become a loner, a mysterious misfit, not that my students noticed. To those attending my lectures and tutorials, which I endeavoured to lace with wit and charm, I was the ambitious academic, peddling his subject with rare passion, intent on becoming Cambridge's youngest history professor. A man with educational accolades and a healthy salary. You might even say, the most eligible of bachelors. Yet Anna was right. Inside, my heart was crying for everything that had eluded me. Wife. Children. Close family. My books, gathering dust as each year passed, had become my life.

In the catch of that enlightenment, as we waited for desserts, I marvelled at the way Anna, a woman I hardly knew, honed in to strike the essence of my being. If truth be told, I gazed into those sparkling eyes and thought primeval thoughts. How her hair would feel to the touch, how the curve of her hips would fit my hand. The heat of her body, the scent of her perfume, her lips against mine.

When I spoke my voice was calm even though my heart ached. "I'm not unlucky. I don't believe in luck. It's a concept people use as a psychological tool. A survival mechanism. If someone beats them to a job they say they are unlucky. But if they land the job they say it was because they were more talented and worked harder. You're right, Anna, I do not have love and romance in my life. Don't get me wrong, I like women, I find them attractive, but there's a difference between finding someone attractive and being attracted to someone. It has little to do with looks. Being single has nothing to do with luck. It's because of decisions I've made, not all of which make me proud."

The desserts arrived, the mood brightened, the ensuing conversation, like the pavlovas, proving light and wholesome. I learned Anna was born in Lithuania.

"In a village outside a city called Kaunas, have you heard of it?" I shook my head. "I was a little girl when the Soviets occupied the country after the Second World War."

"That explains your fluent Russian, but where did your fluent English come from? Your accent sounds almost perfect."

She sat up straighter, preening at the compliment. "Almost! You're right, you can never be perfect. But I tried. My father spoke a little English and all those films I told you about, English and American, I devoured them. We came as a family to Moscow when I was fifteen and I later went to Lomonosov University. That's where I met Rudi. We both joined the film society. I was never away. Every night. Rudi always said I would have square eyes. I wanted to be an actress, dreamed of being Deborah Kerr in *An Affair to Remember*, but I never got the opportunity. Not easy for a Lithuanian immigrant from Kaunas to break into Hollywood. All I got was the hint of an American accent."

"How many languages do you speak?"

"Lithuanian, Russian, Latvian, English, a bit of French."

I whistled through my teeth. "I'm fluent in English only. Some of my students would question that."

"No, Professor, you're being modest, your Russian is excellent. Anyway, it seems all the world right now wants to learn English. Why bother learning another language?"

She spooned a chunk of pavlova into her mouth and I watched entranced as she chewed, eyes closed, jaw, lips and tongue working in rhythm, crumbs clinging to the sides of her mouth, luxuriating in the sensation of sticky meringue, strawberries and cream. *Oh my God. I couldn't recall witnessing a vision as messy, yet as stunningly sensuous.*

"Good?"

Anna nodded, unable to speak, instead purring in contentment like the indulged cat in the adjoining chair. After a while, she smacked her lips, running her tongue around her mouth to clear a morsel of meringue. "I told you this place was good. My little piece of Heaven."

"If you weren't an actress, what did you become?" Everything about Anna intrigued me. I was greedy for more, even though I knew we couldn't stray into her current circumstances.

"A teacher, Professor. Like you." She smiled and was about to pop in another piece of pavlova. I raised my hand to halt her, knowing it would mean another 30 seconds at least of silence.

"What sort of teacher?"

Her spoon hovered mid-way between bowl and lips. "English, of course. At Lomonosov. The students were desperate to learn. It helped me perfect the language, and standing on a stage in front of fifty or more students felt like acting. Don't you agree, Professor."

170

It had never occurred to me. Yet she was right. I took notes into every lecture, but they were no more than cues, stepping stones to assist my travel from one main thought to another. Most of the time I had absorbed the information so completely that the notes lay untouched and unread, even after a lecture lasting more than an hour, during which I'd attempted to inject passion, humour and sometimes poignancy if the lurch of history demanded. It wasn't Hamlet at the Old Vic, but, the more I thought about it, yes, it was acting of sorts.

"Good for you, Anna. We are thespians. I'll drink to that." I raised my glass of sparkling water and she pretended to clink it with her spoonful of pavlova. We both laughed, ordered coffee, chatting some more. Natural. No trace of the overt awkwardness that had constricted my rare attempts at companionship with women in the past. Inside, a warm glow smouldered. I didn't want this night to end. When the waiter brought the bill the glow had turned to flame, burning in my mind. No longer could I contain the feelings I knew I should not utter.

"Anna."

"Yes."

My arm stretched across the table and I took her hand in mine, her fingers soft and warm, nails perfectly manicured complete with silver sheen.

"Anna, when all this is done, can I see you again?"

"I'd like that very much, Professor."

"And you won't call me Professor."

She chuckled. "Not if you don't want me to."

How that might work was for another time, but in that instant my heart danced with a joy that I'd never before experienced. We sat for precious moments, holding hands, gazing at each other, a haunting tune playing in the background that was to be my friend forever. *Blue Moon.*

We caught a cab back to the Four Seasons, saying nothing, but holding hands in the back seat, under cover of darkness and the jacket I was carrying on what had turned into a sultry evening. When we reached the hotel Anna squeezed my hand

171

tight. We both knew that anything more was impossible on this night of all nights.

"Until tomorrow, Sebastian." Her faint whisper barely audible.

"Until then, Anna."

I clambered out and watched the dwindling tail-lights of the cab as it headed towards Red Square. A thought occurred. My impending lecture hadn't crossed my mind once that evening and the knot in my stomach had disappeared.

29

Al struggled to place the woman's voice but he couldn't miss the excited edge in her tone as he answered his phone.

"He's here. If you come right now, you'll catch him."

"Who is this? Think you might have the wrong number."

Al sensed an irritable snort on the end of the line. "You're the guy who came here, aren't you? Looking for Puszkin at number eight."

"Yes, yes, sorry, number eight, that's right, Didn't recognise your voice. Thanks for calling." The image of the woman with the bottle-blonde spiky hair from the Dorchester flats entered Al's mind. He motioned to Emily across the desk, pointing to his phone, casting a thumbs-up gesture and mouthing Puszkin.

Al fished for information. "Is he living there again?"

"Looks like he's clearing his things into the back of an old car. Doesn't look as if he intends hanging around."

"We'll be right over, thanks again for ringing." Al ended the call, grabbed his jacket, beckoning Emily to follow.

"The guy in the white van?" Emily asked the question but she'd already pieced together the purpose of the call, car keys jangling. Al nodded.

It was two days since the near-kiss, although neither of them had mentioned it. In an attempt to smooth any embarrassment, Al had blown her a playful kiss during their most recent transcription session, but Emily wasn't ready for joking. Too confused. Still overwhelmed by Marcus's revelation about Al's mother's car crash. The latest draft of Uncle Sebastian's journal had occupied their thoughts. Now they were certain Anna was the woman in the photo he had shown Katharine. His moving description of the night at Rimsky's had clinched it, as had mention of *Blue Moon*, the song Uncle Sebastian requested for his funeral.

"No one knew why he chose that song," Emily confided to Al. "It had to mean something. Now we know."

Al hummed the first few bars. "Beautiful song. About a man wanting a lover to call his own. The jigsaw's beginning to fall into place."

The revelation had re-fuelled their desire to unravel the journal. Over the last week the task had become more onerous, the code spewing out fewer complete words. Increasingly, the journal contained complexities, such as Russian street names, requiring *The Grapes of Wrath* and the code to build words from individual letters. A time-consuming assignment that led them to agree to read chunks every two days, as opposed to nightly sessions. Sebastian's date at Rimsky's had arrived at the perfect time, invigorating Al and Emily, both desperate to learn what happened next.

They discussed their progress on the way to Dorchester, making good time, parking outside the block of flats less than half an hour after receiving the phone call. Al bounded up the stairs two at a time and when Emily reached the landing he was already knocking on the door of number eight. No answer. He rapped again, this time louder, police-style, rat-a-tat more urgent. Still no answer. The spiky-haired woman's door opened and she craned her neck as before.

"Have we missed him?" said Al

"He was here a minute ago. I could hear him banging around. Lugging a television and an old fridge down the stairs by himself. She couldn't help him."

"She?"

"A long-haired girl, looked like her waters were about to break." The woman made an expansive curved movement against her stomach.

"Where did they go?"

The woman shrugged. Al heard Emily squeal at the top of the stairs. He couldn't fathom what she said, thought it sounded like "Excuse me", but when he spun around she was pointing downstairs.

"Al, quick. He's here."

Bounding to the top of the landing, Al caught a glimpse of a man disappearing around the bend in the stairway. He chased after him, clattering down the steps, creaks and groans from each stride echoing around the bare walls. When Al reached the kink in the stairway the man turned at the bottom step, an anxious glance suggesting he was up to no good.

Al's heart was thumping. A shot of heat coursed through his body, mind assessing the situation, even though his actions were instinctive. He gauged the man around 35, wiry, about the same size as himself. More pertinent, he ran with the athletic gait of someone accustomed to physical exercise.

"Stop! I want to ask you some questions." Al shouted, but the man continued sprinting down the pavement alongside a line of cars.

The man reached an old black Ford SUV, packed solid with white goods, clothes and carrier bags. Wrenching the driver's door open the man computed he wouldn't have time to leap in and pull away before Al intervened. Instead, he reached inside the vehicle dragging out a long baseball bat, smeared in paint stains. He swung the bat behind his head and stood, wide stance, defying Al to stray within swinging distance, snorting a warning in a gruff, unintelligible accent.

Al pulled up sharp, raising his hand in a calming gesture. "I've nothing to do with the landlord. I'm not the police."

The man gripped the bat even tighter, glancing around warily. He shuffled from foot to foot, frizzy brown hair sticking out at the sides, assessing whether Al had back-up. Al feared one false move would prompt him to attack.

"Puszkin. Are you Puszkin? That's all I want to know." Al rapped out the question, anxiety raising the pitch of his voice.

The name seemed to register with the man because while he continued to wiggle the bat in menacing fashion, he spat out a phrase in a foreign accent.

The pregnant woman clambered out of the car, using the passenger door frame to heave herself to a standing position. Her dark hair hung long and lank, breathing laboured, but her weak smile suggested a sweet nature. When she spoke the accent was strong, words fractured, but English fluent. "He's not Puszkin. His name is Henryk and I am Amelia."

The man lowered the bat a fraction but his grip remained tight, eyes darting from Al to the woman.

"Henryk what? What's his other name?"

The man snarled a phrase containing a couple of English words, but still Al couldn't decipher.

"He wants to know why you want to know. He speaks very little English." Amelia walked around the back of the car, positioning herself between Al and Henryk.

"Are you Romanian?"

"Polish." Amelia motioned to Henryk to lower the bat. He complied.

By now Emily had appeared alongside Al, her presence lowering the temperature further.

"Let me explain," said Al. He told Amelia they were searching for a man named Puszkin who had driven a white rental van in Sea View Road, Weymouth, in March. The man's driving licence listed him as living at the flat they were vacating.

"So no police?" said Amelia.

"Definitely not." Al shook his head.

Amelia translated. There followed a lively discussion between her and Henryk.

"Pusznik is Henryk's cousin," said Amelia. "He went home last year. We wanted to stay but don't have a visa or work permit. Henryk finds work where he can. Pusznik let us stay in his flat and we borrowed his driving licence."

"But the picture on it is of you." A perplexed Emily pointed to Henryk.

Amelia shrugged, raising her eyebrows, the gesture unmistakable. Passports, permits, licences, NHS numbers. All were readily available on the black market, some more professionally forged than others, many allowing illegal immigrants to evade the authorities and go about their business. Al had read a recent article on the subject in *The Guardian.* Henryk must have paid to have his picture inserted on Pusznik's licence.

Al had already concluded that Henryk wasn't a Russian State hit-man. Their weapons tended to be more sophisticated than baseball bats, nor did they drive around in decrepit old cars with heavily pregnant women. At least that's what he imagined. "Never mind the picture. What we need to know is why Henryk was in Sea View Road, Weymouth, driving a white van on March the sixteenth."

Amelia translated once more, this time the conversation lasting longer, Henryk not convinced he wanted to divulge more information. Eventually, Amelia turned to Al. "Henryk is a plasterer, a very good plasterer. He works hard. His father was a plasterer, too, in Gdansk. He hired the white van to do some work with his friend."

"Where?" said Al, noting Henryk's jeans and scruffy blue shirt covered in old paint or plaster smears.

"As you say, Sea View Road."

"But which house? What number?"

Amelia turned to Henryk but he had understood. "Eleven."

"Sure? Not number seven?"

"Eleven." Henryk repeated the number, aiming another fusillade of Polish at Amelia.

"He says he remembers he couldn't park outside because of big lorries in the road. He parked down the street and walked up with his tools."

Al sighed. The story sounded legitimate. The white van wasn't mysterious after all. The work appeared to have been done next door to Al's house, probably while he was busy working a double shift at Tasty Treat. Henryk fired off another Polish salvo.

Amelia translated again. "Henryk says his friend asked a man which was number 11 because there was no house number and he pointed them in the right direction."

"Where did this man live? What did he look like?"

Henryk shrugged when Amelia translated. He'd taken scant notice and couldn't remember, but revealed they were no more than a couple of houses away when they spoke to the man.

"When are you due?" Emily piped up, realising the interrogation had run its course.

Amelia caressed her bump, forcing a resigned smile. "Anytime now."

"Where are you going to live?"

"With friends until we can find another flat."

Al fished in his pocket, pulling a couple of notes from his wallet. Henryk immediately raised his palm in a dismissive gesture.

"For the baby," said Al, handing the notes to Amelia to circumvent Henryk's pride. She took them, nodding her thanks.

On the way back to Weymouth, Al and Emily disagreed. Al believed unravelling the white van affair was the end of the matter. Emily thought the mystery man who gave directions to the plasterers was potentially Uncle Sebastian's killer. "He was in the right spot at the right time. That puts him in the frame."

Al took a deep breath. "It's a bit of a stretch. You heard Henryk, or at least Amelia, the road was full of lorries. The man could have been one of the drivers, one of the site workers, or even the dressing gown guy."

"I don't think so."

"Why not?"

"Because one of the workers would have been wearing a high-viz jacket and probably a hard hat, and I think Henryk would have remembered that. And he would definitely have remembered a man in a dressing gown and slippers."

Al couldn't fault the logic. Emily thought some more, assembling a table of pros and cons in her ordered mind, before announcing her conclusion as they turned into Sea View Road. "Henryk didn't remember any details because the man he saw fitted perfectly with his surroundings. Plain. Unremarkable. Mr Ordinary. Exactly the type the Russians would send down a suburban street unnoticed to murder someone."

Al had no reply to that.

30

I was fine until the taxi turned into the Sokolniki Centre and I saw the crowd. Mostly men, hundreds of them, lined up down one side of the main hall, plumes of cigarette smoke forming a lingering cloud.

My knee trembled, as always before a big lecture, although not like this. Jack-hammering up and down, drawing a disapproving glance from the driver. I clamped the knee in both hands, throwing him a weak smile. Security guards with sniffer dogs had held the invited audience outside to give the hall a final sweep, followed by an individual search as each person entered. Routine procedure only for the highest-ranked government officials. They must be expecting Brezhnev, I reasoned. Or knew something was afoot. *How could they?* My mind began to hammer along with my knee. *Had Kalenkov uncovered the plot? Did Kalenkov know I was bait to lure him here? If not, how would the sniper get through security?*

My training kicked in. Divert the anxiety. I wiggled my ankle, closed my fist and flapped my elbow. Three times each. A simple ploy but one I'd learned at Secretarium to reboot my thoughts. I called it my three times stable. Over 20 years I'd learned to associate the process with calming panic. James Bond may not have required such techniques on the big screen, but along with deep breathing and standing tall to open my chest it worked for me in real life. In the real world you learn to use whatever works.

By the time the taxi reached the entrance I'd regained control. The chairman of the Moscow Society of History and Russian Antiquities, a small rodent-faced individual, was on hand to greet me. Squinting myopically through round-rimmed spectacles, he spoke respectable English. "Welcome, Professor, we are delighted you could be here. Everyone is looking forward to your lecture."

We shook hands and an usher accompanied me inside to a small dressing room with swivel chair, desk and mirror, to make final preparations. The organisers even supplied a generous bowl of fruit, sparkling water and a bottle of vodka. I passed on all three.

I sat in the chair, swivelling back and forth, staring at my notes, half an hour to the scheduled 1pm start time. The actual lecture presented little concern. In essence it was the same one I had given perhaps 40 times before during the publicity round of universities and bookshops following publication of *The Two Ivans*. I had memorised it almost verbatim and with no session planned for questions any chance of unexpected events intervening was remote. My mind wandered to Anna and Rimsky's the night before, conjuring feelings of elation and warmth. *How would I see her* again? We'd made what I considered a pact to meet, but without timing, geography, or detail. Her *tour guide* duties were complete, and I was booked on a morning flight to London.

I paced the room, concentrating on my opening remarks, stealing glances in the mirror. Assuming the role. Becoming the character. I imagined Laurence Olivier doing much the same before marching out to play Macbeth at one of London's grand theatres. A knock on the door. "Professor, it's time." I ran through my script from Secretarium one last time. Don't scan the hall. Focus on a central spot in the body of the auditorium. Freeze when the shot is fired. Allow confusion to develop. Act shocked and afraid. I didn't think I'd have any problems with the last one.

I grabbed my folder, checking my hands were steady. No sign of tremor. I managed a confident stride down the corridor, the usher leading me to the side of the stage where I could see the society chairman in the lectern spotlight, relaying background information by way of introduction. The rows of seats stretched into the shadows and every one appeared taken. I couldn't understand the chairman's address, the microphone distorting his words, his Russian proving too fast and idiomatic. But I heard my name.

"From Cambridge in England, please welcome Professor Sebastian Stearn."

The usher tapped my elbow. I strode out on stage, the white noise of applause pounding my ears, senses heightened, spotlights temporarily compromising my vision. Tension and nerves dissipating as I placed my folder on the lectern.

"Spasibo, spasibo." I bowed, accepting the warm welcome.

As I had memorised the script I decided to speak in Russian. Braving the mother tongue always endears one to a foreign audience and employing a strange, unscientific logic, I also felt the guttural tones might isolate me from the events about to unfold. "Thank you for inviting me, Mr Chairman, to talk about my favourite Russian subject in the heart of Moscow. It's a great privilege." The microphone continued to boom. I lowered it slightly, waiting a couple of seconds for my eyes to adjust, a softer light filter reducing the glare, bringing the front of the audience into focus. I couldn't miss them. First row, dead centre. Four men, all resplendent in green dress uniform, although this was anything but a military occasion.

I recognised the top-ranking officers of the Soviet government immediately from my research at Secretarium, as I had done at the first seminar. Andrei Gromyko, foreign minister, Mikhail Sulov and Yuri Andropov, members of the ruling Politburo. Finally, the General Secretary himself, the Soviet leader Leonid Brezhnev, bushy eyebrows unmistakable, shiny medals festooned on the breast of his jacket. My eyes scoured the rest of the row, the brief to focus on the middle section the first casualty. I couldn't help it. Where was Kalenkov? He should have been sitting next to Brezhnev. He must be there. He'd promised to attend and was renowned as a man of meticulous order and routine.

I forced myself to concentrate, launching into the lecture, hiding my confusion behind the rhythm and cadence of my favourite subject, fixing my gaze mid-hall while wondering at the sniper's inevitable perplexity. *Was he here? Did he know about Kalenkov's absence? Was he stuck somewhere in the boughs of the hall with an unsheathed rifle, an itchy trigger finger and a befuddled mind?* The lecture proceeded without a hitch, the audience supplying the welcome ripples of applause that punctuate such an occasion, standing at the end, a sure sign of appreciation. For a moment I revelled in the positive feedback. I bowed, thanked the chairman once more and walked off stage, a flush of elation married with a curious sense of deflation that the mission had gone awry. A few minutes later an usher led me to a foyer.

The rodent-faced chairman was all smiles. "Professor, that was magnificent. Let me introduce you to our important guests."

He accompanied me across the room to a drinks table where the officers stood in line, caressing vodka glasses. I bowed, accepting congratulations, shaking each by the hand until I came to Brezhnev.

I had seen him many times on television news reports and read about his vanity. Hence the military dress uniform and adornment of medals, many of which he had awarded himself. He looked shorter, thinner, paler, a man in frail health. I recalled the conclusion at Secretarium that following a stroke and a heart attack in 1975 he deferred many decisions to a Soviet brains trust of top officials.

Brezhnev spoke in Russian, his voice gruff, yet steady, betraying no sign of his poor health. He twirled a lit cigarette in nicotine-stained fingers. "Very interesting lecture, Professor. I particularly enjoyed your list of Ivan Vasilyevich's many wives. You said six, like one of your own kings. We think it was more like eight." He guffawed and cast a knowing glance at Gromyko and Andropov, who chuckled as if sharing a secret joke.

Brezhnev continued. "Let's just say he had a healthy appetite, although he died from a stroke. I know only too well what that entails. But we have much to thank him for. He was the first Czar, dragging Russia from a medieval state to the path of the great empire today."

I smiled. "I thank you and your ministers for taking the time to come. It feels good to have my work appreciated."

"There would have been more of us, but we had a few unexpected matters to deal with."

"Nothing untoward, I trust."

Brezhnev snorted. "We lost too many fine soldiers in Afghanistan today, Professor. I dare say you will read about it on your news bulletins. Three helicopters down. What do you think Ivan Vasilyevich would have done about that?"

I shook my head, debating for an instant whether to be honest or diplomatic.

"Well?" said Brezhnev.

"I think he would have fought fire with fire, scorched the earth the Afghans inhabit, regardless of how many lives it cost. Vengeance came as naturally as breathing to Ivan the Terrible." I followed my mother's mantra. *Honesty is the best policy.*

Brezhnev's blank expression concerned me for a few seconds, until he chuckled. "You're right, Professor, that's exactly what he would have done. What do you think I should do with Poland and this Solidarity business? Do you think I should invade Poland too?"

"I said that's what Ivan would have done. For my part, I believe violence begets violence." This was surreal. I was standing in the heart of Moscow discussing whether the Soviets should invade Poland, urging one of the world's most powerful men to eschew violence moments after I should have been complicit in the murder of one of his top commanders. Fortunately, Brezhnev turned to speak to Gromyko, allowing the chairman to tug my arm, leading me away.

In the taxi back to the Four Seasons I consoled myself that the mission had failed through no fault of anyone involved, but by a quirk of timing. Kalenkov had obviously swerved the lecture to help deal with the Afghan crisis. I was relieved. No blood spilled. No guilt trip. Nothing to do but pack my bags to catch the morning flight back to my mundane world. Rarely had that prospect seemed more attractive.

When I reached the hotel I snatched a quick word with the desk clerk, requesting a wake-up call. As I headed for the lifts I noticed three uniformed soldiers stride into reception. Two of them carried rifles, all three marched in my direction. Unnerving.

"Professor Stearn?" The soldier in the centre.

"Yes."

The soldier pulled an envelope from his breast pocket and handed it to me. "From Colonel Kalenkov."

The soldiers showed no willingness to leave. I opened the envelope in front of them, scanning the message, written in English.

Dear Professor Stearn,

Unfortunately, I missed your lecture. I was delayed with pressing business.

I would like to discuss The Two Ivans. Please could you meet me for dinner and a game of chess at 7pm. I will send a car for you.

Colonel Igor Kalenkov.

A crushing sensation invaded my chest, knees went weak, but I disguised both by dropping my folder to the floor and stooping to retrieve it.

"Your answer, Professor?" The centre soldier asked when I rose.

Meeting Kalenkov right now was the last thing I desired, but I had no reason to refuse. At least, none that wouldn't cause offence.

"Of course. Tell the colonel I'd be delighted to accept his invitation."

The soldier clicked his heels and left with his colleagues. I waited in the foyer for several minutes before slipping out of the hotel to find a telephone. I walked for miles through the streets of Moscow, trusting my training, switching direction at random, entering a couple of Metro stations, pushing my way through crowds, not knowing if I was being followed. Anna had admitted covert surveillance operatives were scrutinising every move for my protection, which explained the routine search of my hotel room. I hadn't spotted anyone. I suppose I should have found that reassuring.

It was the first time I had witnessed close-up the crumbling underbelly of the city. Dilapidated buildings, poverty, stray dogs, beggars sleeping in shop doorways or drinking ruinous concoctions on litter-strewn wasteland. A sense of desolation. I found it depressing, but when I was satisfied that no one had followed, or at least no one in earshot, I discovered a street phone booth and punched in the number Secretarium had provided to memorise and destroy. The orders had been specific. *Only in case of emergency.* I gauged being invited to dinner by the individual the department had failed to eliminate that afternoon fitted the definition.

Five rings before the line connected. Silence. "Whisper," I said. No answer. Ten seconds later I was ready to put down the receiver when I heard a voice. Anna's voice.

"Yes?"

I wanted her to tell me everything would be fine, I was safe, I'd be on that morning flight out of Moscow. We'd meet again as soon as possible. But I knew I couldn't even say her name. First law of covert operations. No names. No details.

"I've had a proposal I think you might be interested in." I waited for an answer. Another irritating silence.

"We'll be in touch." The phone went dead.

An hour later I'd returned to my hotel room, stomach churning once more. It was late afternoon when I heard a gentle knock at the door. After checking a distorted vision of Anna in her tour guide garb through the spy hole I slipped the security chain and let her in.

No pleasantries. Her manner clipped, professional, as if Rimsky's had never happened. "What is it, Professor?"

I explained about the meeting with Brezhnev, the reason for Kalenkov's absence at Sokolniki, the invitation to dinner and chess with Kalenkov that evening. She digested the information for a few moments before a determined gleam lit her features. Her voice soft but urgent. "Professor, with your help we may have an opportunity to retrieve the mission."

"Pardon."

"Everything seemed lost when the target didn't attend the lecture, but this invitation changes everything."

"How?"

"Do you know how many agents have been inside Kalenkov's apartment within the Kremlin?"

"No."

"Precisely, Professor. That's because the number is zero. Security is impossible to breach. I could find a way to walk into the Oval Office tomorrow. Ten Downing Street no problem. But Kalenkov's personal space? That's by invitation only. This is the first invite I can remember to anyone outside the ruling Politburo."

Anna smiled in response to my perplexed frown. "You're wondering what I'm going to ask you to do, Professor, aren't you?"

"That had crossed my mind."

"I have an idea. I'll be back within the hour. Don't go anywhere."

She opened the door and as she slipped out I called her name. She spun around. "Thank you for last night, Anna." She smiled, a dazzling smile, the sort I knew would make me do anything for her.

***

I spent the next hour brushing up on my chess moves. I learned the game at an early age and had always found the cerebral sparring stimulating. As a student I represented Cambridge at the British Chess Championships in Aberystwyth in 1961 and the following year in Whitby, going out in the preliminary rounds both times to the eventual winner. I competed once more in Brighton in 1977 after students encouraged me to enter, but again failed to clear the first hurdle. I love chess. A game to stretch the mind. Without the obstacle of time, a splendid hobby. In Russia it's different. Chess is the national pastime. An obsession. The home of grandmasters. I knew I would prove no match for Kalenkov, but the prospect of humiliation offended my competitive instinct.

Anna returned, as she promised, an hour later. She seemed tense. I thought she avoided eye contact when she entered the room but I could have been mistaken. I didn't know what to expect, although I suspected my role may be to keep Kalenkov occupied at the chess board. "Okay, what do you need me to do?" I said.

Anna slipped a hand inside her brown leather shoulder bag, pulling out a slim black box, the sort used to present a small gift. The chequered motif of a chess board adorned the top, alongside the inscription in Russian, *Zezulkin's of Moscow*. She opened the box. On a velvet base reclined an exquisite white queen chess piece, around five inches long, carved from a mixture of wood and ivory with a solid silver base.

"Kalenkov is obsessed with chess, Professor."

"Aren't all Russians?"

"Yes, which is why he'll appreciate the gift we'd like you to present to him this evening."

I wasn't following. Surely Anna hadn't raced across Moscow to buy a gift for Kalenkov. For what purpose?

"I'm sure he'll appreciate it," I said. "A lovely piece. It looks like a trophy." I made to lift the queen out of the box to inspect it more closely. Anna snatched the box away.

"Professor, this isn't an ordinary queen. I'll be direct. This is a poisoned queen."

"Poisoned!"

"Professor, keep your voice down." Anna hissed the command. She strode over to the door, checking the spy hole before returning, extracting the queen delicately from the box. She turned it upside down, pointing to the hallmark on the silver base.

"Nice," I whispered. "Are you sure it doesn't look too expensive for a simple present?"

"Kalenkov appreciates the fine things in life. He adores chess. He'll love this."

"You said poisoned."

Anna turned the base towards the light. She placed her thumb nail directly on the hallmark, feigning to push it, her teeth biting her lip to demonstrate the force required. She pointed out the location of a tiny hole with her nail, although it was virtually invisible to the naked eye. "When you press hard on the hallmark, Professor, a fine spray will shoot through the hole in the queen's crown. I won't go into details of the substance, but when aimed at someone's face from a distance of two feet it will induce paralysis and cardiac arrest within seconds. Two minutes later the substance will be undetectable to anything other than the most rigorous autopsy. Even then doubt will prevail. All reasoned analysis will conclude the target died of a natural heart attack. Especially in someone like Kalenkov, who has a history of premature heart disease."

For a moment my brain refused to compute. We'd been through this. I'd told Porter in Cambridge I didn't want to pull the trigger. I didn't know if I could. The prospect of doing so with a gun, when I'd been trained in firearms with the outcome certain, was one thing. To do so with a contraption direct from some spy novel, no time for practice or training, with little comprehension of how accurate and efficient it might prove, seemed pure madness.

"I don't know, Anna, it doesn't seem right. Poison spray. A nerve agent. Sounds like something the Soviets would do."

"You mean killing my Rudi with a mystery virus is right. Personally slaying upwards of 30 agents is right. Plotting to assassinate the next king and queen of England is right." Anna snarled, her eyes smouldering with injustice.

"Of course not. Please, give me a moment to think."

"This man has to be stopped, Professor. There's no time to think."

My mind whirled with unconnected thoughts, mainly surrounding how Anna had located a killing device suited specifically to my assignation that evening at such short notice. That was my next question. After all, one can't pop out to the shops and buy a poisoned chess piece. Even in Moscow. At least I didn't think so, although I'd never tested that hypothesis. Anna's answer spoke volumes about how deep the Cold War's puerile depravity had plunged. On both sides.

"Professor, the KGB use umbrella tips, gold-rimmed tea cups, smeared door handles, dart guns hidden in newspapers, kitchen utensils, even contaminated children's toys to spread their poison. The more ordinary the object, the better. Does it not make sense to have a factory of our own? And what could be more ordinary in Russia than a chess queen?"

"You mean there's someone, somewhere, whose job is creating deadly weapons from everyday items, in case they might come in useful one day?"

"What do you want me to say, Professor?"

Her raised eyebrows and cute pout indicated I had stumbled on the truth. I rolled my eyes and thought of Henry Winter, traitor cum bland civil servant, murdered by a similar device on a teeming Tube train at the start of Kalenkov's killing spree. If it had been Porter or any of the other spooks from Secretarium asking me, I would have said no. Point blank.

But it was Anna. Husband killed. Child left without a father. Life ruined, yet still she faced danger with noble defiance every day to try to make the world a safer place. The prospect of walking into the Kremlin to murder one of the Soviet regime's most dangerous, well-protected, men filled me with foreboding beyond panic and fear. But I couldn't say no.

"Okay, I'll do it. But how am I going to get that close to him?" My throat felt dry with dread, voice hoarse from the lecture. I grabbed a bottle of water off the bedside table and took a swig.

"You'll figure a way, Professor. You're a brave, resourceful man. Kalenkov will be off guard. He likes a vodka or two with his chess."

"What if the queen doesn't fire?"

Anna didn't say anything. Her silence provided my answer.

31

"There's no such thing as a seagull."

Al's eyebrows raised, his expression doubtful as he studied Emily sipping a fizzy drink through a straw, gazing at the hypnotic swell of the ocean during a break from the latest deciphering session.

"I beg to differ. I'm looking at roughly a hundred of them right now. I'd count them if they didn't keep flying around."

"No, Al, you're looking at one hundred gulls, they just happen to be on the sea at the moment."

"So they're seagulls."

"Herring gulls actually. The sort that scavenge for food, pinching your chips on the prom."

"Rats with wings, you mean."

Emily chuckled, the conversation typical of their developing relationship, neither of them quite knowing where they stood or where it was heading. Emily the pedant, focus narrow and unyielding. Al easy going, ameliorative, pertinent quip never far from his lips.

Emily had her bone and she was determined to keep gnawing. "People call them seagulls, but there's no such species, and they turn up everywhere these days. They might as well call them urban gulls. Or town gulls. Or …"

"No, I don't think we should go to the police. Not yet. Let's wait until we see what happens." Al cut through the gull chatter to address a more pressing matter. The revelation in the journal that Uncle Sebastian was no longer a diversionary lecturer, but a full-blown would-be assassin, supported Emily's contention that he may have died at the hands of the Russians. A revenge mission, according to Emily. Al was dubious.

"But what happens when I'm right?" said Emily. Al noted Emily's skewed thinking, but let it go.

"Then we'll both go to report it to the police, although what they can do without hard evidence is anyone's guess." Al jumped up. "Come on, let's take a walk. We can always finish up here later."

When they reached the end of the driveway Emily caught sight of curtains twitching over the road, followed by Katharine waving at the window. Emily returned the wave in cheery fashion, as did Al. They were about to amble down the hill when Al glanced again, curious. Katharine still waving. Or was she beckoning? "I think she needs us for something," said Al.

They hurried across the street and waited for Katharine to open the front door after enacting the customary four-point Zimmer turn.

"I'm glad I've caught you. I've been trying to catch your attention for days." The door was barely ajar but Katharine was eager, although her voice sounded hoarse, her chest rattling.

"Uncle Sebastian's phone is working, Katharine. You could always have called. The number's in the book," said Emily.

"Don't trust phones, you never know who's listening on the other end."

Al wondered if she needed help with medication or a visit from the doctor. "You sound a bit rough, Katharine. How long have you not been feeling well?"

"What?"

"Your voice. You sound a bit under the weather." Al turned up the volume.

Katharine completed another swivelling procedure, this time a dismissive gesture waving away Al's concern. "A little cold, that's all. Never killed anyone."

They stepped in, traipsing slowly behind Katharine along the hallway.

"What is it, Katharine, what can we do for you?" asked Emily.

"It's what I can do for you two."

Katharine pottered to her kitchen drawer, the one by the worktop that she used as a desk, and pulled out her diary. Edging over to the table, she slumped in one of the kitchen chairs, breathing heavy. Al and Emily shared a concerned glance.

"I'm not getting any younger, am I?" Katharine paused for a few seconds to regain her breath. "Right, let's look."

Katharine trawled a finger down the page until she found the entry she was searching for. "Here we are, what do you think of that?"

Al and Emily leaned over Katharine's shoulders. Al read the entry out loud. *Large red car. NJP 358. Parked outside 8pm-Midnight.* The entry bore yesterday's date.

"Okay, what's unusual about that Katharine?" said Emily.

Katharine stayed silent, her finger sliding up the page to the next entry, dated the day before yesterday. Al read again. *Large red car. NJP 358. Parked outside 8pm-Midnight.*

Emily attempted to say something but Katharine raised her other hand. "Wait, one moment." The finger slid upwards once more and Al read out the same entry from three days before.

"Don't you find that strange?" said Katharine. "Three nights running. Same car, same place, same time."

Al shrugged. "Maybe a friend or relative visiting someone who isn't well. Where exactly was the car parked?"

"Right outside my house, but the driver was looking over the road at number seven."

"What? All that time? Didn't he get out of the car?" Katharine had piqued Al's interest.

"No." Katharine shook her head in exaggerated fashion.

"Not once?"

"No."

"All three nights?"

"Yes, all three nights."

Al scratched his head. The conversation verged on disconcerting.

"Did you get a good look at the driver, Katharine?" asked Emily.

"No. It was dusk by the time he arrived. He was looking away from my house, but he was up to no good."

"What makes you say that?"

"He had long hair in a ponytail."

"Really."

"And you know what you always find under a ponytail?"

192

"What?"

"An asshole. I should know, I've met a few in my time."

Emily giggled. She didn't mean to, but it was the way Katharine had spat out *asshole*, with an American street accent. Al threw Emily an admonishing look.

"Thank you, Katharine, for letting us know," Al said. "It does seem a bit strange but I'm sure there's some plausible explanation. Maybe he's one of the security personnel from the building site on a night shift. We'll bear it in mind and I'll keep an eye open for the car." Al had been careful to employ as neutral a tone as possible but Katharine picked up on the odd patronising vowel.

"You think I'm losing my marbles, don't you?"

"No, not at all, Katharine."

"Liar."

Al adopted his most charming tone. "Listen, Katharine. You were a big help with the white van, although we now know that was on legitimate business. It's good to know the people of Sea View Road have someone looking out for them."

He took a pen from his pocket and wrote his and Emily's names and phone numbers on a scrap of paper on Katharine's table. He didn't like the sound of Katharine's chest. "Katharine, any problems, or any news, give one of us a ring. Any time. And don't get up, we'll see ourselves out."

As they walked down the hallway they heard an undisguised mutter. "William and Kate believe me."

Al and Emily ambled down the hill, bought fish and chips from Bennetts Chippy and sat on the harbour wall, opposite Custom House Quay and The Ship Inn, legs dangling, tucking into the best fish and chips in the south west. At least that's what it said on Bennetts A-sign. Emily agreed. Al pointed out that she'd never had a fish supper in Edinburgh.

"Did you know this is the exact spot little ships set off for Dunkirk to evacuate soldiers in nineteen forty, and where troops embarked on landing craft on D-Day four years later? Makes you think, doesn't it?" Al pointed to a couple of boats in the harbour, owners readying them to sail.

Emily dipped a chip in tomato ketchup and munched. "You've been doing your research."

"Weymouth is full of maritime history. Some of the café's customers know everything about the place. I love all that stuff."

They needed the break, soaking in the sunshine, wind in their hair, hearing children squeal, pensioners grouch, conversation other than the coded journal, the comforting frivolity and fripperies of seaside life evolving around them. Emily appreciated that. Al worked every day in the café, meeting dozens of new people, some stimulating, others infuriating, but all making the general tick of time less onerous. Emily remained stuck in Sea View Road, cataloguing, photographing, deciphering, often seeing no-one but the postman and Al. Yet more than a month had passed since they began work on the journal and at last they appeared in sight of resolution.

Emily's voice was low and serious. "Al, do you think Uncle Sebastian has what it takes to actually kill Kalenkov?"

Al thought for a few moments, scrunching his fish and chip paper into a ball before lobbing it expertly into a waste paper bin 10 feet away. "I don't know, Emily. I've never been in that position and hope I never will be. But if you thought, by doing nothing, innocent people would be harmed, what would you do? Remember, Sebastian believes the lives of the next king and queen of England are at stake."

Emily gasped. "I can't believe this is happening to a relative of mine. Nothing exciting ever happens in my family. I hope Uncle Sebastian does the right thing."

Al jumped to his feet. "Come on. Let's find out."

32

The car arrived at the hotel's front entrance a few seconds before 7pm. Three soldiers, one driving, one in the front passenger seat carrying a machine gun, an officer in the back.

As he climbed out of the car the officer spotted me waiting at the door, alongside the concierge. "Good evening, Professor. Colonel Kalenkov is looking forward to seeing you."

I nodded and smiled. The officer spread his arms wide, international semaphore for a body search. "Before we drive, would you …?"

My pulse shot from around 50 to 200, fearing the officer would feel the thump of my heart as his hands caressed my contours. When his fingers alighted on the hard package in my jacket pocket he stood back, motioning for me to take it out.

"What's this?" The officer's eyes suspicious.

I prised off the lid and held the display box aloft. My voice calm and considered although sirens of panic screamed in my head. "A gift for the colonel. I'm told he adores playing chess."

The officer took out the *chess piece*, inspected it from every angle, shook it, turned it upside down, stroked it for a moment, enjoying the polished feel of the silver base before returning it to the box and handing it back to me. "A beautiful gift," he said.

The car pulled away and realisation dawned that I had no idea where we were going. I knew from my research at Secretarium that Kalenkov, as a high-ranking Soviet officer, owned numerous residences. It became plain when we turned along the Moskva river that Anna was right. We were heading for the Kremlin. More precisely, the Grand Kremlin Palace. If I needed confirmation of Kalenkov's credentials as a serious political player, up there with Gromyko and Andropov, even Brezhnev himself, in the Soviet pecking order, then clinched it.

As the car rolled into the Kremlin fortress through the official entrance at the Spasskaya Tower, I tried to justify what lay ahead. Wagner's *Ride of the Valkyries* blared in my mind and I imagined myself as Prometheus stealing fire from the gods, presenting it to humanity as a force for good. It was no use. The last thing I felt was heroic. And didn't I recall Prometheus paying dearly for his theft, sentenced to eternal torment, bound to a rock with an eagle sent to devour his liver? I shivered. Scrambled ideas. Dark thoughts. The sort my training at Secretarium had anticipated. I employed my three-times stable technique and by the time the car ground to a halt on a gravelled courtyard inside the rectangular palace I surprised myself at how composed I felt.

In normal circumstances this would have been my version of historical Heaven. On the site where the great Czars once resided. Peter the Great, Catherine and the rest. I would have loved to have snapped away with my tourist camera. The officer led me through the grand archways of the ornate Hall of St Andrew, boots clip-clopping on the tiled floor, echoing around the walls, until we reached a side door leading to a stone staircase. We climbed to the next floor, then along a narrow corridor where four soldiers stood guard, holding rifles. Through double doors and there I was, inside Kalenkov's Kremlin hideaway. Oak floor, resplendent Turkish rug, plush furniture and enormous sash windows overlooking the Moskva river as it snaked through the city. It wasn't difficult to imagine this as the epicentre of power. The officer ordered me to wait, disappearing into the adjoining room. A minute later Kalenkov emerged, the officer leaving, closing the double doors behind him.

"Professor. Good of you to come." We shook hands. I was struck once more by Kalenkov's piercing eyes. Sharp, icy, the sort that cut through a man's veneer to read the secrets of his soul.

"My pleasure, Colonel."

"Please, call me Igor." He motioned for me to sit on an enormous settee although he remained standing, a ploy I found unsettling, which doubtless was the intention. "I was disappointed to miss your lecture, Professor, especially as I knew it would be invigorating. There is something about the two Ivans that captures the essence of Russia, don't you think?"

A test. I could tell. Would I take the diplomatic route? Would I recite the accomplishments in generic fashion? I held the facts on the tip of my tongue. Ivan the Great multiplied Russia's landholding three-fold, renovated the Kremlin, laid the foundations of the Russian state. Ivan the Terrible, the first Czar, introduced the first printing press to Russia, constructed St Basil's Cathedral, dragged Russia from a medieval state to a great empire. Such historical blandness had never been my style.

"Yes, they were a bloodthirsty bunch," I said.

Kalenkov fixed me with those cold eyes. For a moment I was uncertain which way his mood would fall. Then he laughed. A loud guffaw resonating around the room. "Professor, I must say you're a breath of fresh air. I am not a man everyone feels comfortable around. I know that. People like to please me. They do not always speak the truth."

"What is history without the truth?"

"Indeed, Professor. My thoughts exactly."

A door opened, a waiter arriving with a tray of drinks.

"I took the liberty of picking out a bottle of Petrus, Professor. You are partial to a drop of wine?"

"Not usually, but in the case of Petrus I could certainly make an exception."

Kalenkov poured two glasses, the hollow glug reminding me of my reputation among students for passing around the port at Cambridge tutorials. He handed me a glass and I felt the solid weight of crystal. For the sake of politeness, I sniffed the complex bouquet, secretly surmising that I probably held the equivalent of a month's wages in my hand. We indulged in wine talk for a short while and then he sat opposite in a grand old armchair, crossing his legs but leaning forward, eager to return to the two Ivans.

"The thing is, Professor, Russia is and always has been a vast and proud nation, requiring strong leadership, the sort few men can provide. If that leads to autocracy, then so be it. Much better a nation with an autocratic leader instilling

197

discipline and organisation, where everyone knows their role, than the chaos and disorganisation that is the alternative. I think in Britain you would call the alternative a wishy-washy government."

"No, Colonel, in Britain we call it democracy." I took a sip of wine. Smooth. Full bodied. Warming. Courage-inducing. I couldn't bring myself to call him Igor.

Another guffaw. Kalenkov was enjoying himself. He clearly possessed a mischievous, as well as a formidable mind. I sensed the night already taking on the cut and thrust of a chess match.

"Tell me, Professor, if you could have dinner with only one Ivan, which one would you choose?"

Russians were clearly obsessed with the Ivans. Brezhnev had asked me how I thought Ivan the Terrible would have handled the Afghan crisis. Now Kalenkov had me dining with the wretched man.

"First, I should say history is not to like or dislike, it is to learn from. But, I admit, I would prefer to dine with Ivan the Terrible, as we refer to him. I find the villains of history more intriguing than the heroes. Don't you?"

Kalenkov nodded sagely as if accepting my philosophy. His mouth pouted and he rocked back and forth. I took it as a sign of agreement. I continued, "Maybe I'd invite Nero, Ghenghis Khan, and Joseph Stalin to join us. We could have a dictators' dinner party. A tyranny of dictators, no less."

I thought maybe I'd gone too far, although Kalenkov's thin smile said different. "Why Stalin?"

"Because while people in the Soviet Union might view Stalin as a popular wartime leader, history shows his government was responsible for ethnic cleansing, thousands of executions, the imprisonment of millions in the Gulag. I would ask him how he could justify that."

Kalenkov lit a cigarette. He chewed hard on it, sucking until little craters appeared either side of his cheeks, before blowing the smoke upwards in one billowing plume. "You appear very certain of your facts, Professor."

"History is my passion, Colonel. It's nothing without dates, facts, and recorded events. I deal only in verified testimonies."

"Even if truth, as you say in English, is the first casualty of war?"

It was a cliched phrase, an old argument. I expected better from Kalenkov, but I humoured him. "Ivan the Terrible was a complex character and history can't make up its mind about him. An intelligent man by all accounts, devout too, but one prone to systematic outpourings of violence."

"Is that so bad?"

"Violence is one thing, Colonel. Torture and persecution quite another. Sixty thousand people are estimated to have died at his hands during the massacre of Novgorod. Men, women and children, chased into the freezing Volkhov river to drown."

Kalenkov, unmoved, sucked a long drag of his cigarette from the corner of his mouth, fixing me with his eyes. "Treason." He paused, letting the word drift along with his cigarette smoke in the void between us. "I'd say that is a crime undeserving of mercy."

"Children don't commit treason, Colonel."

"And historians have the benefit of hindsight and pontificating from their soft armchairs."

"Point taken, Colonel, but the fact is indisputable that Ivan the Terrible showed signs of mental instability, a trait found in many of history's most wicked rulers."

I wanted to add that nothing much had changed since Ivan's reign. Russia, the largest nation on Earth, still appeared intent on expanding territory as it steered the Soviet Union. It spent more than 10 per cent of its national income on defence and a senseless arms race, housing some of the richest billionaires on the planet while many of its citizens resided in medieval-style poverty. It spied and killed indiscriminately on foreign shores. I'd have loved to have said that but my mission depended on holding Kalenkov's interest, not antagonising him.

An aide pushed open the door, informing us that dinner was ready to serve. Kalenkov rose and I followed his lead, but he paused in thought in the middle of the room. "All very interesting, Professor, but perhaps there is good reason why strong leaders are perceived as violent and unyielding."

"Why?"

"Because they understand the necessity to keep enemies in fear and a nation's people obedient." He spat out the words in a tone I found utterly chilling before catching me unawares. "My aide said you had a gift for me."

Suddenly my brain wrenched into gear, the purpose of my mission again clear, a shiver crawling up my spine. I clawed in my inside pocket and pulled out the box. I hadn't intended presenting him with it until we sat down to play chess, when I calculated we would be left alone for a couple of hours at least. Now, busy waiters and attentive aides were running around to serve dinner. I had no way of knowing what he might do with it, but I would have to take that chance.

"A small token of my gratitude for this evening, Colonel." I passed him the box, hoping he would open it there and then, not hand it to one of his aides. He slid off the lid, gazed at the chess piece and his glacier eyes danced a jig of appreciation. He took out the queen, fingers sliding over the ivory, wood and silver, feeling the weight, sensing the quality. I dared hardly look as he caressed the base, making great moment of studying the hallmark.

"What a beautiful piece. Thank you, Professor. First dinner, then we play. The white queen is mine."

33

"We can't leave it there. We can't Al, one more hour. Please." Emily's tone was beseeching.

Al rose from his seat at the desk. "It's one o'clock Emily. I can't keep my eyes open. We've been deciphering since four. The journal will still be here tomorrow and we'll know then."

"But I'll get no sleep tonight."

"Neither will I, if I don't go home. See you tomorrow afternoon." Al flipped his jumper around his neck, pulling it down as he strode down the hallway before banging shut the front door.

Emily walked around the desk and sat in Al's chair, flicking open the computer. She contemplated for half an hour, the only sound the soft tick of a clock, absorbing every nuance of Uncle Sebastian's latest revelations. She yearned to tell her parents but knew Al was right. Much better to work clear-headed, especially when he needed to be leaving for the café at 7.30am. She closed down the computer and sidled through to the kitchen for a calming glass of milk. As she crossed to the fridge, bare feet on the tiled floor, she shivered. For an instant she thought she detected something or someone at the sliding window doors. An emptiness griped in her stomach as she peered at her reflection in the windows. No moon, the night black. Grabbing the milk, she turned to flee the feeling of unease. Uncle Sebastian's painted eyes, created by his own talented hand, followed her every step of the way. As if guarding her. Or perhaps attempting to reveal a dark secret.

Emily was right. A combination of the uneasy feeling, staring at a computer screen, anticipating the finale to Uncle Sebastian's story, meant she endured a fitful sleep. She rose at seven o'clock, contemplated walking to the café with Al, but decided instead to plough on with cataloguing the belongings. She'd made significant inroads, not as swift as anticipated, but that was due to time spent deciphering the journal. Even so, she'd accounted for, photographed and packaged all books, records and cds. There was something discomforting about seeing Uncle Sebastian's most intimate possessions boxed in cardboard, sealed with parcel tape, hidden away, never again to see or hear the wonder and enthusiasm he must have lavished upon them. Emily couldn't identify the emotion. *I wonder if people would call this sad?*

The day began chill, a persistent drizzle, one of those late spring days that doesn't realise summer is around the corner. Emily made a sandwich for lunch and while walking through to the study heard a thud at the front door. The postman. She picked up the small brown package. At the same time, she noticed a man exiting the driveway, wearing a high-viz red jacket, hard hat, carrying a clipboard. Not the postman, but Pete from the building site. She ripped open the package to reveal two USB sticks with a label stuck to one of them. *ACE Security. March 16th.*

Emily muttered to herself. "Thank you, Pete. Could have done with it days ago, but better late than never."

She resisted the temptation to ram the sticks into her computer to trawl hours of recorded CCTV footage. Two pairs of eyes were better than one. She would wait for Al. The white van no longer concerned her, but she believed the footage of Sea View Road, almost certainly on the day Uncle Sebastian died, would somehow help understand his death. She ate her sandwich and waited.

Al was late. Usually, he'd arrive by 1pm but the doorbell rang almost an hour and a half later. "Sorry, couldn't get away," he said.

Emily ushered him in. "Problems?"

"Sort of. One of the older customers came in carrying his umbrella. Don't know why but he pressed the button and the brolly unfolded in the shop, one of the prongs almost taking out Jennifer's eye. She had to go to A&E. As she was on check-out I covered for her."

"Hope she's okay." Emily's wide grin didn't exactly complement the sentiment, but at the same time she dangled the USB sticks, one in either hand.

"From Pete?"

Emily nodded.

"What do you want to do first?" said Al. "View or decipher?"

"View."

"We could be here a while."

"Better get started then."

Al unpacked his computer alongside Emily's, reasoning they could watch both USB sticks at the same time. They took the laptops through to the kitchen island worktop and sat on stools side by side. One stick covered midnight to noon, the other noon to midnight. Emily chose the first one, fast forwarding to sunrise at around 5am. Al began watching his stick from the start.

The quality proved grainy, but the camera covered the entire length of the street, although it quickly became apparent *A Day in the Life of Sea View Road* wouldn't win any cinematic awards. An action thriller, it wasn't. Al spotted half a dozen lorries trundling up to the building site, delivering sand, aggregate and equipment, others collecting debris for disposal. All struggled to negotiate parked cars packing both sides of the street, residents using the road because skips or scaffolding occupied their driveways.

Emily spied nothing for more than an hour, until one resident appeared briefly, walking a black Labrador. Another hour passed, the only stirrings the odd swooping gull. Emily resorted to a secret supply of chocolate at the back of the fridge.

"Want one?" She offered a bar to Al.

"You bet, it's one of my super powers."

"What do you mean?"

"Making chocolate disappear."

Emily delighted in the rush of sugar, sucking her bar slowly as dressing gown man sauntered to his garden gate. She witnessed the young couple's car lurching out of their driveway, the woman gesticulating, an angry domestic greeting another fraught dawn.

As Emily was about to suggest switching to deciphering duties, the first spark of interest arrived. A white van turned into the street, proceeding with caution, apparently searching for a house number. Emily nudged Al. "Here we go, could be Henryk's van."

The van stopped for a few moments outside number 11, but a skip blocked the driveway and cars were parallel parked. The van continued to the end of the cul-de-sac, the driver executing a three-point manoeuvre in the turning area before trundling back down the road. This time it passed number 11, stopping at the first available parking opportunity, two of its wheels spanning the pavement, outside what appeared to be number seven, although blurry perspective made it difficult to judge.

Two men clambered out. While the picture remained misty, the driver had distinctive hair sticking out at the sides. Al pointed. "That's Henryk." The other man wore a red baseball cap. They swung the van's rear doors open, unpacking bags and equipment. As they were doing so, the picture began to flicker, doubtless a seagull or pigeon having landed on the stanchion.

Al and Emily's eyes strained as another fuzzy figure came into view. For a few seconds the three figures appeared to meet. Emily's voice almost screeched with excitement. "That's the third man. The one Henryk told us about. He must be giving directions. Look, Al, I think he's going down Uncle Sebastian's driveway. Or is it number five next door?"

"Who knows? Bloody technology. Haven't a clue if it's a man or a woman."

"They call that Sod's Law, don't they?"

"Wait four hours seeing nothing happen clear as day and when something does we might as well be wearing a blindfold."

After a few more seconds the picture cleared in time to catch Henryk and colleague entering number 11. Al glanced at Emily. "Okay, let's keep our eyes peeled on number seven. If someone went in, he or she has to come out. If and when they do, I want to grab a screen shot."

The burst of action recharged their concentration, Al pausing his computer, both studying Emily's screen. A few minutes later, more movement. This time a person exiting number seven, bushes lining the driveway partially hiding him. The figure hesitated half-way along the tarmacked drive before continuing to the roadway. The image was small, the picture quality poor, but the stocky gait suggested the contour of a man. As the person stepped into the road, the parked van masked his frame. When he emerged his face pointed towards the entrance to Sea View Road, away from the camera.

"Damn. Come on, turn around." Al's fingers ready to take a screen shot. An instant before disappearing behind another parked van, the man's head swivelled to look up the road, face virtually thrust into the camera. The computer shutter clicked.

"Got him," said Al.

Emily gasped. She turned to Al, eyes wide, a mixture of shock and confusion. "Oh my God. Marcus. It's Marcus. He lied, Al. He lied. Why would he lie? Why would Marcus lie?"

"What do you mean? Marcus coming out of Sebastian's house. What's unusual about that?"

Emily's hands trembled, features screwed into a befuddled grimace as she strived to rationalise the potential consequences of the CCTV evidence.

"You don't understand, Al. Marcus told me he was away the day Uncle Sebastian died. Said he hadn't seen him for weeks. Visiting his daughter with his wife. Told me he was upset that he couldn't have been there for him when he needed him most and was sad that the cleaner had to find him."

"Why would he say that?" Al looked puzzled.

"Exactly. Why would he? He's a creepy guy, Al. He seemed really friendly at first. I think he knew Uncle Sebastian well, but there's something about him I don't take to."

"I don't know him. I've spoken to him a couple of times. He seemed pleasant enough."

"Have you ever seen his wife?"

Al thought for a moment. "I've only been here a couple of months but, no, can't say I have."

"Neither have I. Never laid eyes on her, nor has Katharine. Not for months anyway. His house is a tip. Untidy, dirty, no woman's touch whatsoever."

"What are we saying here?" Al's expression grave.

Emily shrugged, eyes switching from Al to the computer screen. "I don't know. But this tells us Marcus saw Uncle Sebastian on the day he died, although his body wasn't discovered until the next day."

"Maybe Sebastian died later that day, or that night, after Marcus had visited."

"If so, why lie? Why not tell everyone how Uncle Sebastian seemed. That's the normal thing to do. There's another thing."

"Go on." Al liked this energised version of Emily. He detected a surge of obsession building within her that wouldn't be sated without convincing answers.

"He professes to be Uncle Sebastian's best friend, but didn't go to his funeral. Made something up about his wife, Mary, not doing funerals. That's if Mary even exists."

"That is strange. What about the cleaner?"

"What about her?"

"I presume the police spoke to her. Would they not have asked all the pertinent questions? Who was his best friend? Did he have any visitors? That sort of thing."

Emily jumped off her stool, scouring the side of the fridge where a heap of notices and memos clung, magnetic figures pinning them to the metal. She tore off a scrap of paper full of names, professions and telephone numbers.

Emily pointed to the words *Cleaner* and *Eva,* and beside them a phone number. "Let's ask her. I don't know her, but she came to the funeral."

"Er … okay then, give it a go."

"Will you ask the questions, Al? You're better at that sort of thing."

Emily punched the number into the cordless telephone, selecting speakerphone. After five rings a woman's voice answered. Emily explained who she was and that she was cataloguing Uncle Sebastian's belongings at Sea View Road along with her friend. The woman offered her condolences.

"I remember you from the funeral. What a lovely service. Only a small gathering, but didn't people say such nice things about him." Eva had an accent that tripped along. Sounded Italian.

Al cut in. "Eva, we're trying to build a picture of Sebastian's last days and wondered if you could tell us if he had any visitors."

"Not that I know of. Kept himself to himself. Didn't see many people. Most days he amused himself with his books and music. But I only worked one day a week for two hours."

"Always the same day?"

"Yes, always Wednesday. Arrived at ten o'clock on the dot. For the last fifteen years."

"I don't want this to be upsetting, Eva, but the day you found him did you notice anything out of the ordinary. I mean, apart from the fact that he wasn't alive obviously." Al's tone was gentle but confident.

"The police asked me the same question."

"What did you tell them?"

"There was nothing unusual. He was lying in bed, looking peaceful. I thought at first he was having a lie-in."

"How had you got in?"

"I had a key. Professor Stearn gave me one years ago when he spent a lot of time in Cambridge. He still stayed over, but not as often. Slowing down after his heart scare. I'd rung the bell, but when there was no answer I let myself in."

"Heart scare?"

"He didn't call it that. Said it was something to do with rhythm. He made a joke, said he'd never had any rhythm, that's why he couldn't dance. The doctors knew all about it. He started taking medication for it in the last few months."

That would explain Sebastian's clue about *The Grapes of Wrath*, thought Al. What did it say? *If you are reading this, I must be gone.* In fact, it accounted for the urgency to purchase *The Wrath* and *The Wind*. Sebastian was reclaiming the key book codes thieves had stolen in the burglary because he realised his heart was failing.

"Eva, did you know Marcus from across the road?" Al careful to maintain a light, relaxed tone.

"Yes. He kept an eye on the professor's garden when he was away. They were good friends. Had their moments, bickered at times, but I remember Marcus's daughter playing the professor's piano. Even did some exams on it."

"Eva, you've been very helpful and …"

Eva interjected. "There *was* something a little odd. I didn't think about it when the police were asking questions and it's probably nothing, but it has been nagging away at me."

"Go on." Al and Emily swapped knowing looks.

"It's not something … erm … that I found, as much as something I didn't." The line went silent.

"Take your time, Eva."

"Every night Professor Stearn enjoyed a whisky. The good stuff. A large one, but only one. A medicinal malt, he used to call it. Said it kept him young. I don't like whisky myself, I prefer …"

"So what was missing, Eva?" Al's deft intervention steered her back on course.

"His whisky glass. I washed it every Wednesday morning, the first thing I did. It was always on the little table by his armchair, pointing out to sea. He liked watching the lights twinkling in the bay. I would put away his bottle of malt, then rinse out his glass. But it wasn't there. I found it in his drinks cabinet. Clean as a whistle. Hadn't been used."

"Who knows Eva, maybe he wasn't feeling well that night and gave it a miss."

"Yes, you're probably right."

"You've been a big help."

Emily jumped in. "Yes Eva, thank you for looking after him."

"It was a pleasure. The Professor was a genuine gentleman."

They bade Eva farewell and after Al explained his theory about the books and Sebastian's heart scare, they sat for a while, staring at the ocean, mulling on what they'd learned.

"What are you thinking?" Al broke the silence.

"I'm thinking Uncle Sebastian was murdered. And maybe not by the Russians. No prizes who's my prime suspect."

"Yes, I think we should at least pay him a visit."

34

"Have you ever killed anyone, Professor?"

I swallowed hard. Had to force a piece of chicken down my throat as Kalenkov's question rattled around my brain. For an instant I wondered if he knew. How could he? If he knew I wouldn't be sat at his dining table quaffing fine wine and eating rich food.

"No, Colonel, I haven't. Why do you ask?"

"Because I detected moral distaste when you spoke of Ivan. As if you didn't believe the readiness and necessity to kill is a fundamental quality when ruling a great nation."

"Quality is a strange word to use when talking about cold murder."

Kalenkov lifted his wine glass, eyes fixing me as he sipped, another move doubtless employed to disconcert. It succeeded. He licked his lips, replacing the glass slowly, as if contemplating my comment. "I'm sorry if my English is not correct. I spent only one year in Oxford as a student, but I have visited the United Kingdom on many occasions."

"For what purpose, Colonel?"

"Many reasons. Some of them to visit old friends." Kalenkov smiled.

He was playing with me. A cat with a mouse. I'd read the reports at Secretarium. I remembered Porter telling me about Henry Winter, the double agent the department believed Kalenkov killed on The Tube with scant regard for the safety of scores of commuters. I recognised the conversation hovered at a delicate stage. While I didn't want to alert him, I needed to explore his inner being. What made this man believe killing was an acceptable mode of government? From all that I'd read and gleaned, Kalenkov was the Minister for Murder.

"Let me ask you the same thing, Colonel. Have you killed anyone?"

He put down his knife and fork as if the question had curtailed his appetite, sat back in his chair, clasping his hands against his chest, twiddling his thumbs.

"Professor, have you heard of the Thirteenth Directorate?"

Of course I had, through Porter on the roof at Clare College. Again at Secretarium, where intelligence types had explained the harrowing and hideous nature of *executive action* and *wet affairs* under the command of Kalenkov. The 13th engendered fame and infamy in equal measure, but I shook my head, denying all knowledge.

"Professor, there are those who believe the Thirteenth was and always will be the most important department in the defence of our great nation. It controls no tanks, missiles, or submarines. From time to time the number of the department might change but the ethos of the Thirteenth remains the same. Root out our enemies, some of whom masquerade as old friends. Treachery is a disease that requires radical surgery with the sharpest of blades. Does that answer your question?"

"Not exactly, Colonel, but it will have to do."

He studied me again with that thousand-yard gaze. Did he suspect my pretence, or did years of getting away with murder blind him to his one weakness? Arrogance. I was about to receive the answer.

"Guns, knives, bombs, even missiles, don't kill people, Professor. People kill people. There is only one weapon needed to kill."

"What would that be?"

"The will." He spat out the words in a mocking, dismissive tone, aimed almost certainly at my moral distaste, as he had described it. That was the moment I decided. Until then I hadn't allowed myself to fully weld with the purpose of my mission. I know that sounds unlikely, weird even, when I was sitting in the world's most fortified location with a hidden vial of lethal poison, but the mind has strange coping mechanisms. Kalenkov's arrogance slipped the safety catch in my brain. I knew there was no turning back. From that point my words tracked his conversation, but my innermost thoughts concentrated on completing the mission.

"And you possess the will?" I said.

"Yes, Professor. I'm not ashamed to admit it. Have you finished?"

"Erm, yes, of course." I laid down my cutlery and Kalenkov clicked his fingers. The waiters cleared the plates. He motioned to an aide, who bent his head, Kalenkov whispering in his ear. A few minutes later the aide returned carrying a hard-back book, which he slipped to Kalenkov.

"I would like you to accept this, Professor, read it and let me know what you think. There's a chapter on the *will* we talked about." He handed the book to me.

"*Iskusstvo Zashchity. The Art of Defence.*" I read the title out loud in Russian and English, Kalenkov's name appearing in a modest font size in the bottom right corner of the dust cover.

"You are not alone as an author, Professor, although I wrote this book many years ago."

"I don't know what to say, except could you sign it, please." I plucked a pen from my jacket and handed it to him. He scrawled an indecipherable squiggle.

"I'm ready to play chess. How about you?"

He didn't wait for me to answer. Instead he picked up my gift box and walked into a cavernous study with a window overlooking the Moskva, shimmering silver in the moonlight as it slalomed without effort or care through the silhouetted landmarks of the capital. A huge desk dominated the room. In one corner a chess board, complete with pieces in place, adorned a polished mahogany table, a gold lamp casting an intimate light. Two soft-backed winged chairs with ornate embroidered cushions were positioned either side.

Kalenkov motioned me to take the chair nearest the black chess pieces and he sat on the other. An aide entered, carrying a tray containing a decanter of clear fluid and two glasses. He deposited the tray on a small table. Kalenkov dismissed him with a wave, ordering him to shut the door as he left.

"Vodka?" Kalenkov said, already standing to pour a glass.

"Just a little. I find I need all my wits to play chess." I'd had two glasses of wine. I wasn't drunk but could sense the

211

alcohol's warming effects. I felt emboldened, but not compromised.

"What is that old joke, Professor? I drank so much vodka last night that I woke up with a Russian accent. Nonsense, I wake up with a Russian accent every morning." Kalenkov laughed, loud and hearty, throwing back his vodka and pouring another. He sat down and reached for the gift box, cradling the chess piece in his hand for a few moments before substituting the usual white queen, which he lay on the wooden floor. My gift stood an inch taller than any of the other pieces, Kalenkov appearing to revel in its prominence. As if it posed a challenge.

"Magnificent. I hope I can do this bright new queen justice. She is regal and grand but not, how would you say, fussy. Rather like your own queen, don't you think?"

I nodded. "I'm honoured that you are playing with it."

"I don't think we need the clock, do you? This is a friendly game, after all." Kalenkov removed the timing device, placing it on the floor by the old queen. He advanced his queen pawn two squares. I countered by doing the same with a bishop pawn.

"Ah, the Sicilian Defence. Very traditional, but also combative. I like that. The fight for the centre of the board begins. You see, Professor, chess is much like invading a country. Sweep in ruthless and decisive, stick to your strategy, leave the enemy guessing, keep worrying, don't let them regroup. End it fast."

"Doesn't seem to be working too well in Afghanistan." I wanted to bite back the comment. It was provocative, unnecessary, especially given the news of the downed helicopters, but Kalenkov let it go, mind focused on his strategy.

We parried for a while, swapping pawns, studying the board, consolidating positions, but always with Kalenkov in control. One move ahead, forcing me to defend. All the while I struggled to concentrate, knowing I had to stay in the game, to maintain Kalenkov's interest until an opportunity presented itself. He sank three more vodkas in rapid succession, without noticeable effect on his sobriety.

"You play well, Professor. Where did you learn the game?"

I explained about representing Cambridge, but falling short when it came to national tournaments.

"Chess is about memory, clarity of mind, strength of purpose." Kalenkov conveyed his knowledge freely, yet I detected a disparaging edge to his tone, as if weakness of any sort affronted his uncompromising view of a world in which coercion and murder were not merely tolerated, but essential government policy. If he detected weakness in me then so be it. That right now could be my strength.

Kalenkov continued, "Some players know all the moves but struggle when it comes to competition. They doubt themselves. They fear winning itself. Maybe you are one of those people, Professor."

We swapped knight for knight, a tense skirmish, the outcome not as favourable as I anticipated, allowing Kalenkov to strengthen his attack. We'd been playing for more than an hour when his aide tapped on the door, enquiring whether we needed anything. "No more interruptions," snapped Kalenkov. The aide shuffled backwards with an apologetic bow.

Kalenkov sank several more vodkas, although I resisted his attempts to fill my glass. For the first time I detected a slight slur in his speech, a mellower expression. No longer did he harry me, as he had done at first with shrugs, nods and grunts, to take my next move. His movements were slower, though strategy still faultless. I sensed the opportunity nearing, knowing there could be only one attempt and it must prove decisive. The similarities with the board game in front of us were inescapable. Kalenkov was protecting the white king and somehow I had to find a way to manoeuvre the white queen into the perfect position for my own attack.

Without warning, during a phase of prolonged inaction, Kalenkov rose from his seat and stretched, before walking over to the enormous window to take in the spectacular vista. He beckoned me to join him and I contemplated grabbing the poisoned queen. I didn't. Too much ground lay between us, the chances of him detecting an awkward movement, a glimpse of white, too great. I stood shoulder to shoulder with

213

him at the window, lights twinkling, river shimmering, Kremlin backdrop silhouetted dark and eerie in the moonshine. He puffed out his chest, nodding as if surveying his kingdom. I wondered what cogs propelled his malevolent mind. A sweep of his arm heralded the view.

"Look, Professor, doesn't it feel like we are standing at the nerve centre of all humanity? Let us not be in any doubt. Russia, the Soviet Union, with its great minds and its military might, this is the nation that rules the world. With such power comes great responsibility."

"What do you mean?" I detected the vodka had loosened Kalenkov's hold on reality. The guard was dropping, his mood boastful.

"We are leaders in space technology, the first to put a man in orbit. We are pioneers in atomic and nuclear technology. It is early days but we are developing robotics and missiles that can intercept missiles. This is all for the good of mankind, despite what the American president might say. The Americans spend more on the military than we do, ten times more and yet they try to paint us as aggressors. Mark my words, Professor, the next century will be the era of the sickle and hammer."

I shrugged, a simple gesture but I could tell Kalenkov disapproved.

"You think my head is in the clouds, Professor. That I am rich, powerful and talk from my position of privilege. Tell me, what is the inscription on the crest of our great union?"

I didn't know. I'd studied Russia down the centuries. I could tell you the names of Ivan the Terrible's six wives. I could spout Catherine the Great's family tree and talk for hours on the nuances of Russian politics, but at that moment the founding ethos of the Soviet Union escaped me. Kalenkov spotted the void in my knowledge, the smuggest of smiles playing on his lips.

"Proletarians of the world, unite!" he said. "That is what it says, for all the world to see. We are not a union for the privileged few. We value our workers, champion the ordinary man, protect the common people."

214

One word came to mind. I wanted to open that enormous window and scream it across the Moscow rooftops. *"Bullshit!"* Instead, I said, "A noble inscription indeed, Colonel."

"Come on, to our game. I can sense the crucial thrusts are near."

On his way back to the board Kalenkov poured another vodka, insisting on offering a toast.

"To the workers." We clinked glasses, he threw the drink down his throat, although I was careful to take the merest sip.

When the opportunity arrived, it owed much to a cocktail of good fortune and strong vodka. Kalenkov captured a rook, a bishop and two knights, as well as a bunch of pawns. My king was in retreat and our queens battling, mine in a vain attempt to stave off defeat, his sweeping through my defence, anxious to supply the winning thrust. In desperation, I sacrificed my remaining bishop, hoping to benefit from a territorial gain but the outcome proved disastrous, his queen, aided by a rook and a knight, surrounding my king. Maybe the excitement at scenting victory threw him off guard. Most likely, the vodka had finally soaked through to the aspect of his brain controlling co-ordination, but as he slid the tall white queen to put my king once more in check, he fumbled, knocking the piece off the board onto the polished table. He grabbed but missed. The poisoned queen rolled off the table, luckily on my right-hand side, landing at my feet.

No time to think. Instinct kicked in, the subsequent events taking place in apparent slow motion. A curious trick of the mind. I snatched the queen, manoeuvring it until my thumb located the silver base with two fingers grasping its neck. I made as if to hand it to him. He smiled, leaned forward, offering his hand. I can't be sure, but I think he mouthed *thank you* as I thrust the poisoned queen towards his face, at the same time pressing my thumb hard into the silver base. His brow furrowed, features betraying momentary astonishment. I detected a hand raising as if to protect himself. Too late. A crack sounded, not dissimilar from the snap of a Christmas cracker, propelling a shower of fine mist into Kalenkov's face. He didn't recoil. Instead, his mouth dropped open, features contorting into a mask of shock and disbelief. For a fleeting moment he grasped my wrist, but already strength had drained from his bony fingers. I heard him gasp, twice, maybe three times, though nothing intelligible emanated from his lips. His grip released, cold stare fixing mine as I slumped in my chair, sleeve across my mouth, holding my breath to nullify the effects of any stray droplets of aerosol. We sat like that for what seemed like hours but was probably no more than half a minute, those evil eyes bulging and burning but no longer with threat or purpose.

I hadn't prepared a speech for the occasion. Why would I? If truth be told I never believed I could accomplish such a mission, but somehow as Kalenkov's life ebbed away, the poison paralysing his respiratory system, inducing a heart attack of almost instant consequence in an already-weakened organ, I whispered, "Who knew it, Colonel? You were not the only one who possessed the will. This night is for Henry Winter and all the rest."

I won't lie. Watching a man die, having broken bread, drunk wine and debated the fine points of history together so recently, was grotesque. The sight of his bemused leer and sound of his final grunts will haunt me forever. But the catch of conscience didn't weigh heavy at that moment. My heart was bouncing, body tingling from the sudden infusion of adrenalin. I felt relieved. More than that, elated that the job was done. I sensed the last vestiges of consciousness disappear from Kalenkov's eyes, the lids close and his body fall limp before beginning to tip forward. His head would have crashed into the board, sending chess pieces clattering in all directions, alerting his staff, if I had not caught it in my bare hands, holding his weight, anchoring his body in the chair. I could feel the drool at his mouth, the prickly texture of his stubble, as I counted the seconds, remembering what Anna and Secretarium had taught me.

Within minutes, the arteries would relax, the poison dissipate, no trace would remain of the queen's lethal contents. I sat like that with his head virtually in my lap for at least five minutes, staring at the double doors to the office, praying the crack of the mechanism hadn't alerted Kalenkov's aides.

When I deemed sufficient time had passed I rotated his head in my hands, levering his body once more into a sitting position, rocking him backwards. His body collapsed into the winged chair, head lolling to one side. Instinct saw me grab to support him. I arrested the fall of his head, my hands holding his cheeks, my face no more than a foot from his.

He gasped, his eyes jerked open, and my heart almost leaped out of my chest.

35

A clang aroused Emily from a sleep that proved beyond fitful.

She felt nauseous, a pulse drumming at her temples, foggy brain thickened by the dread of dreams laced with malice, danger, and the recurring image of Kalenkov's accusing eyes. She staggered out of bed as the doorbell rang again, pulling on her dressing gown, padding barefoot to the front door.

The hall clock ticked towards 10 o'clock. After trawling through the CCTV and phoning the cleaner the evening before, Al and Emily had embarked on a marathon deciphering session. Two sessions in one, mostly due to Emily's desperation to discover details of Uncle Sebastian's mission to the Kremlin. The more Emily unveiled the more eager she was to continue. A bleary-eyed Al left for bed at 4am.

Emily opened the door expecting to see the postman. Instead, a young woman filled the doorstep, long brown hair swept back, fixed in place with a twisted material head band. She carried a heavy rucksack, forcing a stooped demeanour, but her face was fresh, smile open. A student perhaps, thought Emily, noticing the frayed rips and tears in her faded jeans.

"Hello, sorry to bother you, but I wondered if you knew where my dad was?" Her voice carried the innocent trill of youth, head bobbing enthusiastically as she spoke.

"Your dad?" The fog was clearing but Emily's thought processes were still clunky as she attempted to fathom a connection with a caller who looked barely out of her teens.

"Marcus. From across the road. He was Sebastian's best friend. I've come down for the day to surprise him and forgotten my keys. He doesn't seem to be in and isn't answering his phone."

"You must be Helen, his daughter."

"That's right. And you must be Emily, Sebastian's niece, Dad told me you were staying here sorting out all the belongings. I wondered whether Dad was here. He used to spend so much time in this house, or in the garden, doing a few odd jobs, with Sebastian. He also used to leave his keys with Sebastian."

Emily pulled an embarrassed face and gestured at her dressing gown. "No, not seen him today, only just got out of bed actually. Why don't you come in?"

They went through to the lounge, Helen's eyes widening, a glow of nostalgia pinking her cheeks as childhood memories surfaced. She sidled over to the piano, running her fingers along the keys.

"This brings back memories. Good times. If it wasn't for Sebastian, I would probably never have got into music. I used to love coming over here to play. He was always so supportive. Helped me get through my grades. I can hardly believe he's not here anymore."

The affectionate mention of Uncle Sebastian focused Emily's thoughts. The CCTV footage of Marcus exiting number seven had convinced her he was implicated in her uncle's death, although there was no proof. Here, by pure chance, lay an opportunity to test at least part of his story, although it called for astute and gentle handling. Not Emily's domain, but she warmed to the pitch and tenor of this young woman's demeanour, and she'd always valued first impressions.

"I was surprised we didn't see your dad at the funeral as they knew each other so well. You and your mum too."

Helen looked puzzled, fine eyebrows almost meeting as they danced a perplexed jig. "Sorry, but I thought the family had requested a small, intimate gathering."

"No."

Helen seemed taken aback by Emily's directness. "O … kay. Dad said he would have loved to have been there."

"What about your mum?"

"What about her?"

"I know she didn't do funerals, but she must have known Sebastian quite well too."

"Mum and Dad split up three years ago. Mum lives in Wales now and she's not in the best of health. Waiting for a hip operation." There was a smidgeon of suspicion in Helen's tone. She tried to hide it but she'd detected a harsh ring, an ulterior motive maybe, in Emily's questioning.

"I'm sorry, I didn't realise that. So they don't see each other?"

"Never, as far as I know. Dad was devastated when Mum left."

"That must be hard for Marcus."

"He's good at finding things to do. He enjoys walking and he's obsessed with photography. Always taking pictures, some of them are pretty good. He's quite the professional."

"He's shown me some of them in his study. I've seen him down at the harbour at the crack of dawn waiting to snap the trawlers come in." Emily's voice rang with enthusiasm and Helen smiled, guard relaxing. Emily beckoned her through to the kitchen and grabbed two drinks from the fridge.

Helen snapped the ring-pull, taking a couple of swigs. "Thanks, I needed that. I was up early for the first train this morning. Nothing hits the spot like cold fizz."

"You're in Bristol, aren't you?" said Emily.

"Yes, in my final year at University. I worry about Dad being on his own sometimes but he can always come to stay with me for a few days if he wants to. It's not a big place, only a student apartment not far from the Clifton bridge, but I've got a put-you-up bed and it's comfortable."

"When did you last see him?"

"Not that long ago. Six weeks. A bit longer perhaps. He stayed quite a time. I think he was coming to terms with Sebastian's death. Seemed pretty cut up about it."

"That must have been the middle of March then?" Emily fishing for information, having discovered that Marcus had lied when blaming his wife for not attending the funeral.

Helen's tone was crisp and assured. "I can tell you exactly when it was because I play keyboards in a band. We had a big Irish gig on St Patrick's Day at the Students' Union. Dad arrived the day before. I remember being late for the rehearsal that night because he was telling me about Sebastian's heart attack. Even shed a few tears. Set me off as well, to be honest."

"That's the day before St Patrick's Day?"

220

"Yes, definitely. Dad came to the gig the next day. I dedicated *The Wild Rover* to Sebastian. He used to play that song to me in this house when I was a little girl."

Little thought grenades exploded in Emily's head. Helen seemed sweet, likeable, talented and intelligent, but although she didn't realise, she was slowly incriminating her father. If Helen's meticulous dateline proved correct, and Emily could imagine no reason to doubt it, then Marcus had informed her of Sebastian's death the day before his body was discovered by Eva the cleaner. To Emily, that could mean only two things. He was responsible for Sebastian's death, or discovered Sebastian's body the morning he was caught on CCTV but for some reason chose to stay quiet and flee the scene. Both criminal acts, in her opinion.

Emily dragged her fingers through straggly hair, swishing it up and down as if to demonstrate it needed urgent attention. "Look, why don't you make yourself at home while I take a shower."

"Thanks, do you mind if I check the cutlery drawer? That's where Sebastian kept the keys to my dad's house."

Emily motioned to Helen to go ahead, but no keys materialised. As Emily showered she heard the piano strike up, something classical played with delicate authority. The music brought vitality and warmth to the bungalow. Emily remembered Marcus recalling how much he enjoyed hearing Uncle Sebastian playing when he rang the doorbell.

Emily dressed, watching and listening for a few minutes from the lounge doorway as she towelled her hair, the strains of *The Wild Rover*, in classical style, transforming an Irish drinking folk song into something far more ethereal.

"That was beautiful," said Emily when Helen finished playing.

"Thanks, it's lovely to be able to play here one more time." Helen's smile of appreciation seemed genuine and heartfelt.

Helen revealed she'd made contact with her father. Marcus had picked up her messages, texting her while Emily showered to say he was on his way back from an early-morning photographic expedition.

"He'll be home in five minutes, so I'll be off. Thanks for being my port in a storm."

"Any time. Lovely meeting you."

When Helen left, Emily walked into town, bought an ice cream and pondered the latest information. How her life had changed. Little more than a month ago she was lamenting the mundanity of her existence and the betrayal of her only proper boyfriend. Now her thoughts surrounded assassins, complex relationships and potential murders on, or at least near, her own doorstep. She soaked in the warmth of a cloudless day, people-watching, killing time until Al clocked off.

She hijacked him at the café entrance, anxious to convey the latest news.

"Holy shit. That does seem to put Marcus in the frame," said Al. "I'd like to hear him explain how he knew Sebastian was dead before the cleaner discovered the body. Sounds like something out of Agatha Christie."

"Can a daughter testify against her father?"

"Good question. I think the answer is yes, but whether she would do so when she knows what's at stake is another question. Helen might just row back a touch from being so certain on her dates and timings."

"You may be right."

They walked up the hill to Sea View Road, Emily gasping from the effort to match Al's walking pace while Al ruminated on the meeting with Helen. As they turned into number seven Al turned to Emily.

"We'll go to see Marcus tomorrow when his daughter has left. Put everything to him and see what he has to say. But first, I can't wait to see how Sebastian's going to get out of his fix in Moscow."

36

"Pomoshch! Pozhaluysta. Pomoshch! Please. Help!"

I had waited more than 10 minutes, using part of that time to recover from the fright of seeing the rolling whites of Kalenkov's eyes, provoking an uncontrollable tremor in my hands and legs. For a couple of seconds, I was desperate, believing the colonel still alive, the mission dead, my own fate sealed. As my heartbeat eased and panic abated, I realised the dissipation of the paralysis-inducing chemicals that had killed Kalenkov was almost certainly also responsible for the belated gasp and hideous death twitch.

I closed his eyes before wiping clean the poisoned queen, its retractable mechanism ensuring no outward sign of its deadly purpose, returning it to the velvety bed of its gift box. I placed it in a glass wall cabinet containing Kalenkov's prizes and chess paraphernalia. It looked perfectly at home, sharing a miniature dais with a black king, as if Kalenkov had treasured his gift. I replaced Kalenkov's original queen on the appropriate square on the board, a move or maybe two at most from securing the checkmate he'd never achieve.

When all that was done, I knelt by Kalenkov's chair and yelled. Shrill. Urgent. Repeating "Pomoshch!" like some religious mantra, loud as I could muster, until I felt my throat cracking. Four soldiers burst through the double doors, boots clattering, two carrying rifles, two bearing pistols. I fumbled with Kalenkov's shirt buttons, pretending to help, but two soldiers grabbed my collar, dragging me away from him. One of them thrust a rifle barrel in my face. He ordered me to lie prostrate with my hands on my head, a persuasive nudge from his boot confirming the command.

A few moments later the room filled with aides, one calling for a doctor, several arriving within minutes. As the doctors worked on Kalenkov, injecting drugs and administering CPR, one of the aides ordered the soldiers to let me sit. The aide asked me what had happened.

"We were playing chess. The Colonel was drinking vodka, many glasses of vodka." My voice faltered as I feigned a breathless tremor of shock, an easy task amid the tension and emotion of a surreal night. "Suddenly he went grey. He said he had a pain, a dull pain."

"Where was this pain?" One of the doctors spun around.

"In his arm, left arm." I grasped my own left arm for emphasis. "It seemed to get worse very quickly. He clutched his chest and I knew it was serious. Then he collapsed. His lips turned blue. There was nothing I could do. That's when I yelled for the soldiers."

The doctor returned to treating Kalenkov while the aide, a neat man with a bald head and robotic manner, showing no outward sign of shock, ordered me to stand. He spoke in Russian, beckoning me to follow him. Two soldiers accompanied us. "Professor, come with me while the Colonel is being cared for. You must understand you will be detained until we discover what has happened this evening."

"What do you mean?" I knew exactly what he meant. Until I could be cleared of any involvement in Kalenkov's demise, but I asked the question anyway.

The aide was patient. "Colonel Kalenkov is a very important man, strategic to the defence of our nation. As such he has many enemies. There have been many attempts on his life."

"But we were playing chess. He'd invited me here. He missed my lecture and we chatted through it over dinner. I hope to God he's all right." Even I thought I sounded convincing. Exactly the right mix of shock and concern. Anna was right. Lecturing is akin to acting. Maybe my entire career, all those lecture tours and seminars, the tutorials when I'd forced myself to inject enthusiasm even when flat and jaded, had prepared me for this moment. I was acting for my life and had rarely felt more energised.

"I understand, Professor, but please wait here." The aide led me into a study off the main corridor, a big room with several desks, an impressive bookcase, but no windows. He left, the soldiers taking up station outside on either side of the door before shutting it with a thud.

I sat at one of the desks, sinking into a soft leather chair, shaking, the swirl of endorphins producing the giddiest of feelings. Time once more for my three-times stable technique, as well as running my eyes over the bookcase to distract from Kalenkov and the next possible gambit in this freakish game of life and death. I even spied a copy of Dva Ivana, the Russian version of *The Two Ivans*. Strangely, spying the tome that had demanded four years of my life, utilising more midnight oil than any project before or since, returned me to something approaching reality. It reminded me of who I really was. Sebastian Emile Stearn. Professor of History. Lover of learning. Champion of students. Chairman of Cambridge's Society for Lost Causes. The latter an honorary title lightly conferred on university fellows who remained confirmed bachelors. I wasn't Sebastian Stearn, assassin. Yet, now, I was. As the hours drifted and I sat musing in that leather chair, orchestrating my past life as it floated slowly by, stable yet cumbersome like a punt on the River Cam, I fell into a fitful sleep.

The doors swung open with a clack of boots and a click of heels. Six o'clock. Half a dozen soldiers, bearing rifles, followed by a man I recognised and one I didn't. The familiar face belonged to Andrei Gromyko, Soviet foreign minister, who sat alongside Brezhnev listening to my lecture the day before. I thought his crumpled features too gentle, wrinkles too kindly, for a Soviet. The other man introduced himself with a damp, limp handshake as Sir Curtis Keeble, UK ambassador in Moscow. I'd have preferred to sink a beer with Gromyko, but Keeble's presence heralded the moment I dared hope I might soon be on my way home.

"Professor Stearn, please accept my apologies for your detention overnight." Gromyko spoke in English.

"Colonel Kalenkov? How is …"

Gromyko shook his head. "The doctors did everything they could, but it appears Igor suffered a devastating heart attack. So young and such a great servant to our nation. You were the last man to speak to him. I hope you see that as a privilege."

"Of course." The lie, embellished with a solemn tone and sombre expression, came easily.

"We'd like to see you in our country again in happier circumstances. You are free to leave." We shook hands and he gestured for me to follow Keeble.

This was going well. I'd driven into the Kremlin, completed my mission, and was now heading for a diplomatic limousine complete with a cordial invitation to return from one of the Politburo's main men. As I walked through the great halls, with Keeble chuntering inanely about Byzantine architecture, I half-expected to hear the scrape of scurrying boots and the clank of metal, soldiers sprinting to arrest me. The face of the officer who searched me at the hotel, who fondled the poisoned queen, pervaded my thoughts. Would he work it out? No, I told myself. The Soviet regime doesn't operate like that. No officer would admit to having facilitated an assassin entry to the Kremlin.

A sudden commotion behind us. Shouting. A man's voice, the sound of running feet. I hardly dared look as it came nearer, an electric impulse standing my hairs to attention. "Professor, Professor." The call more urgent. I turned and recognised one of Kalenkov's aides. In his hand a book. *Iskusstvo Zashchity. The Art of Defence*. He handed it to me. I was leaving with a gift. For the first time as we exited to a cold and murky Moscow morning I felt a fleeting pang of guilt.

On the short journey to my hotel, Keeble informed me that the embassy had rearranged my intended flight for later that afternoon. Relief. I was going home. On reaching my room I showered, luxuriating for 20 minutes or more under the jet of water, as if swirling the sickening memory of Kalenkov's death twitches from my mind. I ate eggs on toast as usual in the breakfast buffet, packed, and listened to the news for any mention of Kalenkov's demise. I didn't expect any, and there was none. There wouldn't be anything in the Press either. Pravda, Russia's premier newspaper, might translate as *The Truth,* but I'd always viewed that as the most inapt of media titles. As I had an hour to kill before leaving for the airport I took a stroll, winding through the streets of Moscow, arriving at the same phone booth I'd used the day before. I punched in the contact number. No answer. I dialled again, letting it ring until the network disconnected. Never mind, I thought, I'll see her soon enough.

I returned to the hotel, finished packing and cast a final eye around the room. I was heading for the door and my waiting taxi when a gentle knock sounded. Probably the bell boy. I threw the door open and there she was. Anna. She brushed past me, agitation in her manner.

"Professor, I don't have long. Who knows who is watching and listening? There are suspicious glances everywhere, but I had to come." She turned around and the deep pools of her eyes glistened, almost full to overflowing with a complex mixture of elation, sadness, concern and gratitude.

"What is it, Anna?"

"I want to say thank you for Rudi. He was kind and brave, like you Professor. I will never forget what you have done."

"Anna, when this all blows over will you come to see me in Cambridge?"

She didn't answer. Instead, she tottered towards me like a little girl, flung her arms around my neck and kissed me full on the lips, hard and sensual. I could taste her minty fresh breath, feel her probing tongue, the heat of her body, sense the ardour in her caress. In that moment something profound and powerful stirred between us, a wild and giddy pleasure that I had never experienced before, but was desperate not to end.

"Yes."

That's all she said when the clinch broke, a crack of emotion in her voice. Then she was gone, bustling past me, her sweet fragrance lingering as she scurried down the hotel corridor.

37

Emily almost skipped along the promenade. Light and jaunty, a burden lifted by a good night's sleep and the realisation that Uncle Sebastian had completed his mission, apparently unscathed. She still yearned for the journal to see him home safe and remained intrigued by his relationship with Anna.

She knew no permanent overt liaison blossomed, her dad confirming Uncle Sebastian had remained a confirmed bachelor, but that didn't mean they couldn't enjoy a relationship of sorts. Maybe by correspondence. Perhaps by mutual holidays. She'd read somewhere that Winston Churchill's preferred manner of keeping secret trysts involved trips to the south of France for a week or two of sun, sea and sex with his socialite lover. Maybe Uncle Sebastian and Anna had arrived at a similar arrangement. His lecture tours provided the opportunity. She hoped that was the case. He deserved more than one snatched kiss.

Emily nodded to the ice cream seller in his kiosk, then shook her head as if to say "Not today" when he tried to entice her, cheekily raising a cornet as if making a toast. The lady pushing a little dog in a pram passed by. Emily smiled, wondering how something she'd deemed certifiable a month ago now seemed quaint, almost normal. She spotted an empty bench. Five minutes with her eyes shut, face thrust towards the sun, listening to the relentless lapping of waves and the distant squeals of happy children. *What could be more relaxing?*

She'd arranged to meet Al for a coffee after his shift ended before they returned to Sea View Road to confront Marcus, a meeting she didn't relish. Emily may at times have appeared brusque, almost rude, but that was her way. The prospect of actual confrontation rendered her nauseous. Always had done, right back to her schooldays and that embarrassing faux date with the boy on a dare. Her sweary altercation with the call centre supervisor, as empowering as it felt, was not Emily.

She mused on that now, experiencing a wave of heat, disturbing thoughts surfacing like molten lava from somewhere deep inside.

"Hello there." A young woman's cheery greeting snapped Emily from her day-dreaming. Helen, arm in arm with Marcus.

"Oh, hello, I was miles away."

"You looked so content we almost walked on by, but I wanted to say thanks again for yesterday." The smile on Helen's face matched the warmth of the sun and majestic sweep of the bay.

Marcus added a reverent nod, draping his arm around his daughter, giving her a fatherly squeeze. "And thank you from me too. For some reason I'd switched my phone to silent and missed Helen's message. But once again, Sebastian, or in this case his niece, comes to the rescue."

"No problem, glad I could help. Pity we couldn't find your keys," said Emily.

Helen piped up. "I asked Dad about that. He said his house keys are no longer in the cutlery drawer. He took them back a few weeks ago."

Marcus nodded. "There didn't seem any point leaving them with no one in the bungalow."

"Do you still have any of Uncle Sebastian's keys?" Quite why Emily asked the question she didn't know. Perhaps a griping sense of vulnerability, or a scratching in the eaves of her mind that many people experience when staying alone in unfamiliar surroundings. It could merely have been Emily. Blunt and direct as usual.

If Marcus was affronted, he didn't show it. "I do actually. I've got a full set, including to the garage and shed. I must return them."

"What time's your train?" Emily turned to Helen.

"Not until tomorrow morning. I've decided to stay an extra night. Tidying up a bit. Dad hates throwing anything away. He's one of life's worst hoarders. It will give us the chance to catch up a bit more."

Marcus shuffled, averting his eyes, although a weak smile played on his lips. Someone adept at reading body language may have calculated he had something to hide, or was concerned his daughter might spill a dark secret. The pretence of the wife he no longer lived with, for instance. The signs flew over Emily's head like the gull that left its calling card on the bench beside her.

Emily shuffled along the bench, fixing Helen with her sweetest smile. "Have a good night then and good luck with your studies."

They shook hands, although a vexed thought crossed Emily's mind. Helen's presence meant any interrogation of Marcus would be delayed at least 24 hours.

38

The flight from Sheremetyevo was unremarkable, apart from discovering myself in first class, sipping champagne and dining on smoked salmon. Expenses in the British diplomatic service more generous than in the university world.

I caught an underground train from Heathrow into London followed by a train from King's Cross to Cambridge, arriving at my study studio a little before midnight. Going home seemed surreal. The sight of carefree students staggering back to their accommodation after a night out, chip shops doing brisk trade courtesy of the munchies brigade. The distant sound of Kim Wilde belting out *Kids in America* from a late-night bar. Suddenly, life appeared free of worry, joyful, uncomplicated, as if Kalenkov never existed. I fell into bed and slept the sleep, if not of the righteous, then at least of the exhausted.

Yet when morning came the black dog was nipping in my brain. Porter had scheduled no official debrief. The orders from the nameless ones at Secretarium amounted to carry on as normal. Seek no contact. Hide in plain sight. Fine, when my mission involved nothing more than giving a lecture. But now I required reassurance. I needed Porter to confirm my actions had kept the Royal Family safe. That Kalenkov's passing had made the world more secure. No contact materialised. A week drifted by, two weeks, a month.

I embarked on research into a forthcoming book on the Rurik dynasty, Prince Vladimir the Great and his son, Yaroslav the Wise, but devoid of my usual vigour. The wonders of the past no longer intrigued as once they did.

I watched the royal wedding on television on July 29th, Charles dashing in his military uniform, Diana so young and innocent, the pomp quintessentially British. I watched it all, right up to the teeming crowds lining The Mall, a swell of excitement in front of Buckingham Palace anticipating the iconic picture. The kiss on the balcony. When it came, it appeared awkward, as if this couple knew little of each other, even less about love and relationships. It will never last, I thought, and wondered if that was being uncharitable. But it happened. Life went on and I bathed in the notion that my actions one summer night in Moscow helped in some way to make it all possible.

That inclination didn't last. As the weeks wore on I concluded that perhaps the royal plot had been a figment of the spooks' imagination. A product of a Cold War feeding on menace, nervous tension, distrust and paranoia. A war that saw huge sums squandered on defence with nuclear submarines from both sides careering around the oceans, taunting each other like schoolboys in the playground, one false move away from triggering Armageddon. Kalenkov wasn't a threat to world peace, as Porter had suggested. He was a murderer, pure and simple, if a murderer can be described as pure. In that respect, not unlike Ivan the Terrible. But, in reality, Kalenkov was little more than a small cog in a machine of madness that during the long years of the Cold War knew no borders.

Not that the colonel's fate troubled me. I came to terms with my actions soon enough. No, it was Anna who consumed my every thought. I phoned the contact number I'd memorised. A hundred times, maybe more. It always rang but no one answered. Whenever my own phone rang I would hear her voice in my head before I picked up the receiver. Wishing it was her. Imagining her sing-song notes, that subtle lilt. And when it wasn't her my heart would ache with disappointment. No, more than that. Sadness.

I had no address for her in Moscow, or anywhere else for that matter. I considered contacting Lomonosov University, but reasoned that would bring attention upon her. In the Soviet Union of the 1980s that was not advisable. Driving out to Secretarium remained an option, but I knew well enough that visits to that isolated location were by invitation only. I'd have reached the clinical gates only for some faceless, nameless security guard to brighten his day by turning me away. A visit may have prompted a reaction from Porter, but I realised there must be good reason why the department had gone dark.

All I had was the photo, the one on my tourist camera that I took to Boots the Chemist to be developed. Anna astride a hire bike, long hair blowing in the breeze, cheeks pink, laughing into the camera on that carefree day when she had the crazy idea of riding through the Moscow traffic.

39

The hill tugged at Emily's calf muscles and she wondered how the numerous residents around Uncle Sebastian's age coped when fragile nerves and failing eyes put paid to their driving days. Taxis probably. That would explain the constant clunk of car doors opening and shutting at the end of Sea View Road.

Emily swung two heavy shopping bags from either arm. She'd walked into town for provisions, planning lunch at the bungalow with Al following his shift, after which they intended to confront Marcus. On reaching number seven, she dumped the bags in the porch and rummaged for her keys. That's odd. The sound of a piano emanated from within. Not the tuneful tinkling of Helen. More staccato, rhythm aimless, notes stumbling and grinding as if requiring lubrication.

A puzzled frown untidied Emily's features as she turned the key and eased open the door. "Hello." Her greeting accompanied by an upward lilt at the end to affect surprise and, hopefully, disapproval. Her first unsettling thought had been an intruder. But, while she wasn't an expert on petty crime, she was fairly certain burglars didn't halt, mid-heist, to practise the piano. The playing stopped. Emily heard jangling and footsteps in the lounge, before a man appeared in the hallway. Marcus.

"Oh." Emily took a step back, a disturbing chill settling between her shoulder blades. If she'd compiled a list of people she'd least like to have encountered at that moment Marcus would have been up there. Number one, probably.

"Hello Dear. I'm sorry if I alarmed you. I didn't mean to. I brought round Sebastian's keys." He dangled the bunch in front of him, a loop of string connecting them to a key fob of his own. Emily noticed a crack in his voice and when he stepped forward into the light his eyes were misty and bloodshot.

"Thanks Marcus. Did Helen catch her train on time?"

"Yes, she'll be back in Bristol by now. She enjoyed meeting you and seeing this place again. It holds special memories for her, for all of us to be honest."

"Marcus, are you all right?" Emily's question prompted by a strange look in Marcus's eyes. Distracted and melancholic, as if the visit of his daughter and the return of Sebastian's keys had unlocked emotions too powerful to hide. He didn't answer, but wandered through to the kitchen, trudging around the island worktop, gazing at the picture of Sebastian. Emily followed.

"Do you ever wonder what he was thinking when he painted himself?" Marcus's tone was weak and forlorn.

"I imagine he was concentrating on the mechanics of art. Absorbed in the colours, getting the angles and likeness right. That sort of thing. He did a pretty good job. Marcus, what's this all about? Are you unwell?"

"Mary left me." The revelation, in matter-of-fact tone, hung in the air for a few seconds, Marcus tilting his head away from the picture to gauge Emily's response.

"I know. Helen told me." Emily saw no reason to deny knowledge.

"I've been lying all this time."

"I know, Marcus, but why are you telling me now?"

Marcus leaned his head to one side like dogs do sometimes when they are trying to work out their owner's instructions. His brow knitted, face contorting in a bewildered grimace.

"Helen knew after talking to you I'd been hiding the truth. I can't lie to Sebastian anymore." His voice was almost a whimper.

"Pardon." This was not how Emily envisaged a confrontation with Marcus evolving. She'd expected to knock on his door later that day with Al, strong and protective by her side, framing the questions, presenting the evidence, outlining their suspicions, ready to nail Marcus's lies with the aid of CCTV. But here he was, seemingly on the verge of a confession.

"Lie about what, Marcus."

"About Mary. I told Sebastian she'd gone to look after her mother. For three years I dodged his questions and his concern and …" His voice trailed away.

"You mean you kept it a secret and all this time you were living by yourself?"

Marcus nodded. "My little secret."

"These things happen, Marcus. Lots of couples split up."

"After 40 years?"

Emily didn't know the statistics, but she had to concede Marcus had a point. There couldn't be many decrees nisi granted after four decades of marriage. "It's nothing to be ashamed of," she said.

This was surreal. Emily had convinced herself Marcus was responsible for her uncle's death, yet here she was comforting him as he slumped onto the low settee underneath Sebastian's artwork, cradling his head in his hands.

"I could understand if she'd left me for another man. Chasing a thrill. The thought of a better life with someone else, but there was no one else. Mary admitted she was just bored. She didn't want to live with me anymore. I was ashamed of that more than anything. Too. Boring. To. Live. With." He spat out the words slow and deliberate, shaking his head. "I couldn't admit that to someone like Sebastian who'd travelled everywhere and led such an exciting life. Too boring. It's not something you want on your gravestone, is it?"

Now the secret had wormed itself out, Marcus appeared content to wallow in the slurry of self-pity pooling in his mind for the past three years. The repeated mention of Uncle Sebastian and Marcus's apparent desire to compare their lives set Emily's antennae twitching.

She'd felt pressure building for days. The revelations in Uncle Sebastian's journal. Late nights. The search for white van man. The CCTV. The knowledge that Marcus had lied. The last time she'd felt overwhelmed, when the old man was fighting for his life on the pavement outside the pie restaurant, she'd closed down. This time her brain focused on her latest obsession. The man sitting in front of her. Creepy at best. At worst involved in Uncle Sebastian's death. She knew the wise move was to soak in the information and retire to consider the next move with Al, but instinct told her to seize the moment. Be bold. Even though she'd rehearsed how to confront Marcus for days with Al, her line of questioning leapt out more by accident than consideration.

"Marcus, Helen told me something else."

"What?"

"She said you told her on March the sixteenth, the day before St Patrick's Day, that Uncle Sebastian had died."

"So?"

Emily had moved to the end of the island worktop and Marcus fixed her with a quizzical expression.

"Uncle Sebastian's body wasn't discovered by Eva the cleaner until the next morning," said Emily, surprising herself with her clarity and composure.

Marcus shrugged. "Helen must have got it wrong. We've never been good with dates."

Emily nodded slowly as if considering Marcus's reply. No nausea. No fear. If anything, for the first time in her life she felt like one of the barristers in those big screen courtroom dramas she enjoyed, the adrenalin of the moment supplanting her lifelong anxieties.

"I wondered about that. But Helen was quite precise. She remembered you turning up at her flat on March the sixteenth, telling her the news and making her late for her band rehearsal. She even recalled both of you shedding a tear."

Marcus clasped his hands in front of his chest and they began to shake while his eyes darted around the kitchen, a window to the turmoil in his mind. His desolate glance emboldened Emily.

"There's another thing, Marcus. The building site's CCTV cameras at the top of the road caught you entering Uncle Sebastian's house on the morning of March the sixteenth, nine o'clock actually, around the time doctors believed he had already died."

The shaking in Marcus's hands spread throughout his body and he slid off the settee, kneeling on the ceramic floor as if in prayer, little gasps and convulsions emanating from his nose and mouth, as if the information administered a toxic shock to his system.

"What are you saying? Sebastian was my best friend." Marcus's tone shrill and scratchy, wavering between denial and painful acceptance.

Emily sensed Marcus on the precipice, a final nudge required. "I don't doubt you were friends, Marcus. But we saw you on CCTV the day Uncle Sebastian died. Giving directions to two workmen. Going into the bungalow. You said you were away. Said you hadn't seen Uncle Sebastian for weeks. Yet you were here all along. Why would you lie? The only logical reason is because you had something to do with his death."

Marcus didn't speak. He averted his eyes, lowering his head, as if searching for a crevice to hide from the truth.

"I have to tell you, Marcus, Al and I have decided to go to the police." Emily moved to the other side of the worktop, picked up her mobile phone, punching in Al's number. She turned away from Marcus with her phone to her ear but before it began ringing Marcus approached from behind, grabbing her arm.

"Please don't do that."

Startled, Emily let go, the phone smashing on the ceramic floor, screen shattering into a mosaic of shard-like shapes.

"Marcus!" Emily's tone shocked and angry.

Marcus slumped back on the settee. "I'm sorry. I didn't mean to … I didn't mean to. It was an accident." At first Emily thought he meant smashing her phone, but Marcus's expression was grave, his thoughts distant. Reality slowly began to dawn. For several seconds nothing happened, Emily motionless, fearing what she was about to hear, paralysed by the tension of the moment. She sat on the opposite side of the settee to Marcus. They stared at each other, Marcus gasping for breath, neither knowing what to do next or whether life would ever be quite the same again.

***

Emily spoke first, a tremor in her voice. "What did you do to him?"

238

"I loved Sebastian. I really did. He was the only person I could talk to. Properly, I mean. A real conversation. He was gentle and wise. Helen loved him too when she lived in Weymouth. She spent more time over here than she did in our house. Adored listening to Sebastian talking about history." Marcus's eyes misted, for a moment lost in the memory of happier, less complex, times.

"Go on." Emily, desperate to seize the moment.

"When Mary left, Sebastian was there for me. I was in a mess and he listened. I made up some story about her going to help her infirm mother. If he knew it wasn't true he was too kind to let on. He'd never married but he always seemed to know the right thing to say."

Emily sensed a ring of truth in Marcus's earnest delivery, but the grainy CCTV image of him leaving Uncle Sebastian's house remained fixed in her mind. "So what happened that day?"

Marcus still wasn't ready. "It goes back much further. I enjoyed talking to Sebastian. He had so many stories. He told me about winning his blues at Cambridge. Being chairman of the debating society. He had so much going for him. Why he never married I'll never know. We'd talk for hours about his student days, usually in the garden, but then we started having a whisky together in the evening. He liked his whisky. Only one each night. Sebastian always liked to stay in control. He had a large tumbler, but never more than a double measure, I'd say."

"So you didn't get drunk."

Marcus shook his head. "No. Never drunk. That was the problem. If Sebastian had got drunk, it might never have happened. He might have told me all about his adventure."

"What adventure?"

Marcus's eyes shut and he ran a hand through his thinning hair. He looked sad. "That was the problem. Each night he'd tell me a bit more about his trips, one in particular. It sounded so exciting. He'd met a woman he adored, I think in Moscow, but would never tell me why it hadn't worked out. He dropped a few hints that it was all a bit hush-hush but there were never any details. I teased him about being a member of the Portland spy ring in the sixties, but he wouldn't bite. It was infuriating. I'd worked in the same boring shop in Weymouth for more than thirty years. The most interesting thing to happen all day was opening and closing the shutters, while he'd been around the world, staying in top hotels. Living the life of a celebrity, or at least that's what it seemed like to me."

Marcus stood, edging over to a cupboard to grab a glass, before filling it with water and quaffing it down in one. He motioned with the glass to Emily, offering her a drink also. She shook her head. Emily knew exactly the tale Uncle Sebastian had hidden from Marcus, but she stayed silent. She wanted to know where his story may lead. He seemed intent on unburdening himself.

"With each night, each glass of whisky, I became more frustrated. I started to resent our chats, instead of treasuring them." Marcus gasped, shoulders shuddering as if recalling a hideous event.

"What happened Marcus?" said Emily.

"I wish I could change things. If only I could turn the clock back." For the first time Marcus sobbed. Not a wail or a flamboyant gesture. A chest-heaving sob, one he tried to arrest, but only succeeded in inducing a choking fit that provoked spit, snot and splashes of vomit. He dragged a sleeve across his nose and mouth and composed himself.

"Marcus, tell me what happened." Emily tried again, ensnared in the moment, at the same time pondering how Al would have handled it, her tone calm and measured, gentle even.

"It was Monday night. I was due to come over for our usual whisky about nine o'clock. I'd been thinking how I could coax the real story out of Sebastian. I'd become fixated on it, so I decided to help him along." He paused.

"How?"

"I've been a chemist all my life. I knew what I was doing."

"What are you saying?"

"I have lots of medications in my office over the road. Stuff I've hoarded over the years. I chose sodium amytal."

"You mean you drugged him?" Emily looked perplexed.

"They call it Amobarbital now. A truth serum in the past. They used it in World War Two to lower anxiety in soldiers suffering from shell-shock. Patients with insomnia take it. It's not dangerous, honest, if you know what you're doing. It has no odour, just gives you a good night's sleep, but has a hypnotic property that encourages you to tell the truth."

Emily's eyes widened, her mouth open, as she listened to Marcus describing, justifying, how he had laced Uncle Sebastian's drink. "Go on."

"I didn't even give him the maximum dose. Half a gram at most. I slipped the powder into his whisky when he went to the toilet. He never realised. But it didn't work. He wasn't in the mood that night. Not as chatty as normal. Think he had something on his mind. He seemed sad. We called it a night earlier than usual, about quarter past ten. I left and said I'd see him the next day."

The image of Marcus staring into the CCTV lens once more filled Emily's mind. "So you went to see him around nine o'clock?"

Marcus nodded.

"What did you find?"

Another choking sob as Marcus grabbed a tissue from a box on the worktop and blew hard. "I let myself in when there was no answer. I've always had a spare key. I found him lying there in bed. I knew he was gone straight away. He looked peaceful, but my mind was in a whirl. It couldn't be the drug, surely. Could it? I only slipped him a half-dose. I convinced myself it couldn't be. I didn't know he had a heart problem. An arrhythmia. I only found out later. He was always so private about his health. Private about everything. I'd never have given him a sedative if I'd known."

"So what did you do then?"

"I saw the whisky glasses on the table by the window. I panicked. I took them through to the kitchen, washed and replaced them in the cabinet with the bottle of malt. I wasn't in the house more than ten minutes."

"That doesn't sound like panic, Marcus. That sounds like someone who knows they've done wrong and doesn't want to be found out." Emily's tone was even and reasoned.

Marcus's voice strained with emotion. "It wasn't like that. I kept telling myself it couldn't be the drug. He was eighty-three. It must have been natural causes. I almost picked up the phone to ring nine, nine, nine, but he was gone. There was nothing anyone could do for him, so I went home, got in my car and drove all the way to Bristol. To Helen's. I couldn't face coming back until it was all over."

Emily joined Marcus at the worktop, albeit at different ends. They stood in silence for several minutes, looking out to sea where all appeared calm, normal life continuing, tiny sail boats with white sails tacking back and forth as usual. Between intermittent sobbing fits and silences, Marcus had been telling his story for an hour and a half.

Emily broke the silence. "You realise you'll have to tell all this to the police, Marcus?"

Marcus nodded, a grateful peace descending after exorcising the secrets he'd fretted over these past months. He turned towards Emily, picking up a carving knife from the worktop, and cut the string to release Sebastian's keys from his key fob.

***

Al's phone rang. As he didn't usually take calls at work and failed to recognise the number, he refused the call. A few seconds later, another ring. Same number.

There were no customers in the check-out queue. This time he connected.

"Hello." A frail woman. Hoarse. Al couldn't place the voice.

"Hello. Are you the young man?" It dawned. Katharine.

"Hi there, Katharine. Everything all right? How's that cold coming on?"

"Never mind that. I want to know about that young lady of yours. Is she all right?

Al took a deep breath, wondering if it was a good idea leaving their phone numbers with Katharine. She'd perhaps taken his advice to stay in touch a little too literally.

"She's fine, Katharine. Probably having a lie-in this morning. Had another late one last night."

"I've been trying to ring her and can't get through."

"Probably still asleep."

"Doubt it, not with a man in the house."

Al wondered whether he'd heard correctly, or maybe Katharine was experiencing a confused episode. He'd read about infections, mini-strokes and low blood sugar levels triggering sudden delirium in the elderly.

"Sorry, Katharine, are you sure you're okay?"

"My marbles are rolling in the right direction, if that's what you mean. And I think it's impertinent of you to ask."

"Sorry."

"Almost two hours ago I saw Marcus skulk across the road to number seven, and let himself in. I thought that was odd, but ten minutes later the young lady arrived and followed him in. She was carrying shopping bags. I've not seen Marcus leave. He's still in there. That's why I ..."

Al stuffed the phone into his pocket without disconnecting, tasting the panic as a plug of bile rose in his throat. He shouted to one of the young assistants to take his place. Then he dashed out of the café, bumping into customers, dodging pedestrians, sprinting down the promenade, cursing his decision that morning to walk rather than cycle. It was around a mile and a half to Sea View Road. He settled into a manageable gallop, his mind awash with sinister thoughts. If Marcus was responsible for Sebastian's death, then Emily could be in danger. She had been obsessing on Marcus for some while, not in a good way. *Oh God, what might she have said to him? What might he have done?* Al reached the hill and gulped oxygen, forcing his legs to pump even faster. When he turned into Sea View Road his lungs were burning, shirt stained with sweat, but he mustered one last effort to sprint to the bungalow.

Instead of ringing the doorbell he dashed around the side of the property to the steps that connected the back lawn with a large paved balcony leading into the kitchen through the sliding glass doors. Emily almost always left them open in the mornings to let in the day, taste brine on the sea breeze. He bounded up the steps two at a time and when he reached the balcony his heart plunged. The doors were shut. A second glance detected two figures in the kitchen, although the sun's reflection distorted the images. One was Emily, the other a man wielding a large carving knife.

Al had never experienced such dread. His brain scrambled. Time for instinct, not reason. He picked up the nearest object, a large terracotta pot containing an azalea, resplendent with brilliant white blooms. He ran at the glass door, hurling the pot with all his strength. The glass exploded. Thousands of fragments hurtled in every direction, the pot smashing on ceramic tiles with a thunderous crash, spilling soil and a confetti of blooms across the kitchen floor. Al strode through the carnage, flinging himself at Marcus, felling him with a crunching rugby tackle. The knife spun out of Marcus's grasp and Al sat astride him, pinning him down in a bed of debris, still in his Tasty Treat uniform, peaked cap proclaiming *The Best Breakfast in Weymouth*.

Al glanced up and saw Emily staring at him, shock and bewilderment clouding her face.

"I do have a doorbell, you know." Emily's deadpan delivery was borne of astonishment rather than an attempt at humour, but as it slowly dawned on Al that she wasn't hurt or frightened, and Marcus wasn't struggling, a surge of relief coursed through his exhausted body. And he laughed. A slightly hysterical laugh.

After Emily confirmed her life wasn't in danger and Marcus had been using the carving knife to release Sebastian's keys, they all went through to the lounge where Emily explained the gist of Marcus's confession.

"We'll need to inform the police," Al said. "In fact, I think we should all go down to the station together. They'll want statements. It will be cleaner to do it right now." Marcus nodded, his mind lighter, shoulders less tense after shedding the burden of his secret.

Half an hour later, after Al had phoned an emergency window replacement company, they walked into Weymouth police station. The desk sergeant escorted Al and Emily to separate cubicles, where they gave signed statements. Two detectives, a man and a woman, listened to Marcus's story in the main interview room.

"Does this mean I'll go to prison?" Marcus asked as he completed his statement.

The male detective, a middle-aged man with a bored expression, had already demonstrated his disinterest by leaving half-way through to deal with a scheduled appointment, while the woman's tone was official, as tightly clipped as her hair. She sounded as though she was revising for detective examinations.

"Preventing the lawful and decent burial of a corpse is an offence in the UK, and it's also a criminal offence not to register a death. But I don't think either of those apply in this case. The admission of spiking the professor's drink, however, is serious. You will be officially released under investigation today."

"What does that mean?" Marcus's voice was steady.

"It means you have been interviewed under caution on suspicion of manslaughter and we want to make further inquiries before deciding whether to refer your case to the Crown Prosecution Service. You are free to leave here today and the custody sergeant will explain the terms of your bail. But I should warn you that you must not contact anyone linked to your case. We will be speaking to the professor's GP and to the coroner. Officers will accompany you home to collect the relevant substance, as well as your hoard of chemicals. We need to ascertain whether the drink being spiked led to the professor's death. Do you understand?"

Marcus's eyes closed but he nodded.

The woman officer's brow knitted and her voice grew graver. "Spiking someone's drink, in malice, in jest, for whatever reason, is illegal. It happens too often these days, usually in nightclubs with vulnerable women the victims. As a former pharmacist you should know the dangers only too well. It carries a maximum sentence of ten years in prison depending on the circumstances. The maximum term for manslaughter, on the other hand, is life imprisonment, again depending on the circumstances."

Marcus stood, his mind numb as the consequences of his stupidity dawned. Al and Emily watched him leave, shuffling down the corridor in the wake of the custody sergeant, eyes glazed, spirit broken, the realisation that he may have hastened the death of his best friend a weight he would bear forever.

"I feel a bit sorry for him." It wasn't usual for Emily to voice an emotion but the prolonged confessional with Marcus had struck a nerve.

"Why?" said Al.

"Don't get me wrong, He deserves whatever happens, but after his wife left, operating in Uncle Sebastian's shadow must have been frustrating."

"I wouldn't waste too much sympathy. Marcus's actions were probably responsible for Sebastian's death. If a Russian agent had killed Sebastian in some revenge mission, as you thought, it would have been dreadful, yet almost understandable from what we've read in the journal. But Marcus was his friend, his confidant. What he did was betrayal. I'd say that was unforgivable."

"I suppose so." Emily sighed.

"If he hadn't spiked that drink, I might have got to know Sebastian better," said Al.

"That's strange." Emily picked up her bag, ready to leave.

"What?"

"For me, it's exactly the opposite. If Marcus hadn't spiked that drink, I wouldn't know the real Uncle Sebastian at all."

"Come on, Emily, let's decipher the rest of the journal."

"Don't you mean, after you've cleaned up the kitchen?"

"Oh yeah, I'd forgotten about that."

40

When Porter eventually surfaced, almost a year to the day since I'd first set eyes on him, we took a stroll on Parker's Piece in Cambridge. I realised then that all I would ever have of Anna was that grainy photo.

"She's not been seen or heard of since the week Kalenkov died. Never arrived home one night after visiting one of her hotels. Believe me, we have turned Moscow upside down, used every contact, compromising our agents as much as we dare. It's bloody, Professor, bloody awful, but there's only one logical conclusion." Porter tried to break the news gently, sparing me graphic explanation, but the words struck me physically, or that's how it seemed. Punching me in the face. I felt dazed, confused, nauseous.

"What about her daughter, Lena?"

"With her grandmother. No longer in Moscow. No longer in Russia, I believe."

"Am I to blame?"

"We'll never know for sure, Professor. You spent a lot of time together the week you were in Moscow. After Kalenkov's death the KGB would have investigated his movements, the places he stayed, people he met. Despite Kremlin diplomacy admitting Kalenkov had suffered a heart attack, you would have been high on the Soviets' list of suspects once doctors had completed their autopsy, even if they found nothing incriminating. As would Anna, if only by association. She knew the risks and would have taken every precaution, but it seems she may have paid the ultimate price."

I gazed at Porter, half of me wishing I'd never met him, the other half computing the obvious logic. That would mean I would never have known Anna either.

"Can you let me have her mother's address, at least I could write to her daughter."

"I'm sorry, Professor. Even if I was in possession of such information, you know that's not possible."

Porter shuffled on the spot, hands in pockets. I could tell he appreciated my desolation, yet wanted to be on his way. He warned that I may still be in danger, but I didn't take notice, nor did I care. A strange numbness enveloped me, tinged with grief bordering on terror at the thought that somehow my actions had contributed to whatever fate had befallen Anna. When I arrived home that evening I took out the bicycle photo and stared at it for what seemed like hours while emptying a bottle of 18-year-old Macallan single malt.

Every year since, on the anniversary of our night at Rimsky's restaurant, I have done the same. I am recording my thoughts here on one such occasion simply because what Anna and I had in those brief few hours, was too good, too powerful, too beautiful to die with me. On each anniversary, as I study the picture reminding me of her fresh face and film-star looks, there comes a time when I can smell her perfume, feel her warm fingers entwined with mine, see the smouldering glint in her eyes, hear the girlish giggle in her throat as she tells me about her dreams to be an actress.

"My little piece of Heaven," I hear her say of the restaurant where we ate. I always agree, because the flame ignited in me that night felt as near to Heaven as my awkwardness could ever envisage. Anna, that week, was everything to me. Guide. Protector. Interpreter, not merely in the vagaries of the Russian language, but in how two people with idealistic minds, honourable ambitions and a gaping void in their hearts, connect. Anna was the warmest soul and the brightest star. She confided the tragedy of her husband, the pride in her daughter, her hopes for grandchildren, lots of them, to grace the years when her mission was done.

Before the Macallan dulls the hurt too fiercely, I always turn on the record player and reach for *Blue Moon*, the vinyl version by The Marcels, the first three lines crackling in my ears, encapsulating to perfection how I felt the day I met her. I sit back, close my eyes, and luxuriate in the memory of our only kiss. Tasting her lips once more, the feeling as real and passionate today as amid the danger and uncertainty of that hotel room so long ago. It was our kiss, our song, our time. There is much I don't know and will never know about Anna, but in the briefest of moments at the most chilling of times she taught me to live and to love. For that, I am forever in her debt.

41

Katharine took a while to answer the door, but when she did her smile was sunny, although her greeting contained an admonishing lilt. "What took you so long?"

"Sorry, Katharine, we've been busy with the garden. That time of year. Throwing a few plants here and there." Al glanced at Emily, who cast daggers in his direction.

They had cleaned up the kitchen the evening before, although it took longer than either of them expected, glass and terracotta shrapnel having scattered to every corner of the bungalow. Emily kept finding annoying shards stuck to the bottom of her thick socks when she walked down the hallway. A repair man had boarded the window but the replacement required bespoke fitting and would take at least a week. The cost? Estimate around £2,000. An expensive doorbell, although Al assured Emily the house insurance would take care of it.

"We thought we should explain, Katharine," said Emily, as they began the slow trek to the kitchen table. When they arrived, William sat with a haughty expression on the washing machine while Kate curled up on a chair. Al shooed her off to allow Emily to sit down.

"Where are your manners?" said Katharine.

"Don't worry, they're good cats." Al grinned.

"I wasn't talking to Kate. I was talking to you. Don't just shoo her away. Ask her nicely to move."

"Sorry," said Al.

They described the events of the previous day. Marcus's confession. Al's dash to Sea View Road after receiving Katharine's phone call. Plant pot through the window and trip to the police station.

"I knew it. I knew there was something about Marcus. Didn't I tell you I hadn't seen his wife for years. I had a funny feeling when I saw him enter the bungalow yesterday." Katharine shivered, shaking her face, lips pouting, as if she'd eaten something sour.

"Well, I'm glad you phoned." Using only his eyes, Al gestured to Emily in the direction of the door and began to rise.

"Not so quick. I've not told you about the asshole yet."

"What?" Al sat down.

"The asshole. The pony-tail in the red car. He was back again last night. Looking at number seven. Stayed until all the lights went off."

"Are you …" Al was about to say *sure* but realised he rarely came off best when he questioned Katharine. "I mean did he get out, walk around or anything?"

"No, just watched as usual."

"Okay, thanks Katharine. I'll keep an eye out for him. Maybe ask the guys up at the building site. We'd better be going. Lots of planting to do."

They bade their farewells and returned to the bungalow, sitting on deckchairs on the balcony in the warm sun. A flotilla of sail boats basked in the bay. Emily licked an ice cream she'd dug from the freezer even though it was a year out of date, while Al fiddled with the focus wheel on a pair of binoculars.

"Do you think we should report the guy in the red car?" Emily's question came out of nowhere.

"Maybe." Al raised the binoculars to test them on the boats in the bay.

"Who to? The police?"

"First, we should get a good look at him, then we'd have something to report."

"How are you going to do that?"

Al wiggled the binoculars in the air. "My eyesight just improved by a factor of eight."

"Good thinking." Emily's phone rang. "Mum. Hi. Not heard from you in ages." Emily slid out of her chair, heading inside to reduce wind noise. When she returned she sported a wide grin and a jaunty step.

"How do you fancy a trip to Cambridge tomorrow?"

"Why."

"That was Mum on the phone. Dad has supplied the documentation the university wanted to release Uncle

251

Sebastian's belongings. Can we pick them up? I'd need to produce my passport or driving licence as proof. What do you think?"

"Great. I'm up for that. I'll ring the café to swap my day off."

"She asked about Uncle Sebastian's journal. I told her we were almost finished and we'd drop by to tell them all about it."

"You'll need a week to do that."

"I know. Maybe we could do that on the way back from Cambridge."

"Better get deciphering then."

Emily nodded vigorously. They went inside, assuming their regular seats at the office desk to work on the final chapter of Uncle Sebastian's journal. They had become a formidable team over the past month, rattling through the codes with practiced efficiency. For Emily it had been a journey of enlightenment. At first, she'd expected it to prove a chore, believing her uncle a stranger, a misfit, a loner, a boring man who could teach her about history, but nothing about life. Yet now he occupied a seat at the centre of her existence. She had listened to his hopes, his fears, his adventures. Some nights she had clung on his every word. Worried about him, dreamed about him, watched his eyes as he followed her around the kitchen. She would miss him terribly when this chapter ended.

They broke for half an hour for supper at around seven o'clock. Nothing fancy. Left-over sandwiches Al had brought from the café. Then it was back for another three-hour stint until Al remembered the binoculars and his tryst with the red car driver. He went to check on the road, looking out of the front window. Sure enough, Katharine was right, the *asshole* was back. "I'm just going to nip out, back in five minutes."

He exited via the kitchen door that wasn't shattered, vaulted the fence between the properties, entering Jim and Jean's house through the back entrance. It had one crucial advantage over the bungalow, a dormer bedroom in the roof section, allowing a raised vantage point. A few minutes later, he was in position, assisted by a sliver of light from a half-moon, even though the car was parked in the dim no-man's land between street lights. Al trained the binoculars. Damn. The driver wore a baseball cap with the peak pulled down. His own mother wouldn't recognise him.

He continued watching the man watching whatever he was watching. Five minutes turned to 10, to 15, still no movement. Al was inclined to ditch the surveillance, concluding spying as a glamour profession overrated, when a flame glimmered. The driver lighting a cigarette. As the man raised the lighter to the cigarette in his lips the back of his hand turned towards Al, his shirt sleeve riding up his arm, the light from the flame revealing a tattoo. A distinctive drawing of a spider that Al remembered from somewhere. The man in the Eagle pub in Cambridge.

42

Time's a great healer, the saying goes. I don't agree. Time allows wounds to fester and sadness to linger.

All the mind can do to cope is apply sticking plasters and bandages. My work became my sticking plaster. In the 10 years following my trip to Moscow I wrote five books, visited 20 countries, presented hundreds of lectures. Embarked on a fitness programme bordering on obsession. Running, cycling, gym work. I even took up rowing and tennis again.

The strategy was fervent. Keep doing, stop thinking. My way of dealing with sadness. Thinking meant hurt. I'd heard all the theory. Move through your grief, don't put off dealing with painful emotions, suffering only leaves when it's ready. I didn't need arty-farty theory. I needed practical help, self-help. Without realising, the students supplied it. There's something about being around young, gifted, intelligent human beings that lifts the spirits and nurtures the soul. Like spending time in green spaces, on mountains, or by the ocean, watching rolling waves propelled by the force of nature. Lends existence a wondrous sense of ebb and flow. That's why I owe a debt to Corpus Christie College, my strength and emotional stay for so much of my working life.

Without my work I know not what might have become of me. Around the tenth anniversary of the events in Moscow I received a letter in a plain white envelope, addressed simply to *Professor Sebastian Stearn, Cambridge University*. Not that unusual. My books had continued to sell briskly in academic circles. One or two had even gained a measure of traction in the commercial world. Not J. K. Rowling success, but the odd fan letter made its way to my door. This one was written in a delicate, womanly hand. No postmark, no date. In fact, it contained no identifying features.

Dear Professor,

I am writing to you on the occasion of my twenty-first birthday to tell you how much I have enjoyed your books. I lived with my mother in Moscow as a child so I particular enjoyed The Two Ivans. My mother had a copy and I remember her telling me about the time she met you. My recollections are vague, details hazy, but I recall she was a tour guide and you a lecturer in Moscow for the annual history convention. You probably won't remember her, but I know she was very much taken with your meetings and my grandmother tells me she enjoyed showing you the sights.

Unfortunately, my mother passed away when I was young, and because my father had also died in Moscow, I went to live with my grandmother. When I ask about my mother's life, my grandmother always mentions the mysterious professor from England who was famous in Russia. I have read all your books and I think they helped develop my passion for reading, writing, and pursuing and recording the truth. Now I am studying to be a teacher like you and my mother. I felt compelled to write to thank you for being such an inspiration.

Yours in history, a grateful reader.

Lena.

I read the letter many times, delighting in the warm glow generated. Not because of the sentiments, although they were generous and appreciated, more because this was the first and only tangible connection with Anna since I had seen her hurrying down the corridor at the Four Seasons.

At least that's what I wanted to believe. Lena, Anna's daughter, for it must be her, had made contact after all these years because of a seed I'd sown in her mother's mind. Yet I knew from my time at Secretarium that everything was not always what it seemed.

Could the letter have been intercepted? Could it be a KGB lure, hoping for a reaction to suck me in, induce me to make a false move, incriminate me in actions long gone, but never forgotten? I racked my brains. There was no address, so I couldn't reply, but still may it not be an opening gambit, a ploy to encourage further correspondence that might reveal location details and secrets down the line?

I realised then that is what the complex world of Secretarium had done to me. My first reaction to a kindness was suspicion. I kept the letter and although I heard no more it provided the impetus to write a memoir. Not a dry autobiography. I had read enough of those by indulgent academics to know that they are interesting only to the writer. That didn't appeal. I wanted to write the truth, but knew that revealing secrets, however insignificant or ancient, would betray the ethos I'd sworn to uphold. That's when the idea of this coded journal came to me. Some might say it is folly, a pointless obsession. There were times the monotony in the mechanics of the coding became so onerous and wearisome that I almost lost faith.

Nevertheless, I stuck with it and for the next 10 years, maybe more, I recorded the memories, emotions and fears surrounding my only mission. It meant reliving the traumas, but allowed me once more to inhabit the world of Anna. I regarded that as therapy. It worked. I took strength from each chapter, in the certain knowledge that concealed in numbers the journal was safe from prying eyes and malevolent forces. I decided to supply the clues to the code only when I knew that time was short. Even then I doubted whether anyone would possess the wit, interest, enthusiasm or stamina to decipher a work that demanded more intricate attention than all my other books combined. If you are reading and understanding this now, then I salute you. I thank you for your time, your intuition and perseverance. I pray that neither you, nor history, will judge me too harshly.

43

There were only two topics of conversation on the trip to Cambridge.

One was the red car man with the spider tattoo. Emily had researched the subject online, discovering in Russian prisons a spider tattoo usually symbolises that the person is a thief.

"Was the spider facing up or down?" Her tone serious and eager.

Al sniggered. "I've no idea. Up, I think. What does it matter?"

"Because if the spider is facing up it means he's an active criminal. Facing down means he's left the lifestyle. Either way there's a Russian connection."

Al rolled his eyes. "Google has a lot to answer for."

"What?"

"Emily, lots of people have spider tattoos. Nearly all of them have nothing to do with Russia."

"Okay, then, what do you think he's up to?"

"I've no idea. If we see him again, I'll ask."

The main conversation surrounded Uncle Sebastian and the conclusion of his journal. Emily was struggling to rationalise a collision of thoughts. Relief that the hundreds of hours they'd invested in deciphering had paid off, proving her dad's £4,000 on *Gone with the Wind* had been well spent. Pride that Uncle Sebastian had accepted and completed his mission. And a strange gnawing feeling she couldn't place. She'd wanted his story to end like all those romantic films she watched as a teenager. She knew it didn't. He'd never married and she remembered dismissing his life as boring at his funeral. *How could I have been so harsh?* Shame. That was it. She felt ashamed that she'd been so quick to judge.

"I hope we find the picture of Anna," she said.

"So do I. She seems a wonderful woman. Sebastian obviously thought the world of her. To see her face would be fantastic."

They pulled in to use the services and enjoy a coffee, but that was their only stop. As the traffic was unusually light they reached Cambridge a little before 11am. They headed straight for Corpus Christie College and entered the porter's lodge. James, the man with the black-framed glasses, was behind the counter. He seemed to remember them from their last visit.

"Oh, hello there, what can I do for you?"

They told him they'd come to collect Uncle Sebastian's belongings. He asked to see identification. Emily dug in her handbag, flopping her passport on the counter.

"Yes, that'll do nicely. We've been expecting you. I'll get the cases." James disappeared behind a wooden partition.

A few moments later a tall, angular figure, wearing a dark suit, emerged from behind the partition. Emily thought he looked vaguely familiar. He smiled, pulling a wallet from his jacket pocket, flipping it open so Al and Emily could read. A warrant card. *Secret Intelligence Service MI6 – 2703 SIS Officer.*

Emily's brow knitted. Al looked puzzled.

"Miss Stearn, a pleasure to meet you. And Mr Andreyevich." The man nodded at Al, while Emily's mouth dropped open. She stared at Al, a blank look of bewilderment.

The man continued. "My name is Stephens, David Stephens. I've been overseeing Professor Stearn's final details. I must say I'm impressed by your tenacity and ingenuity. The journal was a remarkable find. It reads beautifully."

Emily felt as if her brain were about to implode, a torrent of confused thoughts piling on top of her desperation to remember where she'd seen this man.

Al had solved his conundrum. Now he didn't need to ask the red car man what he was doing. Nor work out the significance of the spider tattoo. MI6 or MI5, or whatever satellite service carries out covert operations in the UK, and Al didn't care, had bugged the bungalow. Red car man had been MI6's eyes and ears on the ground, doubtless with a panoply of gadgets. Following them to Cambridge. Monitoring their every move. That was the only explanation.

When Al spoke, his voice was hushed as much with wonder as outrage. "You've been listening in every night. I've been reading you a bedtime story and you've been recording every word."

Stephens neither confirmed nor denied. "I have to hand it to you two. You're sharp. And Alexei, I must say you have a lovely reading voice. But you did leave a trail. The British Library. Carringtons of Chelsea. The Eagle pub. That chap Puszkin, or whatever he was called. It wasn't difficult to put two and two together."

Emily noticed that James had taken up station in the lodge doorway, redirecting students, informing them it was temporarily closed.

"You were at Uncle Sebastian's funeral." Emily spat out the sentence as if it was an accusation. Her mind had cleared. She'd put the silver hair, steady gaze and distinguished air together with the man she'd seen leaning on the big black 4x4 as she waited for the funeral cortege to arrive.

"Yes, I was," admitted Stephens. "It was a privilege to be there. I would've liked to have stood up and spoken about your uncle. Told everyone what a brave, intelligent, selfless, remarkable man he was. A man who taught history and was responsible for changing the course of history, but that's not how we do things. We live by the *S*, if you get my drift."

Emily glanced at Al, puzzled.

"S for secret," explained Al.

Stephens nodded, again impressed by Al's speed of thought.

"Why are you here?" Emily's question, typically blunt.

"Two reasons. First, I thought, after supplying such revealing information, you deserved an explanation. No-one ever fully debriefed Professor Stearn. The atmosphere at the time was fraught. We expected a tit-for-tat reprisal. The powers-that-be decided no contact was the best way, the only way, to protect the professor. It can't have been easy for him. My predecessor, the man you'll recognise as Porter, did manage to see him briefly about a year later, but I'm not sure it helped him fully come to terms with what he'd been through."

"What was the other reason?" said Emily.

"I'm afraid that was to check his personal belongings. The professor learned things that could still compromise the service, even after all these years. It was simply a belt and braces exercise."

"Have you found anything?"

Stephens' smile was non-committal. "Everything has been cleared to go." He called James back inside and asked him to deliver the belongings. James disappeared behind the partition again, this time returning with two cases, a large one on wheels, the other a smaller hand-held version.

"It has been a pleasure to meet you both." Stephens offered his hand and Emily shook it, followed by Al.

"Mr Andreyevich, I trust you have told Miss Stearn the whole story." With that Stephens strode behind the partition while Emily once more looked dumbfounded, staring at Al with suspicious eyes.

Al shuffled uncomfortably. "When we get home. I promise."

44

"Who the F is Alexei Andreyevich?"

Emily stood, hands on hips, in the middle of the lounge in Sea View Road. Eyes fiery, tongue ready to unpack a volley of abbreviated F words for the first time since she'd sworn her way out of a job. The journey back to Weymouth had been cold. Nothing to do with the weather because the sun shone most of the way. A definite chill permeated the car, Emily quietly seething, mind concentrating on driving and making sense of what she'd heard while Al closed his eyes, seeking solace in sleep. They ditched the idea of swinging by to visit Harry and Eleanor. Sorting Uncle Sebastian's belongings and the latest revelations much more pressing.

"That's my full name," said Al. "Before I came to Britain. When I lived in Latvia. It's not a big deal, Al Andrews is who I am now."

"Well, it's a big deal to me. Feels like you've been lying to me all this time. I hate men who lie."

"No, Emily, don't think that. I have a complicated back-story, that's all. It's not what you think."

"Okay, tell me about it, while we go through these things. No lies."

Emily opened the large case, full of Uncle Sebastian's personal items. A couple of caps. A pipe. A multitude of trophies and awards, some presented by the Society of Authors for his books, others from the university, marking teaching accomplishments. A selection of pictures protected by bubble wrap, mostly pen-drawings of Cambridge landmarks such as King's College chapel, Clare Bridge, Trinity College quadrangle and the Bridge of Sighs. All worthy and fascinating, but not the intimate items Emily and Al were searching for.

Emily snapped open the catch on the smaller case and asked again. "What's the story, Alexei."

"Al." His voice tight. Emily shrugged.

"I was born in Latvia, like I told you. But my mother was a refugee from Russia. She had to leave when she was very young. The Soviet regime was harsh. Her mother died and she was brought up by her grandmother. But my mother was always proud of her roots, so much so that she kept her maiden name also when she married my father. He was from Latvia."

"So not from Scotland?"

"He lives in Scotland now and has done for years. He owns a British passport, but yes, originally he is from Latvia."

"Why didn't you tell me this? And why didn't you tell me your mother died three months ago?"

Al gasped, face contorting in an agonised grimace. He fixed Emily with a look of despair. "How do you know that?"

"Marcus. He'd been in touch with the owners of the house and they told him."

Al's eyes danced around the room as if seeking a way out. "Why didn't you tell me you knew?"

"Oh no, don't do that, don't turn it around on me. It's a terrible thing to happen, Al, but how was I to know why you were keeping your mother's death a secret."

Al's voice choked. "I wasn't. I would have told you, but I got so wrapped up with the journal and work."

"That you forgot your mother had died?" Emily's tone incredulous.

"No, of course not. It was more that I'd found something here that took away the pain, if only for a while."

Emily needed time to think. She needed a plausible explanation. She needed a drink, so went to the fridge, returning with two bottles of beer. She cracked them open, handing one to Al. She started to sift through items in the small case, on her knees with the case laid open on the floor. A bunch of keys, a watch, an alarm clock and a thick audit pad containing a list of every lecture Uncle Sebastian had given stretching back to 1970. Then she spotted a book. A meaty hard-back book with a striking dust cover.

"*Iskusstvo Zashchity*," she said slowly, making a stab at the Russian title.

"*The Art of Defence*." Al translated. His spoken Russian was almost non-existent but he retained an understanding of the Cyrillic alphabet.

"Isn't that …?"

"Kalenkov's book." Al finished Emily's sentence. "The one he gave Sebastian the night he died."

Emily clutched it to her chest. The book provided a tangible piece of the puzzle they'd unravelled in the journal. It was there when Kalenkov and Uncle Sebastian duelled at chess. A witness to history, or assassination, whichever way one looked at it. She opened the cover and inside discovered a squiggle in black pen. She thought she could make out two Ks. Kalenkov's signature.

"Al, I wish you'd told me the truth," said Emily.

"So do I, but the absolute truth is I didn't come here to work at the café, or to commute to Bristol, or even to earn some holiday cash."

Emily fixed him with a bemused stare.

"I came here to meet Sebastian."

"To meet Uncle Sebastian? Why?"

As Emily stared at Al, engrossed in their conversation, she flicked aimlessly through the pages of Kalenkov's book. A piece of paper or card fluttered to the floor. A bookmark perhaps. Emily picked it up, studied it for a moment and her eyes danced, her face a canvas of excitement.

"Al, look at this. We've found it. At last we've found it." She turned around the card so Al could see. A photograph of a beautiful woman astride a bicycle, laughing, wind in her hair.

Al's bottom lip trembled. A single tear began to roll down his cheek. He reached in his back pocket, took out a wallet, pulling a picture from an inner compartment. He turned it around so Emily could see. A woman, a shade younger perhaps, but unmistakably the same woman. Al choked out the words. "Anna is my grandmother."

Emily could hardly believe what she was hearing. She shook her head, as if to throw off the bemusement. "What?"

"Anna is my grandmother. My mum's name is Lena, the little girl Anna told Sebastian about, the young woman who wrote to Sebastian, although I didn't know anything about that until I read it in the journal. When Mum died in the car crash I went through her things and found references to a history professor at Corpus Christie named Stearn that her mother apparently had written about in an old diary. I looked up Cambridge history fellows and was amazed to find a Sebastian Stearn still on active records who fitted the bill."

"What were you going to do?"

Al bowed his head. "I needed to make sure he was the right man. If so, I wanted to meet him properly. He seemed such a nice guy. I wanted to ask him about my grandmother but, thanks to Marcus, never got the chance. When you told me about the journal it was another way to get to know him, perhaps even learn something about the grandmother I never knew. I have done, more than I could ever have imagined. I now know she wasn't merely a brave lady. She was a true heroine. Without you I would never have discovered that, Emily. I owe it all to you."

He brushed away the tear, looking up, gazing through blurry eyes at a vision no-one had seen before. Something had stirred deep within the girl who never cried, who rarely showed emotion, something profound. Tears were streaming down Emily's cheeks.

"Come here," she gasped, shuffling clumsily across to Al, both still on their knees. Then Emily Stearn, so recently betrayed in love, did another thing she thought she'd never do again. She threw her arms around Al's neck, pulled him close, and through a tearful giggle kissed him full on the lips.

When they broke their clinch Emily gazed at Al with a longing she never thought possible, as if she'd thrown open a window to a new world.

Al grabbed his beer. "A toast."

Emily snatched her bottle also. "To what?"

"To Anna and Sebastian."

They clanked bottles, before again hugging each other tight, croaky voices mirroring the emotion and sentiment of a dramatic month. The promise of new romance emanating from a love that could never be.

"To Anna and Sebastian."

Acknowledgements

The inspiration for *The 13ᵗʰ Assassin* came from a holiday trip to the English seaside resort of Weymouth with its spectacular views of the Isle of Portland where the Royal Navy once tested equipment for undersea warfare.

This gave rise to the infamous Portland Spy ring of the 1950s, most notably including Harry Houghton and Ethel Gee, who before being caught passed secret naval documents to the Soviets, ensuring the Portland area would forever be synonymous with spying.

In true espionage fashion I must keep some of these acknowledgments anonymous, but I have to thank the man at the British Library who can track down the location of any story ever printed in a British newspaper, and the woman at the London rare book shop whose codebreaking help was invaluable.

A big posthumous thank you also to the former Cambridge graduate who inspired the character of Uncle Sebastian. I wish he knew how much his influence lives on in the serene ambience of his holiday home. In his books, his music, his paintings, and his obvious joie de vivre.

Many thanks, of course, to the team at Sharpe Books for having faith in the project.

Most of all, love and gratitude to my family. To Michael for his encouragement and perception. To my wife, Carole, a tough critic but a generous and staunch supporter, and the perfect sounding board for my flights of fancy.

Printed in Great Britain
by Amazon